Wink a Hopeful Eye

Wink a Hopeful Eye

Denise Danks

You can hear them sigh and wish to die,
You can see them wink the hopeful eye
At the man who broke the bank at Monte Carlo.

St. Martin's Press
New York

Library of Congress Cataloging-in-Publication Data

Danks, Denise.
    Wink a hopeful eye / Denise Danks.
        p.   cm.
    "A Thomas Dunne book."
    ISBN 0-312-11355-2
    I. Title.
PR6054.A524W56   1994
823'.914—dc20   94-31313
                                                   CIP

First published in Great Britain by Macmillan London Limited

First U.S. Edition: December 1994
10   9   8   7   6   5   4   3   2   1

FOR VASILIA LILIKA
WITH LOVE

Acknowledgements

Many thanks for their help and advice to:

David Manners and his colleagues at *Electronics Weekly*, Steve King of Datrontech, Tamás Sápi, Detective Sergeant Graham Saltmarsh, Barbara Ellis and Gary Simmonet.

Chapter One

Charlie East invited me for a weekend in Las Vegas and didn't show up until we were boarding the flight home. He was late, too, crumpled and dishevelled, smiling a little crazily as he strode past the silver palms towards me across the lounge of the glass-walled, neon-lit, McCarran Airport, the only casino in the world with baggage carousels. He grabbed my elbow and hurried us towards the gate.

'This'd better be good,' I said.

'It's bloody good, flower, but I can't talk about it right now.'

'In your own time, then, Charlie, in your own time, but just remember how short that could be.'

I had good reason to be sour. Not only had Charlie stood me up but he'd made sure I hadn't got much sleep. He had called me twice since I had got to Vegas, both times in the early hours of Sunday morning and a day and a half late. The first time his voice was businesslike.

'Hi, George, it's me. You awake?'

'What do you think?'

'What's the spot price on drams?'

'About fifty dollars.'

That was it. No apology, no 'How are you?', no 'See you'. The phone went dead. I fumbled the receiver back into its cradle and snuggled back into my sugar-pink pillow. Seconds later, I was propped up on one elbow, looking around the darkened bedroom. I switched on the side light and asked myself if the phone *had* rung and if I *had* answered it. Drams. Dee rams, stands for dynamic random access memory chips. That's what he had said. If I'd been awake I would have said, 'It depends,' and explained why, but before that I would have told him what a great time I was having

1

on my own and thanks for nothing. I couldn't get back to sleep for thinking about what I could have said and why he had said what he had. What was worse I had no cigarettes, not one, not even for emergencies. It had been two months since I had given up the weed. I only smoked now when Shinichro asked me, and when I drank, of course, and I'd given that up as well. More or less.

I'd really wanted to hang on in California, maybe go to Disneyland and then up to San Francisco, but Charlie told me that there was nothing to beat Las Vegas. He had booked us into Bally's, a slick liner of a hotel opposite Caesar's Palace on the Strip. We were going to share a room with two double beds, one apiece, which was no big deal since we had nothing too intimate in mind. We were just good friends, and it was cheaper that way. So Charlie arranged it and I flew eastwoods across Death Valley to meet him, but he wasn't at McCarran Airport to meet me. I waited for him for over an hour while the piped Sinatra and the clank of one-armed bandits worked on my psyche. By the time I got to the hotel my stash was already thirty dollars lighter, and, as I checked in, the metallic music of a thousand slot machines reverberated in my ears, enticing me to the lush carpeted round of twinkling lights, spinning wheels and crowded tables. Bally's was a cool, cavernous, timeless zone that negated night and day. I had to check my watch to get my bearings. Eleven a.m., that was all. I had a shower, I swam in the pool, I showered again, lunched, slept, but still no sigh of Charlie.

By suppertime he still hadn't shown and I'd started getting angry. I left a curt message for him at reception but the moment I stepped out of the busy air-conditioned foyer on to the six-lane forecourt and into the furnace heat of the desert evening, my ill temper was exorcized by a rush of electrified neon. It was as if the Sorcerer's Apprentice had the night shift but he'd been told to stick to the point. Primary colours gushed upwards and outwards illuminating the black sky with bright, brash, flickering invitations to the glowing casinos that lined the straight highway to nowhere they call the Strip. As art imitating high life, it was impressive. Even so, there was better to come. In downtown Las Vegas, old Glitter Gulch in Fremont Street put it in the shade. There the night was as hot and as bright as lava, glowing volcanic red, yellow,

Bunsen blue and bubble-gum pink. The streets hummed to the rattle of slot machines and the clack of wooden roulette wheels. Downtown, you didn't need a car, you could walk between the older, shabbier casinos and meld with the intimate din of people pumping one-armed bandits, paper cups brimming with silver coins as insignificant as jellybeans.

Under the shimmering chandeliers of the Golden Nugget, the Dice Palace, the Mint and the Horseshoe, I went looking for Charlie, holding my Dixie cup like a child in a demonic chocolate factory. The walls were alight with numbers, racetrack conditions, horses' names, so as the punters reeled away from their fate at the tables they could redistribute their wealth, or recoup it with their last dollar, at the racetrack. I played electronic poker for the first time in my life and could hardly tear myself away. I fed the hot slots of the bittersweet fruit machines, too, right next to a big, beehived woman in tight, white jeans who thumped her machine and yelled 'C'mon, keep it coming, keep it coming!' whenever a trickle of silver started into the metal bowl by her plump crotch. She won but I lost about twenty-five dollars at the machines before moving on, a little fuzzy with complimentary cocktails, through the flanks of metal to the central tables. There, cards fell softly on to green baize like love letters in a hallway. The game was blackjack and I watched a solitary, expressionless man bet $1500 a card, losing every time, to the contemptuous groans of a crowd leaning over the wooden rails that penned him in like a sad circus exhibit. A Texan in a big hat said the guy couldn't play shit, but the Bedouin squeezed in beside him said that the man had wanted to lose, *wanted* to. It was some sort of public self-annihilation that I found hard to watch, so I wandered off to where quick hands shuffled chips on to the boxed pattern of the roulette tables. Silent faces stared at the capricious platter of solid African wood, spinning on its steely spindle, and studded with a circle of metal diamonds as treacherous as rapids. The round white acetate ball bounced around the track and settled into a cup that satisfied no one. Its thirty-eight pockets were numbered from 00 to 36, alternately high-low, odd-even and coloured red and black except for numbers 0 and 00, which were green. Its gyrating pattern illustrated the laws of probability and chance and the game could have been fair too if the house paid thirty-eight to one instead of thirty-five. Those odds given the house a profit of between 5.26 and 7.89 per cent, better than the 1.25 per cent it creams off blackjack or craps. Easy, like taking candy from an anorexic.

The secret of Las Vegas is that its casinos are all noise and dazzling distraction, but no information. The machines ding and dong, rotors clatter, waitresses call, dealers' hands clap, card players riffle chips, dice roll and crapshooters whoop. The money shakes out of your pockets and all around. Watching the flow are big men with keen looks, bull-shouldered pit bosses in dark suits standing guard. Above them are the mirrored Eyes in the Sky, the hidden banks of cameras and computers which scan the floors, looking for misfits and miscreants in the moneybags empire, searching for those who might think to hassle a high roller, or rob it, in any way, of a single, silver drop of the torrent of money that ebbs and flows through the bejewelled canyons of Las Vegas.

I got back to my room at 2 a.m. on Saturday morning, more than a little drunk, just shy a hundred dollars down, and wondering why the hell I thought I had had a good time. The truth was, I'd found it pretty easy going to be a woman on her own in Vegas, which was fortunate because it was another twenty-four hours before Charlie called.

The first time was to price the drams and the second, a couple of hours later, was to ask me to book us a flight home, and to make sure it was first class.

'Sod off,' I said through clenched teeth.

'We've got to go.'

'You go. This place is Blackpool with great big knobs on. Tomorrow I'm going to see Nudes on Ice. Can't miss that, can I?'

'Georgina, I'm hot.'

'That's because it's a hundred degrees out there.'

'Hot, as in someone's blowlamping my bum.'

'OK. I'll book the tickets, but, Charlie, don't ever, ever call me friend.'

Charlie never took me seriously. He settled back happily in his seat having stowed his overnight bag, clutching his briefcase. He had the exhausted, wild-eyed look of a man who had been smiling too long and too widely. He took my hand and squeezed it hard but I snatched it back and Charlie laughed.

'Pinch me, someone, pinch me,' he said.

'I'd rather punch you instead, you creep.'

'Georgina, be nice. I am a seriously rich man.'

'Charlie, don't tempt me. At this moment you're *this close* . . .' I pinched my fingers in his face '. . . to being a seriously ill one.'

Charlie tapped the side of his nose and then tapped my leg reassuringly, pushing his seat back so that he could sleep. I pushed mine forward so that I could drink my coffee and watch the daylight spreading before us, the dark and all its magical twinkling lights far behind. I couldn't relax. The dull drone of the aircraft irritated me. Las Vegas had got to me like a good whore gets to a kind-hearted policeman. It was crooked, but it was honest. By packaging itself into kiddiescapes of tacky Roman palaces and one thousand and one Arabian Nights, no one could feel remotely guilty about turning away from a culture that wasn't there and focusing their attentions on what they were really there for – the taking of chances in the hot, single-minded pursuit of cash.

As I watched the clouds form a treacherous mattress underneath, out of the corner of my eye I could see someone watching me. He was across the aisle from Charlie, a tanned, well-built man with dark hair thinning at the temples and a whacking great moustache spreading thickly the length of his wide grin. We were in a no-smoking section but he clearly had a pack of Marlboro and a Dunhill lighter on his tray. I looked over at him and he tapped the pack and smiled. The spirit of Las Vegas was clinging to me still, the wheel spun, the ball landed in the cup, and I nodded at the cigarettes. The man jerked his thumb backwards and I squeezed past Charlie to follow him down the plane.

'Pal Kuthy,' he said, proffering a broad, gold-ringed hand when we'd both lit up. He had a strong European accent but not of a country I could place.

'Georgina Powers,' I said, squeezing his hand and exhaling at the same time. I closed my eyes and savoured the strong fresh taste. I was going to take my time with this one, and then never again.

'How was Vegas?' he said. 'Treat you good?'

'Read 'em and weep, as they say. And you?'

'I lost a lot of money. I am a lousy player, I think.'

'What do you play?'

'Poker.'

'Oh.'

'You play cards?'

'No, he does,' I said, nodding in the direction of my dozing companion.

'He wins?'

'All the bloody time.'

'Your boyfriend, eh? Husband?'

'He's a friend,' I said. 'Just.'

Pal ordered champagne for our breakfast and we stood in the aisle drinking it. He was one of those overweaningly confident men, who liked to stand with his arm over your head so he could look down on you like some benevolent smiling god. Though his Balkan moustache would have matched a baggy peasant's shirt and matching trousers, he wore a Rolex watch and a fashionable lightweight cotton-mix suit, the arms of which he'd pushed casually past his wrists as was the fashion for plain-clothes policemen, drugs dealers and all-purpose wide boys of the day. He kept raising his dark, fine eyebrows as if every word I uttered was weighted with the heady aroma of sexiness. I hung in there for the champagne and the cigarettes until he said, 'I love Western girls.'

My shoulders dipped to take the dead weight of ennui that was descending fast, but I held up, lifting my glass for a top-up. I asked him where he was from that he would find us so fascinating. With a loud laugh, he said he was a mad Magyar, from Budapest.

'So what have we got that the girls back home are missing?' I said.

'Western girls are much more interesting.'

'In what way?'

'They are so free.'

'In mind, in body, or just with credit cards?'

'Hah. Everything. Western women can do as they please.'

'That's not true.'

'No? How so?'

'We don't have power, that's why. And any power we do have is swaddled in social restraints that masquerade as biological ones.'

'Oh, you are feminist, then. They all say the same thing. At home, they say the same thing.'

6

'Pity no one listens.'

'No one listens because they have no power.' With that, he chucked me under the chin.

It was not a good start. But he and Charlie got on well. They played stud most of the way home, Mr Kuthy ahead by Heathrow.

Chapter Two

I liked Charlie, but I didn't trust him. He was smart but he could screw up. The two of us used to work together on the same trade newspaper, *Technology Week*. That was where he had screwed up last and he'd left the paper under a dark cloud of shame. I had followed, holding a slightly chewed apple of morality. We were just like Adam and Eve, a tainted double act cast out of media Eden. Still, neither of us original sinners were too bothered about that any more. I had come into a little pile of money that I hadn't asked for, or deserved, and Charlie hooked a job that paid him twice his old editor's salary. We were doing OK, except that I was as bored as a cricketer's wife just sitting around, not unhappy, mind, just stretched out and bored. I was so bored I had started smoking more than the Marlboro man himself. I'd wintered with a Japanese lover and taken a three-week spring holiday, both of which had helped pass the time most agreeably, but Charlie's invitation to Vegas had broken the monotony like the sound of glass shattering in a pavilion window.

He gave me a whole day to recover from the trip before calling. When I heard his voice I flicked the speaker button on the telephone and rolled over my pillow to pull the last cigarette from its pack. The sunshine was defying the drawn curtains with dusty shafts of daylight and the numbers on the clock radio were creeping towards midday. I got out of bed while Charlie asked how I was, and drew back the curtains on a dispiriting London tableau of two tatty tower blocks to the front and a ratcheted city skyline to the right, its burgeoning buildings misted with smog, like oily, overheated pistons. Charlie's excited voice echoed from the telephone as I ambled about the room looking for clothes that I'd discarded the night before. He'd won a card game, he said. I said that I'd gathered that much, so he tried to tell me how. The game was a form of seven-card stud, he explained, a weird version called 'lowball', where the worst hand wins.

'Something I should get into,' I said.

'Oh, come on. You're not going to whinge about Vegas?'

'I wouldn't have missed it for the world.'

'It's OK?'

'It's OK.'

'What's up, then? Eddie?'

'Nah. I'm a happy divorcee.'

'Not the job, then, surely? Christ, Georgina. It's been months.'

'Not the job. I'm all right.'

'Look, stuff *Technology Week*. I can get you in here.'

'No thanks.'

'No thanks? Listen to it. Do you realize how much I'm making?'

'Yes, and, Charlie, you *still* owe me fifty grand.'

'Well, listen up, flower, now I can pay you. Come over tonight. I'll explain everything. Can you make it?'

'You bet,' I said.

Charlie disconnected. He'd won a bundle for sure but something else was cook-cook-cooking, and it had to do with his fast exit from Las Vegas, I was sure of that. I picked up my brush from the dressing table and glanced at the business card that had been underneath. It was plain white with black writing, English on one side and Kanji on the other, with a man's face, smiling broadly, also printed upon it, in black and white. My fingers stroked the picture. Shinichro Saito, senior manager, components division, NC Corporation. He had been bored, too. Bored of karaoke evenings with the boys, with Japanese air hostesses in dismal, upmarket London nightclubs, and with being altogether too Japanese. His *wa*, his harmony, had wavered a little on this overseas trip, and he had met me. I'd seen his handsome, bemused face staring at baggy-shirted ravers in a steamy little club in Charlotte Street. He only looked at me because I wasn't dancing either. I'd spilt my beer down the front of his trousers while squeezing past and he'd apologized for being in my way. Oh, Shiny, you were something. I put the card down. Maybe I should call, I thought, now that I was back.

*

9

Charlie let me into his untidy apartment and made me feel at home. He swept a pile of old newspapers and unpaired black socks to one corner of his sofa and hauled a briefcase out from underneath it. Gesturing to me to sit, he bounced down excitedly next to me, sucking his breath in and out like an ape on ice, the dark, metallic case balanced on his bony lap. As he gazed at the smooth surface his long hands roamed lovingly over its rounded edges.

'Would you like to be alone?' I said.

'What?'

'She's perfect for you – smooth, cool, big mouth that doesn't talk back – but, as a rule, I don't like to watch.'

'Georgina, gaze on this and be humble,' he said and spun the combination lock.

Several round, see-through containers lay inside the case. They would have looked like a job lot of fancy frisbees to anyone who didn't know, but I did. They were what are known in the electronics trade as waffle packs. I looked silently down at them and then at Charlie. He nodded, allowing me to hold one pack up to the light and gaze on the circular wafer within it, a matrix of thousands of semiconductors, what the modern world knows more familiarly as silicon chips. They glittered within the transparent, round sandwich like miniature maps of golden cities with shiny streets of silver. Chips. They all look alike to me, little grey squares of intense, intricate circuitry. One would have balanced easily on the tip of my finger but I would not have known if I held the brains of a computer, a microprocessor, or its doodle pad, its memory; or if I held the notes and instructions for a Cruise missile or a Zanussi washer/dryer. To touch one would have destroyed it anyway, which is why these were locked in plastic, shielded and safe from fatal flecks of dust and dirt that would seize their secret functions like clots of blood seize a living organic brain.

'Drams?' I said.

'Dynamic random access memory. You want. I got.'

'How big?'

'What's the largest amount of memory you can get on one chip nowadays?'

'These are one megabit?'

'Yup. State of the art.'

'Are you sure? They could be 256K, 64K. They could be any-
thing. What have you got, X-ray specs? Less memory, less money.'
'Certificated. Bona fide guaranteed factory fresh.'
Charlie sat back and smiled smugly. I tapped the waffle pack.
'OK. So how many in this?' I said.
'2K.'
'Two thousand. OK. How many in the case?'
'Ten.'
'You know the "spot" price?'
'Like you told me, today's price is fifty dollars rising.'
I paused for some mental arithmetic.
'A million dollars, then.'
'The worse way.'
'In a poker game in Vegas?'
Charlie tipped at the brim of an imaginary stetson and crinkled
up his eyes like he'd spent too long under a hot sun eating rattle-
snakes on rye.
'Shee-it. It's a tough way to make an easy living, ain't it?'
Ain't it just. I was holding $100,000 in one hand in a round the
size of a make-up mirror. I counted the packs in the case and
remembered my pathetic mothering of the machines in Vegas,
feeding them endless coins without so much as a regurgitating
burp to reward me. I had spent my time lurching from one system
to another, wagering on unfavourable odds, but Charlie, the poker
player, had bet only on favourable ones and had won a fortune
in silicon chips, the shifting sand of the computer industry. The
win wouldn't always be worth this much. The price was high as a
neap tide mark because we were at the top of a typical four-year
cycle that drams seemed to follow. Demand for these memory
chips was booming, supply reducing, technological advancement
promising new product but not just yet, and, to cap it all, a tetchy
trade agreement between the US and Japan, the latter which,
along with the Koreans, just so happens to dominate the work
market in these chips that were the fundamental components of
every computer in the world, every electronic machine from a
calculator to a Cruise missile. The outcome was a shortage that
made grown components buyers cry. Memory chips weren't my
speciality but everyone in the computer business knew that manufacturers were going crazy for the things. Grandmothers had

11

already been hog tied and sold. These guys suddenly had Japanese quotas to contend with at a time when they needed more chips than ever to build products: computers. calculators, sewing machines, robots, cellular phones, talking baby dolls and ballistic missiles – products that the whole world seemed to want, like yesterday. In the past six months, drams had been as hard to get hold of as snowballs in a Jacuzzi. The prices had soared from seven dollars to fifty dollars for one-megabit drams, and from three dollars seventy-five to between five and seven dollars, for the previous generation of chips, the less capacious 256Ks. The situation had got so bad that some personal computer manufacturers were sending out product with microprocessors but no memory. Let's say the machines had brains enough for sums but nowhere to hold the formulas or the numbers while they did the working out. Computers were being packed up and sent off with a note saying, 'If you can find some memory, buy some and bill us.'

The press had run the story all year, everyone from *Technology Week* to *Business Week* had had something to say about it. That's how come I knew the price. I hoped these were one-megabit drams, but all I could see on this pod was a serial number and a familiar logo.

'I discounted, of course. Gave him ten cents to the dollar,' Charlie said.

'And he took that?'

'The guy had a winning hand. He had to have the money.'

'If he had a winning hand, how come he lost?'

'Doubt, my dear. I sowed the seeds of doubt in his mind. In the end, he bottled.'

'So who is this poor sod?'

'Jap. Called himself Al Sony. Must have stepped out from the electronics fair for a moment.'

'Sony isn't a Japanese name.'

'My Walkman says it is.'

'Morita developed it from the Latin "sonus" as a trade name for the Western market and added a "y" because it sounded like sunny. It's like you calling yourself Mr Pepsi.'

'Hmmm, I like that. Ah so. Ah ... So ... ny. Perhaps the poor sap had a sense of humour. Beer? G 'n' T?'

'Beer.'

Charlie went into his kitchen and brought back two cans of Budweiser, no glasses. He burst the tabs and we clicked tin.

'So, got any buyers?' I said.

'That guy on the flight. Pal Kuthy.'

'You must be joking.'

'He said he was in the electronics business, outfit called AO Electronix. I said, "Do you need drams?" He said, "Like yesterday." '

'Where's he based?'

'Budapest.'

'Forget it.'

'Why?'

'You know why. Cocom rules. Eastern bloc. Denied parties for this sort of chip.'

'Where have you been, George? That's shit. We have *perestroika*, we have *glasnost*. The whole world is changing fast, Reagan's going to Moscow.'

'He's not high tech.'

'Kuthy's OK, all right?'

'You could sell this lot by putting an ad in *Exchange and Mart* the way things are. Why take the risk?'

'I told you he's OK. He sells PCs in Hungary, that's legal. He's got a subsidiary in California, and he assembles in the Far East. How different is he from anyone else?'

'Suit yourself.'

'I will.'

I let it be and the silence cooled us down.

'The game was legal, then?' I said.

'Yup.'

'Why didn't you stay in Vegas, go to that electronics show, sell them there?'

'Will you listen? I didn't want to hang around in that town with a million dollars' worth of drams and all those brokers selling their sisters for them. Talk about fear and loathing. Some of the guys are ... *heavy*. I can sell these to Kuthy now, nice and easy, while the price is peaking ... and the quicker I sell the chips, the quicker you get your money back.'

'You could have paid me before ... on what you're getting paid.'

'I had more than just the one debt.'

'And I was bottom of the heap, I suppose.'

'George, the worst you could do to me is drop by and bad mouth me from time to time when you've had a few. You're not about to make a call on any valuable parts of my anatomy.'

'I wouldn't give you two bob for them,' I said. Charlie snapped down the lid of the briefcase and whizzed it under the sofa. We didn't speak for a while, we just drank and pretended nothing was bothering us.

'Your security stinks,' I said, breaking the silence again. Charlie stood up and reached into the back pocket of his jeans. His expression was businesslike.

'I haven't had time to make arrangements. But listen now. Here's my card and on the back is a number. It's a safety deposit box. This is the key and here's the key to my flat too.'

'Why are you giving these to me? Give them to Debbie.'

Debbie was Charlie's sometime girlfriend, a production assistant for a small publishing house off Poland Street who dressed mostly in different shades of black and white, a uniform that would be a fashion editor's interpretation of what an art student would wear if it wasn't for the tiny matter of the grant. Her face always carried a look of pouting resentment, as if her intellect had been submerged by the huge weight of philistinism that she had to bear while in the company of others.

'I don't want to worry her,' Charlie said.

'You mean you don't trust her.'

'Take it. Just in case anything happens.'

'What's going to happen?'

'Nothing. It's just in case. I trust you.'

'How come?'

'Because I owe you fifty grand.'

Once upon a time the girls in the office used to call this man 'sweet'. Many slept with him on account of his spanked puppy look and discovered too late that he weren't nothing but a hound dog. Charlie watched me drain the last drops from the can and got up to fetch another. He offered me a cigarette, which I took. I noted how easily I'd reached out and taken it, after struggling for months for tobacco-free sainthood. Maybe the tingling under my tongue and the smokes went together. Charlie flicked a light from his windproof stainless steel lighter. I breathed in and blew out, hoping the keen look I was having difficulty keeping off my face would be obscured by the smoke. There were bubbles fizzing inside me and it wasn't the beer. The tension was beginning to tug and tweak. OK, so as they say in the theatre, I was resting, but was this a good story, or what?

'Aren't you afraid of losing? What if *you* had lost a million?' I said.

'I'd be physically and financially embarrassed.'

'That's it? Embarrassed?'

Charlie looked at me, his face clear of doubt. 'I am afraid of losing but not of losing a million. Anyway I didn't lose. Ah So Al Sony did.'

'How come?'

'I read him better than he read me.'

I put myself in Al Sony's place. Charlie was tall and lugubrious looking with his dark hair and dark eyes in a pale, slack-jawed face. Sometimes he looked as if he had no brain at all, or at best a very small one with the synapses burned out. In fact, you could have put him in a straw hat, plaid shirt and dungarees, given him the name Seth and generations of inbreeding would come to mind. But Charlie was a sharp. He liked to gamble, with people, with markets, at arms' length now, and cards, too. He'd been a good journalist, but as the deputy City Editor of *Technology Week* he'd combined the job with the untenable position of amateur fund manager of the paper's covert investment club. He'd been trading in electronics stock at the time of the Crash and acting on what was, technically, inside information; he had staked our fund, and more, on bid stock. He'd traded in the account and lost £50,000 by the time the market had slid into the abyss. I managed to bail him out thanks to an unexpected windfall. But the editor, Max Winters, found out, and Charlie got the boot. I had my own reasons for leaving. But since those L-plated days Charlie had done very well for himself and had learned some lessons about how to stay in the money game and win, and to fold when the time was right, just like he had in poker. I hadn't won anything, ever, well, nothing that I had really wanted, and here was Charlie tempting me with more of what I thought I wanted to leave behind, namely: duplicity and intrigue. I hardly wavered. I couldn't help myself. I wanted to know who Al Sony was. I wanted to

15

know how *he* had got his hands on a million dollars' worth of computer chips, and gambled them away. Now that *was* a story, but it wasn't going to be the first one that I was going to write.

'So, are you lucky, Charlie, or are you just good?' I said.

'I'm good. Bloody good.'

'How did you beat him?'

Charlie's face brightened and his eyes glazed a little from the exquisite memory of the moment and, speaking in the present tense, as if it were happening all over again, he gave me a detailed account of the hands that were played. When he'd finished he sucked on his beer and said:

'George, I get hard just thinking about it.'

'Not so anyone'd notice.'

Charlie waited and then lunged, grabbing me close and squeezing me manfully against his chest.

'One day I'll make you eat those words.'

'Mercy,' I sighed and he let me go with a puppy dog grin. We slumped back into the large soft cushions of his untidy sofa, still holding our beers, and Charlie sighed contentedly, patting my leg with the bony knuckles of his clenched fist.

'It was beautiful, really. He'd won a few pots early on and mistook it for a roll. But poker isn't about who wins the most pots, it's about who wins the most money. Some people can't see that.'

'Well, the Japanese tend to go for market share first,' I said.

'Right. And they go for all that group stuff. Poker isn't a team game, see? The man was culturally unsuited to it.'

'Sumo isn't a team game, nor's Go. Maybe he was just a loser.'

'Maybe, but they're *their* games, George. On a more subtle level, they *are* team games, vertical ones. Uniquely Japanese. Conventions, rituals, ancestors, Shinto . . . all that. Poker belongs to no one. It's a riverboat game, a maverick game, for individuals to play.'

'Individuals like you.'

'Like me,' he said, pausing for a moment. 'Hard to believe, isn't it?'

Charlie crushed the empty can in his hand and chucked it over to a bin on the far side of the room. It landed spot on with a clatter that suggested he'd been practising, then he got up and loped into the kitchen.

16

'Not if you cheated,' I called after him.

'Well, thank you for your support. Remind me not to call *you* as witness for the defence,' he called back.

'He must have been sure to bet that much. Maybe *he* was cheating,' I said when Charlie came back, a dripping magnum of Dom Perignon in his hand.

'No one cheated.'

'With a million dollars at stake, I can't think of anyone who wouldn't, except, perhaps, Mother Teresa.'

'So canonize me. I didn't cheat.'

'So what happened? Didn't he take note of the cards?'

'Yes indeedy, but, more's to the point, he didn't take note of the bluffs. Fancy a pizza with this, flower?' he said, and the cork hit the far wall with a crack.

Two days later the story ran in *Technology Week*, a couple of nationals, and got syndicated pretty much around the world. I was quids in, which was just a bonus compared to the satisfaction of sweet revenge. Charlie was going to have a rush on. I couldn't wait for him to call.

'You bitch,' he said.

'Hey, I thought it was a pretty good picture of you.'

'Where'd you get it?'

'From Debbie.'

There was a terrible groan down the phone, like someone was dying. Charlie came on the line again at full volume.

'You've dropped me fucking right in it. I can't believe you did this. Why?'

'I couldn't believe you dumped me in Vegas.'

'Oh, Jesus.'

'Revenge is sweet.'

'Oh, Jesus.'

'Look. I said the guy was Korean. No comeback, see? Come on, it was a laugh.'

'Well, you can die fucking laughing while I try and fucking stay alive.'

'Do you know something I don't?'

'A million dollars is a million dollars. Jesus. People have been killed for less, Georgina.'

'It has been known for less than a fiver in change and a pension book around here.'

'What a comfort you are.'

'Relax, Charlie. Sometimes a high profile is better insurance than a low one. Anyway, has the phone been busy with eager buyers?'

'Bloody inundated I was, and the Jap called too. That's what really worries me.'

'Why?'

'He isn't a pro.'

'Neither are you.'

'No. Well, not yet.'

'So why does he bother you?'

'A pro isn't concerned with the money, George. A pro just doesn't like to lose the game.'

'So why do they play with money?'

'To keep score.'

'So how come they don't use matchsticks?'

'Don't be stupid. They've got to make a profit, they're professionals.'

'You just said money doesn't matter.'

Charlie's voice was pitched high with frustration. He was half screaming at me. I was loving it.

'It doesn't. The profit does. God. Shut up a minute and listen, will you? You'll never play a great game if you're terrified of losing your wedge. You'd never make the right decision, you'd make a decision based on what you can bloody well afford.'

'OK. So big Al found losing a million dollars' worth of chips hard to take. I can empathize with that.'

'He's unpredictable, don't you see?'

'So how come you beat him?'

'George, for fuck's sake, never mind that, he *cares* about losing the chips *and* he lost face. Japs hate that.'

'Charlie, has he threatened you?'

'No. He wants it back.'

'He wants you to give it back, just like that? A million dollars?'

'He wants to win it back.'

'So what're you saying: that you care about the money now? That you don't want to lose it?'

18

'I won't lose it. He's a loser. He's gambling to get out of deep, deep shit.'

'And you say he won't.'

'No.'

'So what are you worried about?'

'Well, then what, you daft tart? Then what?'

I thought about it for a moment.

'Another picture caption, Charlie?'

The expletive was followed closely by the phone disconnecting. Then what? What does a man who cares how much he loses do when he loses absolutely everything? I picked up the phone and dialled Charlie.

'Sorry,' I said. 'What do you think he'll do, kill himself?'

'Fuck him. What about me?'

Chapter Three

Shinichro called me first. I'd missed him but I hadn't called to say I was back in town. He called me. After Slimeball Eddie, my two-timing toad of a husband, my dear friend Warren Graham, who left me the flat, some money and shit on my shoes, and all the variations of manhood in between, I wasn't in any mood to form what the women's mags called, non-judgementally, 'a relationship'. What I liked best about being with him was the carnality. When he called, I have to admit to almost fusing with the phone. It was as close to love as I had been in a while, and it was the nice kind, warm, a little sleazy, and just painful enough to keep you interested.

No question about it, I had picked Shinichro up that first night and not the other way around. But I had done the decent thing and left him fully dressed and unmolested on my sofa. He had been too vulnerable and melancholy to tamper with, adrift as he was from the familiar twine that kept him anchored in a veritable kelp forest of Japanese manners and inhibitions. He had danced vigorously with me, and when he wasn't dancing hard he was drinking hard, like a man with empty legs and an empty heart. He was so drunk that he came willingly back to my place, which was as far east as anyone would want to go in London at three in the morning. Once I'd shut the front door, he held me against it and told me that I was not very beautiful but my skin was wonderfully pale and my eyes bluer than cornflowers. I had nice teeth too, he said, before kissing me with welcome passion and feeling horny hard against my leg. Nothing else happened. He drew back his hands and staggered away from me, uneasy and unhappy, waltzing from one piece of furniture to another before sinking down on the sofa. He held his head and groaned aloud, saying he was ashamed, ashamed of wanting to sleep with a white woman like his colleagues did, or talked as if they had, swollen-headed big mouths. His accent was terrible and he smelt of beer and fried seaweed. I laid him down, put a bucket by his head and went to bed, leaving him moaning in the dark, alone.

The next day he spent a long time in the bathroom, and fretted so much about his crumpled suit and demeanour that I convinced him to call in sick, if he could stop being so for as long as it takes to dial a number. I offered to call for him but the hard stare from his deadpan face made me back off and withdraw the offer immediately. The call he made to his office was brisk and assured, though he was very unsteady on his feet.

'How are you feeling now?' I said, after he had slept the morning in my bed and showered. It seemed like a simple question at the time, something unprovoking to break the awkward silence over the tea and toast. He did not reply immediately. It was as if he was waiting for my words to permeate past a spongy layer of shame, to some acceptable level from which he could dredge an appropriate response. I gave him time. Who knew what hangover hell he was enduring? Well, frankly, I did, but not that morning, thank God.

'Your enquiry is most kind. I am well, thank you, and you?' he said, with the quaint politeness of a man who had possibly learned his English from *The Tales of Beatrix Potter*.

'Not too bad.'

There was another protracted silence.

'Are you ill?' he said finally.

'No, I'm fine. Not too bad means all things considered, pretty good.'

'Not too bad means good?'

'Not always, sometimes it means bad, but not as bad as it could be. Sometimes it means very, very good indeed.'

'This is most confusing. If I ask buyer how is business and he says not too bad, I cut his credit.'

'Oh. How long have you been here?'

'Six months.'

'Very bad for your buyer, then.'

The stunned look of astonishment on his face was followed by the merest pursing of his lips and a hostile silence.

21

'Joke. That was a joke, not an insult,' I said.

'The famous British sense of humour.'

'Right.'

He looked around my unprepossessing little kitchen with its low-rent view and store of empty wine bottles by the bin. I got the feeling my housekeeping wouldn't pass muster in any Tokyo home but there didn't seem any point in telling him it wouldn't get a star rating in this town either. Poor Shinichro, he must have been wondering what the hell he was doing bunking off work to pass the time with a strange foreign woman who lived in a grubby hutch on the fifth floor of a housing association tenement in Bow.

'My mother doesn't like it either,' I said.

Shinichro lowered his eyes, embarrassed, though I wasn't sure whether it was for me, or himself. He drank a little tea from his cup before stretching around and feeling in his jacket pocket.

'My card,' he said.

The Japanese like business cards. I inspected the photograph, his title: senior manager, components division, NC Corporation, and smiled, nodding approvingly. If I had been working he would have been a good contact, especially with the world chip market beginning to boil. But I wasn't working, except at having a good time and somehow that just wouldn't come.

'I've got one somewhere. Excuse me,' I said.

He gave a tiny bow and a polite little smile as I rose from the table and proceeded to rummage in my desk in the living room. I found a dusty old box of *Technology Week* cards printed with my name and previous title and took it back to Shinichro at the breakfast table. He was well pleased until I said that I didn't work there any more, but that he could contact me at that number in an emergency and I would write my home number on the back. He gave me the card back and tried to sound patient by speaking slowly.

'Please. Where do you work now?' he said.

'I don't. I'm a freelance but I haven't done any work for a while. Still thinking about it, but if and when I do I'll work from here. Do you smoke?'

He shook his head but said he had no objections when I asked if I could. I lit up and blew a few smoke rings into the air.

'I'm trying to give up,' I said.

No answer. I smiled reassuringly, and then he did, a real tight-lipped one this time, followed by another long, awkward silence until I asked a question which widened his eyes in the expectation of yet another assault on his sensibilities.

'Are you familiar with the chaos theory?' I said.

'Chaos theory?'

'I thought it might help us at this point. Help understanding.'

'Go on. Please.'

I bowed deeply.

'If you will allow me to speak slowly, it will help me clarify my thoughts,' I said. His shoulders seemed to relax and he gave a keen little bow. I'd learned this sort of sucking up from one press visit to a Japanese printer factory in Wales. The chairman had not been prepared for the female presence in the press corps and had refused to answer any direct questions from me at the time. I took note of how it was done, though.

'First, the theory states that all systems are sensitively dependent on their initial conditions,' I said.

'Hai.'

'Second, it states that differences that exist in the systems will tend to increase over time, giving rise to rapid divergence of trajectories.'

No hai.

'Am I speaking too quickly?' I said.

'I would prefer more slowly, please.'

'OK. This means that small differences in systems compound themselves over and over again until they become very large differences.'

'I see.'

'It's a good explanation of Darwinian evolution, fratricide, computer failures and why I don't live with my parents, or my ex-husband, and how come human beings from two little islands across the world can be so very, very different. It explains why I can insult you when I don't mean to and you have spent the past half an hour looking at me as if I have two heads.'

Shinichro lapsed into silence again, more anguished than disapproving. I began to suspect that silences to the Japanese were as subtly variable as snow to an Eskimo and rain to an Englishman.

'It is very difficult for me, a Japanese, to understand your

ways . . . your philosophy.' Philosophy was a hard word for him to say and he winced with frustration as he attempted it.

'Well, don't worry, we have millions of them, for each and every one of us. Sometimes they coincide, but in clumps, and on big issues, like whether the shops should open on Sundays.'

He stared back at me over the kitchen table, a fierce resentful gleam in his dark eyes. He looked a little better. His well-proportioned face, which had been sickly pale and olive green first thing, had recovered its golden sheen and I was pleased to note that he was as handsome in my kitchen that morning as he had appeared the night before at the club. He was in his early thirties, I supposed, about five nine, and chunky. His black hair was not slicked back as was the typical Japanese businessman's preference, but styled in a neat, modern crop above a high, smooth forehead. He had a strong, well-shaped nose and good cheek-bones but I liked his mouth the best: dark, full, bow-shaped lips that I wanted to reach out and tweak.

'This is another example of the famous British sense of humour?' he said, and I nodded and laughed, giving him a good show of my teeth. I forgot his first refusal and offered him another cigarette. He hesitated, and then accepted with the tiniest of bows, taking the cheap pink lighter from my hand. He was not a smoker, but he managed to stifle the cough that threatened to burst from his burning lungs and drank some tea to calm himself. This man could be tempted, and I guessed that he wanted to be, that's what was really bothering him.

'Do you like it here at all? In London, England?' I said.

Shinichro's hooded black eyes peered through the burning smoke that poured from his nostrils but he said nothing.

'You don't have to be polite,' I said.

I touched his empty cup, he nodded and I took it with the rest of the breakfast plates to the sink, which was half full of yesterday's dirty dishes.

'I am undecided,' he said as I turned around to face him.

'Last night I would have said you were lonely,' I said.

'Thank you but I am not lonely at all. I have many Japanese friends.'

'No one was with you last night.'

'It was an experiment I had to do by myself.'

24

'Experiment?'

'Excuse me. The Japanese way is to be intolerant of outsiders. We have not learned how to get along with foreigners, yet we must. That is what makes life in your country, any foreign country, so difficult. I try, but I find it is something to be endured, not enjoyed.'

'So, pumped up with a couple of beers you were enduring a whole club full of us. What was it like, a visit to the zoo?'

'Sorry. It was not like that.'

'Well what, then? Are you waiting to be pushed, so that you cannot be blamed, or will you jump over the edge in a foolhardy rush, all by yourself?'

Shinichro blinked his eyes and rubbed his hand through his thick shiny hair.

'You are very perceptive, Miss . . . eh . . . Miss . . .'

'Powers. Georgina Powers.'

'Saito.'

'Shinichro Saito. We introduced ourselves last night.'

He looked uncomfortable, wondering what else he might have forgotten. I controlled my laughter. It would have been too much for him. No way out of the shame but *seppuko*.

'You said I was not beautiful . . . but you seemed to like my eyes . . . and my teeth,' I said, tapping my front ones lightly. He rolled the cigarette quickly back and forth between his broad fingers, his hands shaking a little.

'Forgive me, I do not remember. I apologize.'

'You said you were ashamed at wanting to sleep with a white woman.'

Rising briskly from the table, he bowed stiffly and fully and said, 'Please forgive me.'

'What for?'

'For my condition last night and my ill-chosen words and actions. You are most kind. I have imposed on you too much already.'

With that he left the room. I followed him out and sat on my sofa, flicking through a magazine while he stood there, not moving, not going anywhere. I didn't bother to look up as I spoke.

'You know, you're quite a looker, Saito-san. You should loosen up, enjoy a little chaos while you're here.'

I waited for him to leave but he didn't. I had time for at least

25

three drags of my cigarette, some ash-flicking in my Lakeland souvenir ashtray and a couple of turns of the pages before he sighed aloud for my attention. I didn't look up. I didn't have to. His presence seemed to breathe out across the silent room like gusts of air from a slowly beating fan.

'Have you ever made love with a yellow man, blue-eyed Powers-san?' he said.

I kept my triumphant eyes on the glossy magazine, browsing casually through it while teasing the tip of my tongue around the inside of my mouth.

'No, full-lipped Saito-san, I have not. But I'll tell you right now, no condoms, no deal.'

Shinichro was the man I wanted to speak to about Al Sony. He would be sure to know who the mystery poker player with drams in a suitcase was: after all, the Japanese business community pretty much stuck together and chips were his business. The logo on Charlie's treasure trove led me to believe that they could be specifically his business. I just hoped he wouldn't go native and close ranks. I'd have to time it for when I was standing there in nothing but my Doctor Marten boots.

'No. Who is he?' he said, lying back in bed drinking beer. I clumped across the wooden floor, rubbing the last drops of moisture from my hair, and lit up a cigarette, first and only one of the day. Shinichro only liked the aroma of fresh cigarette smoke when it mingled with Madame Rochas perfume on damp showered skin. He said it smelled of old-world decadence.

'He's a Japanese guy,' I said.

'Al Sony? No. Not Japanese. Must be American. Sony is . . .'

'I know.'

His hand dropped down, touching my bare leg where it met the leather of the boot and began working its way up, smoothing the skin on my calf and gently squeezing the meat on my thigh.

'He's in components. I thought you'd know him,' I said.

'Are you meeting him?'

'What do you mean?'

'Are you sleeping with him?'

'If I was, why would I ask you if you know him?'

'To make sure it was safe.'

'I don't even know him. He's a friend of a friend of mine, Charlie East.'

'If you *are* sleeping with him, I forbid it,' he said, letting go of me and swinging his legs over to place his bare feet on the floor.

'You forbid it?'

'Yes.'

'Shiny, you're jealous.'

He put down the beer and took the cigarette gently from my hand, jabbing it into the china ashtray by the bed with measured pressure. I was waiting for something to happen, something pleasurable, maybe his lips and tongue moistening my nipples, but his leg striking out and lifting me off the floor took me completely by surprise. I half flew, half stumbled forward, breaking my fall to the bed with my hands. I tried to turn but he held me down with just one hand and with the other he struck my buttocks hard, several times, with stinging slaps on naked skin. I lashed out and struggled but he had already straddled my back, pinning me to the bed. His knees pressed in against my waist and his warm chest came down on to my skin, his hands cupping my shoulders, and his wicked tongue flickering around the lobe of my ear until I lay still.

'That hurt,' I said.

'I missed you,' he whispered.

'That hurt.'

'I forbid it, Georgina.'

'Fuck you.'

'Yes, me. OK?'

'OK.'

He turned my body over gently and lay beside me, his hand stroking my hip gently, moving around in circles until it pressed in between my legs. I reached over and squeezed his bottom lip between my fingers.

'Now listen, you idiot. Charlie East won a million dollars' worth of computer chips – drams – from a guy called Al Sony, in Las Vegas. It was in the paper. My story,' I said.

'I did not see it.'

'Never mind. Just tell me who walks around with that many memory chips in a briefcase.'

'A broker, maybe.'

'There was an electronics show in Vegas at the time.' He sighed loudly and pulled his hand away.

'There is your answer. The situation is ... how would you say it ... crazy out there. Brokers set up in hotel rooms with faxes and deal these chips from a list of their contacts. This man maybe has access to grey market components. Chips from, who knows where ... Korea, Malaysia ...'

'Japan?'

'Japan, too.'

'You lot are raking it in, aren't you?'

I stopped too late, wishing I had phrased that a little more carefully, or not at all. His eyes darkened like a bruise and his voice clipped out the words, freezer fresh.

'I suspect business will be very good today in Akihabara district,' he said.

'Thanks to the shortage.'

'The West made this shortage.'

'The trade agreement was supposed to stop Japan dumping chips. It didn't say anything about Japan imposing quotas, and restricting production to get a good price.'

'There are no quotas, no restricted production. Prices have risen because of increased demand that production has not been able to meet because of politically inspired export monitoring. US chip manufacturers complain that Japan sells its drams too cheap and they set artificially ...' He stopped to repeat this word which he found almost impossible to pronounce but duty bound to attempt despite his mounting irritation.

'Ar ... tee ... fish ... ee ... ally,' I said.

'... thank you, high floor price. Japan does not want this agreement. Western software designers expect cheap memory in personal computers. They write large programs as if this memory is free. Japanese do not write this big hungry software. The changeover from 256K-dram production to one megabit is aggravating shortage as well. I think also that, typically, Western buyers overestimate demand from their customers. That's why prices rise.'

'Yes, but Japan isn't helping by making sure its internal market gets the drams that *are* there first.'

'Please, I do not wish to talk about this now, Georgina.'

28

'I want to know . . .'

'Enough. I want to make love with you and you talk business. If I were a Western woman I would complain.'

'I want to know how it is possible for a Japanese guy to walk around with a million dollars' worth of certificated drams and bet them on a poker game.'

'I told you. You can obtain these anywhere.'

'Tell that to the computer manufacturers.'

Shinichro stood up abruptly, muttering to himself in harsh-sounding Japanese. I propped myself up on my elbows, swinging my booted feet against the bed.

'What if I brought you a chip. Could you tell where it came from. Eh, Shiny? What do you say?'

Shinichro's smooth broad back was half turned away from me, a muscled arm on his naked hip. He pushed one hand quickly through his black hair and grunted. That meant yes.

'Thank you, honourable master . . .' I said. He wouldn't turn to face me, he was still angry. I lifted my leg and kicked gently at his thigh, tapping at his flesh until he grabbed my ankle tightly, circling it in his fist, and hauled my naked leg up.

'Enough.'

Enough talking, he meant, and I waited for him to succumb and push me apart on the deep, red covers that smelled irresistibly of rice crackers and tea.

All I had to do was get the numbers, Shinichro had said. Every packaged chip has its code: the week it was made including the date, the batch number, which would indicate the fabrication point and the country of origin. It would be all in the certification document. He'd need a microscope to check the individual dies – the raw chips – themselves, to see that they matched up to the document. That was a problem he could get around, but I didn't feel comfortable with the idea of walking out of some security vault and into a London street with a pack worth $100,000 under my arm. It was out of the question. I'd just take my notebook and write the numbers down from Charlie's list. But, as it happened, I needn't have troubled my conscience with the pros and cons of that decision. When I sat down in one of the windowless rooms, provided by Charlie's chosen Oxford Street bank for the discreet inspection of booty, and opened the hefty metal box, there was nothing in it.

I asked the clerk to check who else had signed for the box in the past week and she showed me two signatures, both Charlie's – C. H. East, in a fast, loopy, forward scrawl. She couldn't describe him because she said she was new and worked downstairs filling the money machines most of the time. I signed out and left. It had just rained and the traffic was slushing by, stopping and starting, spitting greasy spray on to the pavement from the dirty pools of water and litter that had gathered in the gutter. I stepped into a newsagent's, bought a packet of cigarettes, broke it open and lit up outside on the bustling street. The taste of tobacco was unaccountably bitter in my mouth. People were pushing past me but I wasn't moving, I was thinking; wondering whether Charlie's haul was still under his sofa, or whether Pal Kuthy already had the lot and Charlie had decided to call off the game. I was hungry too and the sickly smell of cookies carried along in the damp air was making my mouth water. I couldn't stomach them as a rule but now I wanted an oversized coconut one with a luminescent red cherry on top. What was doubly disconcerting was that I wanted it with tuna too.

I ate the cookie and the tub of tuna sitting on a wooden bench in Soho Square, where the cycle messengers hung out in their Dayglo stretch shorts and cut-away vests and the winos liked to lay yesterday's papers on the benches and stare rheumily at passers-by. It was hot now the rain had gone. The pocket-handkerchief park steamed a little in the sunshine as the air sucked up moisture from the damp grass and the pearly green shoots in the flower beds. The flayed trunks of two large birch trees stood to the north of the gardens like the stumps of an old soldier's fingers. These sad giants had been wrecked by the hurricane that had blasted through the south-east of England in the autumn. It had felled forests that had survived a millennium, splintering them to matchwood, twisting trees out from the rain-soaked earth by their ancient roots. The great gale had been a sign of the times as surely as when the heavens themselves blazed forth the death of princes. For while the wind had howled about, the City braced itself against its own electronic storm, as destructive as any of nature. In twenty-four hours the global machines that computed the wealth of nations had crashed with the world stock markets. The financial buccaneering of the past decade had come to an end with a huff and a puff that had all but blown the counting house down.

Shinichro was right. Anyone would think the Japs were responsible for the whole of the US deficit. The unpalatable fact was that the US manufacturers couldn't cut it. The Americans had an overwhelming trade deficit because they managed their manufacturing resources badly and their financial raiders had been allowed to weaken whole industries for short-term monetary gain. The dollar devaluation of '86, which was meant to aid the export of goods to Japan, had all the efficacy of sicking into a stiff ocean breeze. It cut the cost to Japan of US raw materials by two-thirds and cut US income by the same. Japan was number one now, merchant and banker to the whole world, though it left it to others to say it, in raised voices that whined with resentment.

I had whined too. One sentence and he had registered it. Now the spot where a little ditch of xenophobia divided us was muddled with my hasty words.

'George. George.'

I felt a large hand shaking my shoulder and opened my eyes on an almost empty park, and two black-trousered legs and a white plastic Virgin bag partly obscuring the view. There was a tinny clatter as a large shiny shoe tapped at something under the bench. I sat up and grabbed hold of my shoulder-bag that Richard Munroe was handing to me.

'That Special Brew is a bit strong to drink in the sunshine, isn't it, love?' he said.

'Bloody cheek. What time is it?'

'Five-thirty. Fancy a top-up?'

'I just fell asleep, that's all. Special Brew. Jesus Christ.'

Richard laughed and sat next to me, elbows on thighs, bag swinging between his big sporty legs. He waited patiently while I checked the contents of my handbag.

'All there?'

'Yes, thanks. What's with the suit?' I said.

'Interview.'

'Where?'

'Guess.'

31

'Not with Max?'

Richard nodded.

'You're crazy.'

'News editor.'

'Oh.'

That wasn't bad. News editor at *Technology Week* was the job I would have liked had things worked out differently. If I hadn't wanted to write one big story as I saw it, not as Max Winters, the editor and proprietor, had.

'Did you get it?' I said.

'I think so. There's that dead horse, Reggie, from *Computer Weekly*, and Sue Lloyd, fragrant single mother of one from *Computing*, and me. I think I've got it. How's the freelance?'

He knew damn well how the freelance was. There hadn't been any. I hadn't exactly been burning down the phone lines trying to get work and the calls had stopped coming once people got used to me being unavailable.

'Fine,' I said.

'Well. I could use you. You know that.'

'Thanks, Richard, but Max wouldn't.'

'Have you asked?'

I didn't answer him because, of course, I hadn't asked. Pride and indolence combined to prevent me. I'd brooded for months about the big story that had gone down the toilet because Max's best interests would not have been served by it. The last few months I'd just got used to lying in. Richard tugged at his collar, uncomfortable in the unfamiliar shirt and tie.

'Bloody hot for May, isn't it?' he said.

'It's the greenhouse effect.'

'Hippos in the Thames next year, eh? Fancy a jar?'

I did. It was thirsty work sleeping on a bench.

Richard bought the first round and I the second. It was cooler inside the pub and I didn't want to stand out on the crowded pavements. I wanted to sit down and rest my weary, aching legs.

'You're a bit dark under the eyes, you know. Are you OK?' Richard said, pulling up a bar stool to the round table that I'd found by the games machine.

'I'm a bit tired, that's all. Could be jet lag.'

'I thought you'd been away. I saw that stuff you did on Charlie.'

'I was doing him a favour.'

'Sure. It was a good story.'

'Thanks.'

'So where's the other one?'

'Richard, gimme a break. It was just a picture caption. A fun thing.'

'Come on.'

'Cone on what?'

'What about the Korean?'

'What about him?'

'He lost a million dollars' worth of silicon.'

'Ye-es,' I said, as if he were trying my patience.

'So who is he?'

'I don't know.'

'Well, that's the story. Isn't it? That's the one we want.'

'So?'

'So if you're not doing it, who will?'

'I don't know.'

'We will, won't we, dear?'

I thought I'd have time to play around with the story and see if I really wanted the hassle but Richard had already started counting to ten. He was offering me a headstart but not for long. it wasn't a major story, but it could be, and it was one he'd want done for *Datamatics*, the paper he worked for, or for *Technology Week*, the paper he might be going to work for. If I didn't want to do it, he'd find someone who did. I should have thought of that before, but I hadn't. I just wasn't thinking right nowadays. Richard pointed to my cigarette burning away in an ashtray.

'Are you going to smoke that bloody thing?'

'Yes. No. I don't fancy it now.'

'Well, put it out, it's blowing in my face.'

The truth was I'd forgotten I'd lit it. I wasn't enjoying the beer, either, it was making me dizzy. My A-cup breasts felt as swollen as in-season cantaloupes and my back was aching.

'I think I'm coming down with flu,' I said. Richard grabbed my chin and looked hard into my face.

'Yes, it's that greenhouse effect, all right. Viruses replicating in unusual hothouse conditions.'

'Viruses the size of hippos in the Thames next year, then?' I replied.

'I tell you what. They're offering decent odds at Ladbrokes. I'd take them if I were you,' he said.

It had started to rain again as I got out of the cab and took the lift to Shinichro's flat. As a rule we didn't treat each other to surprise visits but I felt guilty about the other night and I wanted to make it up to him. I also wanted to tell him about the empty deposit box and ask him if he had any other ideas, maybe tell him now that the chips bore his company logo. It took a while for him to open the door and when he did he left me standing on the wrong side of it.

'I was not expecting you, Georgina.'

'Didn't I mark your dance card?'

'Pardon?'

'Do I have to book?'

'Of course not. Are you well?'

'Shinichro, let me in, why don't you?'

He pursed his lips and allowed me to pass. I took off my sandals, laid them by the door and heel-toed it brusquely down the hall and into the uncluttered living room, half expecting to see another woman. Instead, I saw a thin, tattooed Japanese man in a Hawaiian shirt pouring himself a large Scotch. Shinichro said nothing as he followed me into the room but took my arm to direct me out of the door again.

'Aren't you going to introduce me?' I said, pulling away. I looked pointedly at him and then at his surly friend, who looked me up and down and then smiled suddenly, exposing a gold tooth in his top set. He spoke with a faintly American drawl.

'Yes, Saito-san. Where are your manners? Aren't you going to introduce the lady?'

Something guttural came out of Shinichro's mouth and I heard the word *gaijin*, the Japanese word for foreigner, 'outside person', in the up and down stream of syllables. His guest replied with a laugh and stepped forward, hand outstretched.

'My name is Hiroshi Sano,' he said.

I didn't take his hand. I knew that, though they tolerated it, Japanese found handshaking repulsive. Mine were a little sweaty with the heat and a palm to palm touch under such circumstances would have made any self-respecting Japanese gag. If he could be Western, I could be Oriental, I thought, and Shinichro would see how much the *gaijin* had learned. I bent my head self-effacingly low, and placed my damp hands flat on my thighs, in the traditional feminine style of a Japanese woman. I could smell the beer on my breath.

'Georgina Powers,' I said.

Hiroshi roared with laughter and when I straightened up he said, 'Very good,' as he might have done to a little performing dog. He was smirking but Shinichro's face was a study in control and within a few moments he bowed curtly to Hiroshi and took me firmly by the arm, guiding me into his kitchen. He stood me by the table, staring angrily into my face. I pulled and pushed at his hands.

'You're hurting me. Don't,' I said.

'You must leave now.'

'Why?'

'Please wait in here while I telephone for a taxi.'

'I didn't get it right, did I? I should have backed out of the room, I know. But that's going a bit far, don't you think?'

'It was not necessary for you to do anything at all.'

'Why can't I stay?'

'I have business to attend to.'

'I'm not interested in your business and I don't understand Japanese. I want a long, hot soak – sorry, a shower, then a soak, then I can watch the TV in your room. Maybe flick through your dirty little magazines and get in the mood.'

'No, not tonight.'

'Being a bit Napoleonic, aren't we?'

'I don't understand.'

'Why not tonight?'

'I cannot explain company business to you.'

'I have something to tell you.'

He waited patiently, hands folded in front of his groin.

'I couldn't get the numbers. The chips weren't there,' I said. Unmoved, he turned away from me and walked into the hall. I heard the men's voices in the living room. Hiroshi sounded most amused by something until some harsh words from Shinichro

35

disabused him. I heard him pick up the phone and call a cab, then he came back into the kitchen with a large icebound Scotch which he placed on the table. I pushed it away.

'Why have you dumped me in here? Just tell him who I am and get on with whatever you have to get on with. I won't bother you.'

Shinichro wouldn't answer and made to leave.

'Tell him who I am,' I insisted.

'You have introduced yourself very well already.'

'I mean, tell him who I am. What I am to you.'

'I have said who you are.'

'A *gaijin*?'

He pursed his lips and narrowed his eyes.

'It is the truth, Georgina.'

'He can see that, can't he?'

I looked hard into his alien face for a flicker of tenderness but there was none. His silence angered me. I wanted to slap him, to hurt him and change the dull, poker-faced expression, with its puffed, hooded eyes and high, tufted eyebrows, hard as a shield.

'Kiss me,' I said.

'Some other time,' he replied and pushed the Scotch back along the table.

I sat alone in the silent kitchen for twenty minutes. The two men in the living room made no sound while they waited. When the doorbell rang, Shinichro's slippered feet padded down the hall to fetch me from my quarantine. I poured the Scotch down the sink, tucked my vest into my jeans and swaggered past him, pushing his chest with stiff fingers as I went by.

'Little shit,' I said.

His hand caught me and turned me around smartly so that he could deliver two hard open-mouthed strikes to my face before holding my arms down, pinning them to my side. Dizzy from the blows and shocked by the smarting pain, I began to breathe too hard and too fast until his low voice and steady black eyes held me to attention.

'Look at me. Yes. Look at me. Breathe in through your nose, one. Out, two. Slowly. One. Two. One. Two. One. Two. Good. Go now.'

Chapter Four

The next morning I felt queasy when I shouldn't have done. I counted the number of drinks I'd had with Richard in the pub. Three bottles of Becks and hardly any cigarettes; I'd been virtually teetotal. I blamed it on the food and the sun. I shouldn't have had the tuna, not with the coconut cookie, or the sleep in the park, in that heat. The telephone's warble disturbed my brooding introspection. It was 11 a.m. and it was Charlie, talking fast and urgently.

'Didn't you get my message?'

'I was too tired to run them back last night. What's up?'

'The chips have gone.'

'Gone?'

'Gone. Stolen.'

'I don't believe it.'

'Someone broke in here, turned the flat over, took the key and the number of the box.'

'When?'

'While I was at work yesterday.'

'Have you told the police?'

'Yes.'

'And?'

'They want to know why you signed in at the bank yesterday . . .'

My heart began to beat a little faster.

'Oh.'

'Yes. Oh. But tell me, Georgina, is that "Oh my God"? "Oh really"? or "Oh shit"?'

'Listen . . . I can explain.'

'They want to know why you signed and whether the chips were there when you did.'

'No, they weren't.'

'So why didn't you say anything?'

'I thought you'd sold them to Kuthy. I saw your signature in the book and I thought you had been in.'

'That wasn't my signature.'

'Could have fooled me.'

'You and the fucking dipsticks at the bank. I want to see you.'

'Charlie, I'm feeling a bit sick.'

'Tell me about it,' he said.

We arranged to meet for lunch. I put down the receiver and immediately ran back the messages on the answering machine from the previous day. One from Charlie, almost hysterical, telling me about the chips, one from Shinichro, wondering if we could meet, and one from Pal Kuthy, saying Charlie'd given him my number and how about a drink. He'd left a number for me to call. I wrote it on a gummed yellow memo, stuck it on my computer and dug out my diary. I counted the dates. Three weeks in California, a week and a half back here, last period six weeks ago. Oh, mother.

Charlie worked near Liverpool Street so it was an easy enough journey on the train from Bow. Pal Kuthy arrived ten minutes late and Debbie, twenty. The doomed chichi champagne bars had had their day and Charlie had never liked them, but I could tell that Debbie was disappointed by the whiskery old pub he had chosen for the occasion. It smelled of hops and tobacco, and the landlady's vision of nouvelle cuisine was a smaller helping of steak and kidney pudding. When Debbie paid a visit to the toilet, Charlie cut the small talk and turned to me.

'OK. Tell me. Why did you go to the bank?' he said in a low voice. I thumbed at Debbie's disappearing back.

'Doesn't she know?'

'Not that you had a key.'

'I wanted to get the numbers. I've got someone who knows about the chip market. He'd have told me where they came from.'

Pal offered his Marlboro around. I took one as an experiment, and as we all lit up the bitter taste that I had anticipated forced me to stub the thing out, breaking it like a twig and spilling tobacco into the ashtray. It looked like nerves and, as I looked up, the two men were staring at me.

'Why do you need to know this?' Pal enquired.

'Where they came from? I wanted to do a story, on the man who lost. The legendary Al Sony,' I said.

The two men looked at me again in hostile silence. Pull the other one, dear, hear it go ding-a-ling. This was tough.

'You think I took them?'

There was no reply. Charlie flicked nervously at the filter of his cigarette with his bony thumb. Pal sat back, legs crossed, grinning smugly, his thick black moustache shining in the daylight that spilled into the dark pub from the doorway.

'I had a key, why should I turn the flat over?'

'To cover yourself?' Pal suggested with a smile.

Debbie had begun to mince disdainfully back to the table, horrified that a gent too old to know better had made way for her to pass and winked at her by way of a greeting and a reward. Her red, crayoned lips were in full pout. If she'd been a pal I would have told her that the lipstick had stuck to her rather large front teeth, but she wasn't, so I let her do one of those teeth-clamping sighs that she specialized in without comment. She looked as if she'd been straining tomatoes. Charlie patted her leg and Pal turned back to me.

'Did you tell anyone else about the chips?' he enquired.

'No,' I lied.

'Not the man who was going to help you?'

'No.'

'It was in the paper,' Debbie interrupted, pointing a long-nailed finger at me. 'She made me give her Charlie's picture. Everyone knows about them, thanks to her.'

The smell of food was driving me crazy. I stretched up to look at the menu board: steak and kidney with mash and peas, with chips and peas, sausages, beans and mash, sausages, beans and chips . . .

'I'm starving. Are we going to eat?' I said, half standing up. The others were still looked at me with suspicion. I sat down again and looked defiantly back at them.

'I'm hungry, for Christ's sake,' I said.

Debbie sighed. 'Actually, so am I.'

She and I sat together without speaking as Charlie got up to order the food and Pal got in more drinks. I couldn't believe that they thought I might have taken the drams from the deposit box.

I was sure that Charlie wouldn't have entertained the notion unless that presumptious Hungarian had suggested it and insisted that he ask. Charlie trusted me. That story I had run about him had just been a joke, not a real betrayal of trust. Charlie would have understood that once he'd calmed down. One thing was certain: I couldn't mention that Shinichro was going to help me identify the chips. The Japanese connection would have been too much of a coincidence.

'Charlie's furious about the briefcase,' Debbie said at last.

'I can see,' I replied.

'They didn't take everything though, *fortunately*.'

She said, 'fortunately' with special emphasis, like it was a big word and ought to have my attention drawn to it.

'Oh?'

'They left some photographs of Charlie and me.'

'Holiday snaps?'

Debbie raised an eyebrow. 'I would have been so embarrassed if anything had happened to them.'

A million dollars had gone missing and the woman was scoring points off me, telling me that Charlie and she had pictures *together*. I could have told her that she had the wrong idea, and the wrong key to the wrong box, but that would not have helped the situation I was in. Looking at Debbie you could see what Charlie saw in her, but listening to her gave you real doubts. I once asked Charlie why he'd been with her for so long and he had said that she wasn't as bad as I thought she was and, more importantly, when she loosened up she enjoyed having sex with him and he with her, and the dirtier the better.

'We were at a party once and she got me to do it in the toilet with her,' he said. 'I like that. It's the arty-farty exhibitions she likes me to take her to that I can't hack, but the drive home afterwards is always great.'

The men sat down and spread the plates and drinks on the round wooden table.

'I believe you, George,' Charlie said.

Pal and Debbie looked stonefaced.

'I believe her, OK? Now, let's look at the situation we're in. We have a poker game on Friday.'

'And no pot,' Pal said. He took a long dark swallow of stout

and sucked the creamy froth from his sleek moustache. No wonder
it looked so healthy, better than a protein conditioner that stuff is.

'Sony doesn't know that,' Charlie replied.

'Maybe,' the Hungarian replied.

'What do you mean?'

'What I say. Maybe.'

'OK. Maybe. But he's going to come and play for a million,
isn't he?'

'Yes, Charlie.'

'And he's going to lose.'

'Maybe, Charlie. Only maybe.'

'I've played him. Whoever wins, you, me, the other couple of
guys, it ain't going to be him, baby. He's going to go out and his
bank roll will be ours.'

'So the game is on?'

'You bet.'

'Lucky about the photographs, though, isn't it?' I said and
Charlie lost a saveloy under the table.

'I can see a brown ring,' Esther said, peering into the clear glass
of urine, yellow as sunflower oil.

'Hold it up to the light and look again,' I said.

'OK, but you're fooling yourself, girl. This is positive.'

Esther put the bottle down on the kitchen table and shuffled to
the sink to fill the kettle with water.

'Tea?'

'I think a stiff drink is in order.'

'Tea, then.'

She emptied my teapot of cold, wet teabags, washed it out and
when the kettle began to boil poured a little hot water into it to
warm it. She peered into my uninspiring kitchen cupboards, sigh-
ing every now and then, stretching up on her solid, slippered feet.
I could imagine what she thought. I'd been next door for supper
many times and Esther's speckled melamine cupboards were
bowed with the weight of cans, bags of rice, noodles, dried peas
and lentils, jars of spices, flour, sugar, and packets of chocolate
biscuits. Esther was an agency nurse and she and her husband,
Bill, a retired railway worker, had got married last year after living
together for ten years. The wedding celebrations had lasted for

about a week until the supplies of rum and Red Stripe had finally run out. Esther and her husband liked to party and they liked to eat. They thought I was way too thin.

'What are you going to do?' she said, placing a mug of hot tea in front of me and sitting opposite. She took the weight off her feet slowly, with the help of her strong, dusty black arm on the table.

'I don't know,' I said.

'You going to tell him?'

'I don't know.'

'What about your mother?'

'It wouldn't help.'

'Your father?'

'Certainly not. It'd see him off.'

'You might be surprised.'

'I don't think so.'

'So what are you going to do?'

'I'll have to get rid of it, won't I?'

Esther took a long, deep breath through her flat nose.

'Well, what else can I do?' I said.

'You could have the child.'

'No way.'

'Why not?'

'I don't want it.'

'Why?'

'It was a mistake.'

'How'd you know you weren't?'

'Probably was.'

'Well then.'

We supped at the tea in silence until I asked Esther to look at the glass again. She got up wearily and did as I asked. Then she pointed vigorously at my belly.

'No change. You got a baby in there, and that's that,' she said.

She didn't know who the father was and she didn't ask. Shini-chro didn't visit my place that often and I didn't talk about him to anyone. He worked too hard and in the evenings he socialized a lot with his workmates. He never invited me out for drinks with them and didn't seem keen to mix with my friends either. It suited me, most of the time, because when we met we wanted to see each other, alone. I might have told him that I was pregnant but I wasn't about to tell my mother. I could imagine her contemplating a half-Japanese grandchild. I remembered her funny little comments when she found out about Warren Graham, the guy whose flat I now occupied. She seemed pleased that he wasn't 'too dark', and *he* had only been a friend. Had been. Not now. Was a time when he would have understood my predicament, helped me talk about it. Not now, wherever the bastard was.

I could have talked about it to my best friend, too, but she was not around either, too busy working the clubs, too busy trying to make it. I knew what she'd say anyway, something like 'get it hoovered'. Sensitive, was my Carla. I'd have to tell Shinichro. But how could I, when the last words I had said to him were 'little shit' and he'd belted me round the face to shut me up?

'You see much of Warren nowadays?' Esther said.

'Why?'

'I'm just asking.'

'No. I never see him.'

'He was a nice boy. A good boy.'

'He was neither, Esther.'

She didn't speak for a while and then she said, 'You got the money?'

'For what?'

'For whatever you decide to do.'

'Money's no object.'

'Just got to decide, then.'

'That's all.'

I had no gin. A bottle of gin and a hot bath was the old wives' way. They knew it wouldn't work. It was a concoction for catharsis and comfort. I had some cold Chardonnay for that and *True Blue* on the turntable, cranked up loud. I drank the wine and I danced, all the time not thinking about the future, just of the past, whirling myself around with my eyes shut tight and my arms flailing like a suicide jump. Some women say they know exactly when they had conceived, the sublime instant of transubstantiation, the earth-moving moment of sea change. Why the hell didn't I? Was I lazy or numb or what? Sperm and eggs, I never gave them a thought. But it was the ebb and flow of that warm primordial tide, the seaweed juices of life that had suckered me, and now, somewhere in the chaos, there had been order. I'd been unlucky, hadn't I? Evolution had got me, caught me in its irresistible cumulative progress through time, and something unbelievably complex was going to come out of the dumb simplicity of it. I tried to think when. Was it the time on the table, or under it, or was it the time with the hat? How did it happen? To me? I never wanted one with Eddie and I married him. We always made sure. I took care. Warren had been out of the question: we'd only just begun and it was over, and I had just passed the time with the rest of them. I'm begging. I need some good advice. *Please, please* . The woman's voice begging. Spinning around and around, over and over, loud music pumped all over me. *Daddy, is this the one you warned me all about?* Warned me about all of them, that was the point, made it meaningless. I'd never depended on anyone and now I was going to have to ask for help. *Was I going to keep my baby? Keep my baby. Mmmmm.* Oh no, I couldn't do that. Could I?

The ringing of the doorbell woke me. I had fallen face down on the sofa and slept. It was still light but it was a dim, yellowish evening haze that illuminated the room.

'Hold on, hold on,' I shouted, staggering towards the door. I checked in the wall mirror; my head ached and my puffy face was red, marked with stripes from where I had rested heavily on my arm. I checked my watch. It was 8 p.m.

'Wait a minute,' I said. I pushed a few short strands of muddled hair back from my face and rubbed my fingers up over my face, straightening my ruffled eyebrows. I looked through the spyhole. I could see dark Zeiss shades and a black moustache, fat as a mole, through the fish-eye lens. I unhooked the chains and opened the door. Pal Kuthy gave me a big friendly smile.

'Hi,' he said.

'Look, this isn't a good time. I'm sorry.'

Pal stepped round me into the living room, taking a good look around.

'You OK?' he said.

'I had a few friends over for a drink, you know.' His blue eyes looked at me with amusement and then at the table. He could see the empty bottle and the one glass.

'Pity I don't come round earlier. Some party, eh? How about I make you some coffee?'

'I was just about to take a shower.'

'Go ahead. I don't mind.'

'How did you get my address?'

'Charlie.'

'Great.'

I showed him the kitchen and left him filling the kettle while I went to the bathroom. Standing under the rushing water, I squeezed my tender breasts and stroked my hand down and around my curving belly, slick and shiny with bubbles of soap. Six weeks, I reckoned, and the little bloated bag of cells that had burrowed its way into the soft walls inside was less than the size of a hen's egg. It had blood red eyes and tubes stretching out so that it could feed and grow, safe in its expansible sac of sterile amniotic fluid. It had little hands and feet, but I didn't want to think about it. I still had time. I dried myself slowly and put on the silky blue dressing gown that Shinichro had given me.

'What are you looking for?' Pal called out. He was in the front room with the coffee he had made us and I was in the kitchen slamming cupboard doors.

'I'm looking for some paracetamol. I've got a slight hangover.' Slight, as in five hundred watts.

'Are you hungry?'

'Very.'

'That's it. You cannot drink on an empty stomach. How about I take you somewhere to eat? It will make you feel better.'

Was this man for real? I knew that you couldn't drink on an empty stomach and get away with it. Who was he to tell me? I was an expert. I'd tried it all, the pint of milk on leaving the house, the two gagging pints of water before retiring. The fact was if you drank a litre bottle of wine single handed, the chances were you were going to get a head banger of a hangover. What I really wanted to know was how to make the aching nauseous horror of it go away. I had to have some food but nothing in the fridge could make the meal I needed. I needed tuna with pasta, followed by strawberry macaroons. I had to go out and find that perfect combination of protein, carbohydrate and sugars that the little creature from the deep needed and made me yearn for, but I didn't want to go looking with Pal. He pushed the ashtray between us and offered a cigarette. I shook my head.

'Nice place you have here,' he said.

'Compared to what? A suburb in Miskolc?'

'A palace compared to anywhere there. I like the velvet curtain. The carpet too is nice. You have good taste.'

'It isn't my taste. The fellow who lived here before thought I might like it. It was his going-away present.'

Pal caught the bitterness in my voice and changed the subject. He pointed at what I was wearing.

'That is very beautiful. It is a kimono, yes?'

'No. It's a dressing gown, a *yukata*.'

'It is Japanese?'

'Yes.'

'A gift?'

'Yes.'

'Sexy.'

I held the front of the *yukata* tight and sat down in the easy chair opposite him to drink from my cup. He was resting his elbow on the wide arm of the sofa and his gold-ringed fingers on his forehead, relaxed, like a cat in the crook of a shady tree.

'Charlie said he didn't think you were with anyone at the moment.'

'Charlie wouldn't know if I was. What's it to you?' I said.

'Are you?'

'It's none of your business.'

'I'm sorry. Have I made you angry by asking this?'

'Pal. What are you doing here?'

'I want to make up to you.'

'What?'

'Sorry. Make *it* up to you.'

'Make up for what?'

'For being tough on you yesterday.'

'It's OK. The coffee buys it. Thanks for popping by. When you've finished you can go.'

Before Pal could make up his mind whether to take me seriously or not, the doorbell rang. I peered through the spy hole again and this time moved a step back. It was Shinichro. I didn't want to but I opened the door. He smelt of beer and he could see over

46

my shoulder. I looked behind me. Pal was standing in the middle of the room, jacket swaggered back, shades tucked into the collar of his Ralph Lauren polo shirt, hands in his pockets, legs apart.

'Come in,' I said, but Shinichro didn't move. His eyes looked down at my *yukata*, his gift to me, and then up at my damp hair. He looked over my shoulder again, at Pal and the bottle on the table, and his face paled with anger, though not so much as a crinkle disturbed the smooth calm of his features. His black eyes glistened and his voice was low.

'Forgive me. You have company.'

'He's just leaving. Come in, I must talk to you,' I said, reaching out a hand, but he had already bowed and turned away from me. I called his name but he walked briskly on.

'Is that your man?' Pal said, offering me another cigarette. I wanted to smoke but I was afraid of the taste, afraid of my delicate stomach. I remembered the health education leaflet I had read in the chemist, about the dangers of smoking in pregnancy. It could harm the baby, in the long term. Drink, too, and bad diet; none of it was any good for a growing child, in the long term, but how could any of it, any of it, compare with what I had planned to do in the short?

'No thanks, I'm trying to give up,' I said. He let the cigarette hang from the side of his mouth and lit it, keeping his laughing eyes on me.

'Is he the famous Al Sony?' he said.

'His name is Saito.'

'Common name.'

'Shinichro Saito.'

'Ah. An eldest son. A man with responsibilities.'

'Whatever, he's not Sony. He won't be going to any poker game on Friday, I can tell you.'

'Will you come? It will be interesting, don't you think?'

'It might.'

'You would see him then, huh?'

'I don't know what you mean.'

'For your story. The man who lost a million dollars. Big story, huh?'

'I'm not interested in that story any more.'

'Because you know where the drams have gone?'

'No. I don't. I told you that yesterday.'

Pal hadn't moved. One hand scratched inside his shirt and I could see the flat dark hairs on his chest and stomach. The other hand pulled slowly on the cigarette. He was still smiling but I felt afraid. Pal Kuthy could mistake a *yukata* for a *kimono* but he knew the roots of a Japanese name. He liked to laugh but not at anything really funny, like he had his own private joke that kept the grin on his face. He wore counterfeit clothes and a phony wristwatch but he had a million dollars to spend on Charlie's drams.

'You want to get changed? Put some clothes on?' he said.

'You'll have to leave first.'

'Tell you the truth, you're right, to be so cautious. The way you look in that thing, a man could lose control. But me, I like more meat on a woman.'

Stick around, I thought to myself, you could get a big surprise. He didn't move as I walked towards him. He stood with one hand in his pocket and his legs apart in the middle of the room. I waited, arms folded and he took a minute or so before stepping to one side and waving me past. I went straight to my bedroom, shut the door and sat heavily on the bed with its crumpled peachy duvet that matched the peachy curtains the bountiful Warren had chosen. My mouth was dry, my head ached and my stomach was a vicious vacuum. I wanted to eat and eat, feed the worm inside. I wanted to talk to Shinichro not to Pal Kuthy. I had to tell him what I was going to do. It was only right. I was in trouble all right, river deep and mountain high. I wished Kuthy had never seen Shinichro. I didn't like the conclusions he threw about in his cool, jokey way and I'd have felt safer with him somewhere more public. So I got moving, hauling on some jeans and a red vest that carried the logo 'Trouble' in white and two arrows saying 'Over Here' and 'Over There'. Every bloody where. I heard footsteps and listened. He was by the door, waiting to come in, maybe catch me in my panties. I grabbed the MA1 flying jacket that Warren had left me as part of the goodbye present and snatched the door open. Pal was where I'd left him, waiting in the middle of the room, lighting up another Marlboro and smiling.

'How'd you like Italian?' he said.

*

48

I was twisting knots and hoops of sauce-sodden pasta into my mouth like I hadn't eaten since Christmas Day.

'You think I'm a bad guy, don't you?' he said. I didn't answer.

'I'm not a bad guy.'

'You threatened me back there,' I said.

'I did?'

'You did. You know it.'

'I'm teasing you.'

'What for?'

He shrugged and grinned. 'I'm not a bad guy. I'm a person, as they say in Hungary, who finds the small gates.'

'A bit of duck and diver,' I said.

'A duck?'

'As in head, not as in bird. Miss the low-flying missiles, seize the opportunities presented.'

'Exactly. A very beautiful expression indeed. It is necessary to be so in Hungary, with our lack economy.'

'Black economy.'

'Lack. People are lacking. Products are lacking. No one works at their proper job, they moonlight. You want a colour TV, you bribe the shop assistant. To get anything more than what the state gives you, to get on, you must find the little gates. To survive, you must do this.'

'That what you do, survive? A million dollars in petty cash is more than surviving, I would say.'

'A million dollars?'

'For Charlie's drams. You offered to buy them, didn't you?'

'I have a good business. I make cheap PC clones and sell them in Eastern Europe.'

'So I hear. How're you shaping up with the big boys selling low-end product into those markets now things are loosening up?'

'No contest. They are too expensive. High quality, yes, but too expensive. I make cheap kit. I make it look like IBM.'

'You're still not supposed to have one-megabit drams.'

'Look, we've been getting high-tech products for years, years. The whole embargo has been a farce.'

'You've been stealing and copying it.'

'And buying. But who cares now? Gorbachev and Reagan wished each other Happy New Year on January first.'

'And East Germany rounded up its dissidents a month or so ago.'

'And in Hungary ten thousand people marched through Budapest calling for freedom of the press and political reform. There were no arrests. Times have changed for us all.'

I placed my cutlery on an empty plate, wiped my mouth and looked up. Pal was not smiling now. He looked rather intense, more sincere.

'I understand what you're saying. The system is going to change and since the whole high-tech embargo might just be lifted, why not move in?'

'Yes, why not?'

'Because Charlie could still go to prison.'

'Because you put his picture in the paper and everyone knows he has these chips.'

'OK. *Mea culpa*. It's done. But now Custom and Excise'll want to know where they went.'

'The police will tell them that they've been stolen.'

'Convenient. So who's got them, Pal? You?'

Pal laughed out loud, showing the gap in his teeth and his gold fillings. He grabbed my hand and squeezed it hard against the gold rings.

'I wish. No, not me.'

'Not me either.'

'And not you. I knew that.'

'When?'

'When you said so. I just wanted to play.'

'So who, then?'

'The very famous Mr Al Sony, of course.'

Chapter Five

The way Pal told it, it could have been true. Al Sony, he said, had to be a grey marketeer. He knew the type, he said, because he had to deal with them all the time. The big computer companies tended to buy their chips directly from the major chip manufacturers, so they knew what they were getting at a scheduled price. They only used the grey market with its system of middlemen, both legal and illegal, when they fell short. This year they all had. Some major computer manufacturers had even bought into chip firms just to guarantee their supply. The small buyer, who was always in a hurry and had little clout anyway, couldn't order in bulk. He used the grey market for supplies and a better price than the 'spot' market where manufacturers legitimately sold their chips for the price of the day. The chip shortage had forced everyone to fall upon his patch like hungry dogs on a carcass. Pal had said that, of course, he had always shopped there, dealing with the middlemen, who distributed silicon chips like wholesalers. If the price in the market was really low the chips had to be stolen, but he had never felt that it was his duty to bring it to the attention of the police, though some less vulnerable buyers might have. Mostly, though, no one asked questions. The fact was, some chips had always made their way out of the back door. The good chips got mixed in with the defective ones, and with the counterfeits, even the partials, those incomplete chips cut from the edge of a round wafer. Who would know once these raw chips were packaged in their black antistatic cases with electrodes leading out of the case like silvery centipede legs? The business had always suffered from this sort of 'shrinkage', only now it was worse than it had ever been because the prices were as high as Timothy Leary. Drams had never been taken on such a scale, nor out of the front door in heavy style, by men with big guns and ugly dispositions. Pal reckoned that five million dollars' worth of drams had been heisted from Silicon Valley in the past few months alone. But it wasn't just street villains at work. Some of the chip manufacturers themselves were lying about their production yields in order to cash in. They'd tell their customers that their yield was only fifty per cent when it was really seventy-five, so twenty-five could go straight out of the side door on to the lucrative 'spot' market. Once the chips got to the grey market, they'd lose their source of origin because the middlemen overlooked it and their customers didn't care.

'You think that over the years a high-tech embargo stopped Moscow getting the chips it wanted? Look at me. I have a US subsidiary. No one ever asked me who my mother and father were. Dollars. That was the problem. Paying in dollars. That's what bled us dry.'

'So you're saying Al Sony could have got them from anywhere. They could have been stolen.'

'Of course.'

'And he's got them now?'

'Sure.'

'So why is he hanging around?'

'*Kao.* You know what that means.'

I nodded. *Kao* meant face, a Japanese concept so revered that some astute businessman had named a soap after it so that no one in Japan could bring themselves to criticize it. They'd praise it or say nothing, even if it left their skin the texture of pumice. We'd call it damn fool pride and think we understood it. But pride is something we in the West shape and discard when it suits us. Japanese *kao* is something more absolute. It is a badge of respectability on which the Japanese fixes his self-confidence and displays his harmony with society. I'd learned a few rules about *kao* through being with Shinichro, but not nearly enough of them, it seemed. It struck me that poker was not the sort of game a Japanese would risk.

'How could he play cards? He'd always have been at risk of losing face,' I said.

'You don't lose face by losing at cards. That's OK. Maybe if he couldn't pay up, that's losing face.'

52

'But he did.'

'What?'

'Pay up.'

'So. I suspect he has lost face not to Charlie but to someone else.'

'To whoever he failed to deliver the chips to?'

'Maybe.'

'Who else, then?'

'Whoever gave him these chips in the first place.'

'I thought you said they could have been stolen?'

'Not necessarily by him.'

I had to think about this but the sight of my empty plate distracted me. I wanted the macaroons, heaped with strawberries and cream. I wanted them badly but Pal had not finished his carbonare. He was toying with it instead of shovelling it into his mouth two-handed like I had my tuna and fettuccine and the oodles of creamy sauce. I slid my fingers along the edge of the table and leaned back on my chair. It was impossible. I felt both bloated and starved at the same time. The egg ball inside probably had a mouth now, and a thumb to suck, its cells multiplying and registering, checking into reception after conception. It was twisting the biological screw as its program instructed, rooting in deep so that it had a chance, a real chance. I felt strangely proud of its achievement.

'Are you OK?' Pal said.

'Yes, why?'

'You seem to be looking for someone, or dreaming of someone.'

'Just the sweet trolley. Sorry. What were we talking about?'

'Al Sony's face.'

That made me smile as it had intended to. Pal wasn't so bad, not a bad guy, but I still didn't trust him. His eyes kept looking at my breasts. They'd never been much of an attention grabber in the past but I was conscious of them now, swollen and tender inside my tight black dress. I put my hand to one and felt warm dampness. I squeezed the material a little and the moist patch was slightly sticky to touch. Leaning forward slowly, nonchalantly, I placed my elbows on the table so that my arms crossed and covered my chest. A blush had begun its slow burn up my neck to my cheeks and I slid a finger, discreetly, into my mouth and sucked it. It was delicately sweet. Sweet as honeysuckle in the summer air. I kept my eyes from Pal's face, hoping that he'd think I was gleaning the last remnants of the cream sauce that I'd so obviously enjoyed, and then wiped my hand on the napkin, a little shocked by the involuntary workings of my now unfamiliar body.

'Why would this Sony want to play Charlie if he has the chips back? I still don't understand,' I said.

'I told you. *Kao.*'

I frowned. I didn't get it.

'He knows Charlie hasn't got the chips because he has them himself,' Pal said. 'Charlie will have to withdraw from the game and lose *kao* to Sony, you see? Big *kao* for Sony in the eyes of whoever he has let down, whoever he has *on* or *giri* to.'

'Obligations. How come you know that?'

'I – how would you say it? – pick these things up when I'm looking for little gates.'

'Losing face to Charlie doesn't matter, but to these guys, whoever they are, it does.'

Pal pointed his index finger at me like a gun and pulled his thumb down like a trigger. The girl had got it. He lifted his beer to his mouth and drank thirstily while I waved at the waiter to roll the sweet trolley over. Pal watched me scan the trays for what I wanted and once I had sat back with my plate piled high, he smiled, wiping his moustache with the knuckle of his index finger.

'You have a good appetite for one so slim. Your metabolism is high, eh?'

'That's it, my metabolism,' I said, crushing my spoon into the crumbly macaroon.

'You are pregnant, eh?'

I kept the spoon firmly in my mouth and swallowed, with steady caution, otherwise I would have choked watching Pal's graceful eyebrows raised in a cheeky question above those blue eyes that mocked me across the table. I smoothed the freshly licked spoon back down into the strawberry mixture and turned it about.

'How can you tell?' I said.

You have a – how can I put it? – a soft, milky look here . . .' his brown hand touched my cheek and moved down my jaw . . . 'around the face, and I see that your breasts are leaking. Your dress is wet. It is not very noticeable.'

54

'You noticed.'

'I did.'

'I'm sorry. Has it killed your appetite?'

He smiled and shrugged. 'On the contrary.'

I smiled to myself at the variety of man.

'So where does a man like you get the experience to notice such things and come to the right conclusion? Are you married?'

He waved his elegant hand about in a lavish, exuberant arabesque.

'Georgina, I have had two wives and children, of course. I am not the peasant that you think I am. I am a true Magyar, an adventurer, a man of the world,' he said.

'A peasant would be able to tell. An adventurer certainly would not.'

Pal drained his glass of beer and looked at me, theatrically shamefaced but obviously unabashed.

'The pregnancy test in your kitchen. It is yours, no?'

That was funny. I laughed with him.

'Bastard,' I said. But when I realized what I had said I pressed my hand protectively against my belly, under the tablecloth where he couldn't see. I wanted to change the subject.

'So everything runs on credit, then?' I said, tackling my dessert again.

'That's right. Sony lost a million dollars' worth of chips that he did not own, most probably.'

'He owes a customer, delivery and the supplier cash. He must have been crazy to risk it on a card game.'

'Sure. He was on tilt.'

I shook my head.

'Tilt. Like the pinball machine. Means you've lost it. A card player on tilt is like this. Losing, but still thinking he can win,' he said. I looked away from his face and down at my dress as a warm trickle oozed again from my nipples. I cupped my hands over them and slouched forward again, elbows on the table, face red. Pal reached over and touched my arm.

'Let me take you home, mama,' he said.

Pal's moustache smelled of beer, cigarettes and mother's milk. He lay unashamedly naked, full length on my sofa holding his penis in one hand and a fresh Marlboro in the other. I kissed him fondly one more time and clambered over his hairy chest to put my feet on the floor.

'You have a nice ass,' he said.

'I thought you liked more meat on a woman.'

'I lied,' he said, pulling on his cigarette, puffing out smoke in a self-satisfied plume.

'It was good, eh? Sexy, like that,' he added as I walked away. Well, at least that was more up front than 'How was it for you?' and it was certainly better than nothing. The man had no doubts in this department. He had done it before. He called the dry land Earth, and the gathering together of the waters called he Seas, and he saw that it was good. It wasn't half bad, I can tell you, and I found myself more at ease with the man than I cared to admit. I didn't mind standing in front of him with his greedy eyes watching my back, watching me step over our clothes to get him an ashtray. I felt satisfied, my stomach was full, my vintage headache had all but disappeared and I felt strong in myself as I sat silently by his feet at the end of the sofa, stroking my hand around my breasts. It was a good feeling, a feeling of completeness, of earthy power and, curiously, of freedom. I hadn't had that little nag in the back of my head when he came in me. The one that was always there, to a greater or lesser degree, like a dwarfish parent warning me of what could happen when you had sex. I was already there. It had already happened so I was free. I could really let go.

'Very good,' I said.

'Little mama with her little *galuska*.'

'Her what?'

'*Galuska* . . . dumplings. Very delicious.'

'Oh, please!'

Other people's music started up from somewhere in the flats. Neighbours were returning from the pubs, cruising back for a little party maybe, a little smoke, diddy-diddy dumping reggae through the walls into our space. It was OK. OK when you wanted to know other people were there. It was OK then, vibrating into our silence. Pal picked up the controller and flicked on the television. Hopping channels, passing the ads for lager, for motors, pausing on some conversation between an angry woman and her man, flipping to the news and holding on for the bit about the US Navy in the Gulf.

'This is the next place,' he said.

I didn't answer.

'After the Cold War. This is the next place. The tension will go and the elastic in the whole world's underpants will give here,' he said, pointing at the screen and then pressing hard on a button to switch the set off.

'Coffee?' I said.

Pal swung his arm over and stubbed out his cigarette.

'After,' he said, leaning over and pulling me between his legs.

I walked out of the dim room into the shadowy kitchen, feeling my hand around the wall for the light switch. I was tired now but Pal wanted a cold beer before he went to bed. Food I may not have had, but cold beers I could always be relied upon to stock up with, especially in summer. The night had cooled a little with the clear sky, and little clouds hung around the creamy moon which shone upon the steel of the sink and the bland pale Formica-topped table. There was a breeze whistling in from the window, which I couldn't remember having left open. I stood for a moment and peered into the darkness, afraid of what might be there. As my eyes adapted to the moonlight, I saw the bulky shape of him, sitting silently in the corner. His hair glistened black and his eyes stared at me like hard dark jewels, goosepimpling my skin.

'Shinichro?' I said, but there was no immediate reply. I switched on the light and he blinked once like a night creature caught in the camera flash and remained as he was, motionless on the chair, his hands flat on his knees.

'Tell your friend to leave now,' he said.

'Shinichro . . .'

'Tell him, please.'

Pal called out from the other room and when I didn't answer he came quickly to where I stood.

'You had better go now, Pal.'

'I think it is a better idea that he does.'

'No, you go. There's a minicab rank around the corner. You saw it. You go, please.'

'I don't think so. I think *this* man should go and come back maybe tomorrow, when he is more calm,' he said.

'He doesn't look calm to you?' I said.

'Are you kidding?'

With that Shinichro rose up and walked towards us, his hands up and spread out, warning us to move back into the other room. Pal seemed to be moving towards where his jacket was on a chair behind the sofa but he stopped when he saw Shinichro begin to unbutton the cotton shirt he was wearing and remove it. He undressed slowly before us, folding and arranging his clothes neatly. His Bass Weejuns came off next, then his pure cotton socks, his khaki chinos with their silver-buckled belt and, finally, the black silk boxer shorts I had given him a while back as a little reward. These he ripped in half and threw to one side. Pal stood waiting with a look of tolerant amazement on his face, one tanned hairy arm crossed over his chest, his hand tucked into his armpit. Shinichro, stocky and hairless by comparison, flicked his fingers at me so that I stood back, away from the centre of the room, and in one slow, strong move he rolled the sofa back so that there was a wide area between him and Pal, with me out of the way.

'I must ask you to leave,' Shinichro said and watched while Pal slowly shook his head.

Shinichro paused and bowed. 'Then I am sorry. I will have to remove you by force,' he said.

Pal dropped his hand and shrugged his shoulders, beckoning to the Japanese man to take a chance and try. In a split second Shinichro did just that, first crouching like a toad, legs squat and apart, elbows between his thighs, arms muscled, fists clenched before sprinting at his opponent in an explosive half-jump, half-run. Pal stepped forward and threw his arms around Shinichro's body, pushing him backwards with all his strength only to find himself sprawling downwards, face down in the soft carpet. Pal grinned, pressed himself upright and bowed.

'*Sukui-nage*? Scoop throw. No?' he said. Shinichro didn't bow, but corrected him.

'No. *Tsuki-otoshi*. The twist-down.'

'Ah yes. Forgive me. I like sumo. But not that much,' he said and threw a promising punch which should have caught Shinichro, but who side-stepped it easily.

'Pal. Put your clothes on and go,' I said from my grandstand place by the table. Pal glanced over at me and then at Shinichro and then held up his hands in surrender. He edged to the sofa and straddled it to reach his clothes, which were strewn about the floor and chairs in direct correlation to mine. Shinichro did not bother to get dressed. He stood where he was, his naked body glistening a little with sweat, watching Pal's every move as he made ready to leave. When Pal finally jerked on his jacket, he checked his pockets for change and his money belt for foldies. He bent down slowly and casually to pick up his cigarettes and his Dunhill lighter on his way to the front door. As he went to open it, he turned round, holding his right hand up to Shinichro almost as if he wanted to shake his hand. Shinichro didn't move, his face didn't alter as mine had, in a jaw-dropping look of horror. His eyes like mine were watching the gun. Pal started to smile like it was all a big joke but his blue eyes were not laughing like they usually did.

'Bye-bye, Japan,' he said and the gun clicked on an empty barrel.

I sat down when the door shut and held my head in my hands. The thumping beat of the music suddenly turned off, leaving an afterglow in my head and the room in silence. Shinichro didn't move for at least five minutes. He stood contemplating some point before him before moving to haul the sofa back to its usual spot. I looked up and watched him walk towards me, feeling afraid, thinking that maybe I couldn't talk to this man. I spoke, almost shouted, 'I'm pregnant,' to make him stop and stand still.

'May I ask if I am the father?' he said.

'You are the father. Who else?'

'I do not know who else.'

'No one. You are the father.'

'And you allowed this man to make love with you. You, my child and this man.'

'He didn't make love to your child. He made love to me.'

He didn't answer. He just kept looking down at me, standing close so my eyes could scarcely take in his real shape, just his smooth masculine bulk.

'It just happened. I thought you were never coming back. It wasn't how it looked when you turned up at the door.'

'I know how it looked very well, Georgina. I know how it sounded very well.'

'I'm sorry.'

'It was good with this man?'

'You heard, you saw, you bastard. What do you think?'

'Good, not "not bad".'

I looked away from him and shivered, naked as I was, sitting by the table in the draught coming in from the kitchen and blowing in the early morning air. My eyelids sagged with tiredness and my body with perceived disgrace. I heard his footsteps move away and the bath begin to fill. He came back, grasped my shoulders and dragged me towards the bathroom where he lifted me and dumped me into the water.

'Wash,' he said and I did while he waited. When I'd finished cleaning myself to his satisfaction he threw a towel at me and I dried myself off, almost helpless with fatigue. I was less worried now that he was working off some steam.

'Come to bed,' he said.

'Look, no way, I'm tired . . .'

'Go to bed.'

I lay down and watched the door, waiting, but he didn't come. After a while I pushed back the cover and walked quietly to the door. Shinichro was sitting quite still, cross-legged on the floor, his back against the sofa. When I walked up behind him and touched his shoulder, he looked up at me and his face was wet with tears.

Chapter Six

When I woke up he'd gone, of course. It was raining hard outside and through the open window I could hear the traffic hissing along the wet roads and thunder rumbling over the City. It was past midday and hot in my room, hot enough to sweat. I knew I'd had some phone calls some time in the morning but I'd been too sleepy to answer them. I reckoned Pal might have called to see if I was OK, see if I'd survived the night. Charlie might have called, too, maybe to invite me to the game. Richard could have called about the story, but the one person I didn't expect to call was Shinichro and I didn't know how I felt about that. I sat on the edge of the bed and gazed at my bare feet, flat on the floor, little shiny pads of hard skin on the toes where my boots pressed a little, the Doc Martens that he liked me to wear so he could contemplate the tight, black laces and the shiny leather that was both smooth as a drum and wrinkled as a walnut. I shook my head and looked up. I felt OK, a bit hungry, but not sick, and not hungover. My blue-veined breasts had stopped aching too; they felt cool instead, heavy and dry, while perspiration slicked down my breastbone and pilled out on my skin. Last night I had felt as strong and free as a goddess but now I was less divine, weak, with hobbled feet of clay. I still didn't know what to do, and the fact that I could make a choice and had to make one scared me more than anything. I was looking for the number of my doctor when the telephone rang. Charlie's voice broke up in a stutter. He was on a mobile.

'I thought it was someone demanding a ransom,' I said, when his voice returned.

'What could they have that you could possibly want, George?'

'My privacy.'

'Too bad. How'd you get on?'

'What do you mean?'

'With Pal. How'd you get on?'

I wanted to say we got on and we got off, Charlie, and then on and off again and what business was it of his, but I said, 'Fine.'

'What do you reckon?'

'About what?'

'Can we trust him?'

'Of course not.'

He said 'shit' and then, 'Thanks, George, I knew you'd suss him.'

'Charlie . . .'

'Come to the game tonight. It's on. I want you there to watch these guys.'

'Charlie, I've got a problem of my own at the moment.'

'George, tonight I've got a problem that's worth a million dollars. Yours can wait until tomorrow, can't it?'

I looked at myself in the mirror. Sure it could.

'Where is it?'

'The Black Horse.'

'The Black Horse is a pub.'

'That's right. It is a pub.'

'I thought you high rollers would have pitched camp in some Mayfair casino. Somewhere classy.'

'No one plays poker in Mayfair, they play roulette and blackjack. The classy casinos aren't interested in card tables.'

'Not even for these stakes?'

'OK, maybe they would lay on a Salle Privée, if they knew who I damned well was, the Sultan of Brunei, perhaps. The Black Horse is better.'

'Since when? Last time I was there they had a tape deck in the corner, flashing lights and a free bar for Martin's leaving do.'

'Martin Davies from sales? He didn't invite me.'

'He didn't invite me either. Never mind. Does this mean I don't get to wear my fringed sequinned moll number?'

'Where d'you get it? Harvey Nicks?'

'Roman Road market.'

'Perfect. Be there at eight-thirty.'

I could tell Debbie thought I looked like a tart. It wasn't so much the dress that bothered her, though, as the way Pal tried to put

62

his hand up it, so much so that she screwed her face up like someone had electrified her fillings. It was only a joke but she couldn't see it. I felt like reminding her who it was took her knickers off in the passenger seat while Charlie was still driving and then proceeded to obscure his vision. Charlie told me everything, like it was almost as good for him to say something about it as do it. Pal wasn't saying anything, content to look the part with his thick moustache gleaming as he leaned on the bar with a smoke and a beer. He wore a braided waistcoat over a white collarless shirt and dark pleated trousers from which peeked a grey Samsonite briefcase that he'd tucked between his legs. I wondered about the gun and whether it was loaded tonight and what Charlie had meant about sussing him out. Charlie was pacing the floor in a black zipped polo shirt and a baggy grey Boss suit. His clothes looked expensive but Charlie didn't look cool or smart, he looked nervous. He held his briefcase firmly in his hand, and he had an unlit cigarette behind his ear and one smoking in his mouth. Danny, the landlord, let a third man in at eight-fifteen, a short man who looked Mediterranean, Greek maybe or a Turk, and a fourth, at eight-twenty, a tall blond man who looked like a Swede and dressed like a tennis player, in an expensive jogging suit. The fifth man came at eight-thirty precisely. This man wore a black and white shirt and a black suit and I could just see the blue scrolls of tattoos curling around his slim wrists. He gave no gold-toothed smile this time. Hiroshi Sano kept face instead and bowed to the company.

If he recognized me, he didn't let on. I didn't either, I just watched as he took his seat around the pool table under the Tiffany-style lights and waited as the others settled themselves, riffling their chips, splitting them into stacks and pushing them back together with a calming click-clack. After a couple of minutes Danny, rotund in his tight white shirt and black bow tie, announced that the game was 'lowball' seven-card stud and began to deal, his hamfisted publican hands, delicate as elephants' toes, elegantly flicking cards across the green baize with a caution to the participants not to lose their chips down the pockets.

I don't know much about poker except that if you don't know much about it it is damned boring to watch. Debbie shared my view although she didn't express it. She was content to read Dostoevsky at a rate of two pages an hour with twenty minutes to recap while I peeled the clingfilm off a plate of cheese and pickle sandwiches and chomped my way through them to ease the dull ache in my stomach. I was half wondering whether to give Shinichro a call when there was a sort of half-time announced after the third or fourth outburst from the Greek. The men decided that their mothers and the Virgin Mary had suffered enough and it was time for a break. Charlie cosied up to Pal once he'd got his beer and said, 'He's fucking got them, hasn't he?'

Pal shrugged.

'Well?' Charlie insisted.

'I told you this,' Pal said.

'We bet, he folds. His play is as tight as a fish's arsehole.'

'He is not playing to win, for sure. Not to win a million dollars.'

'He's playing not to lose the fuckers. Shit. He's been thinking up excuses to leave all night.'

Charlie looked at me and raised his eyebrows. I swung my legs down from the seat and walked over, conscious of Pal watching me move, liking it too.

'When this guy calls a cab, can you make some excuse about sharing it with him?' Charlie said. I raised an eyebrow. Charlie was doing me a favour.

'How about Debbie? She's not doing anything either,' I said.

'Look, you're the one who's so keen to find out who Al Sony is. Why don't you ask him?'

'That's what's in it for me. What's in it for you?'

'I want to know where he's going, where he's staying tonight. The drams are probably in the hotel safe right now. You go, we'll follow. OK? Pal?'

Pal nodded, his eyes laughing at something, at me, probably, like he knew I had a connection. One Japanese may be regarded as misfortune, two looks like carelessness. I knew he couldn't know that there *was* a connection, that I knew Hiroshi Sano, alias Al Sony, but he kept looking at me anyhow, as if he did. I had to admire Charlie. After his call to me he made it clear he didn't trust Pal any more than he did Oriental Al, yet here in the bar he was playing like he and Pal were a team, real buddy-buddies. They drank their beers together, took each other's cigarettes and after about fifteen minutes sat down with the others for another session at the table. I stepped outside to call Shinichro but he wasn't home. Too bad. I wanted to tell him that his friend was here, playing cards for chips again and what did he think about that?

One hour later Sano began to gather up his winnings, about five thousand, a tidy little sum for anyone but these guys.

'Gentlemen, I can see I'm getting nowhere fast. I'm going to get some action at the tables,' he said.

'It won't seem like action after Vegas,' Charlie replied waving at Debbie to call the man a cab.

'I'd like to check it out,' Hiroshi replied.

'That's it, then? I get to keep the drams.'

'You must have been living right.'

Charlie didn't say any more, no one said any more. They just watched the wiry Japanese man walk over to the bar, cool as Sappuro, and wait for his cab, thinking, does *he* know that *we* know. Danny began to deal again and Debbie began to whinge about going home. I couldn't blame her, it was hardly a dream night out for a girl of her predilections. However, I really didn't want her to jump me in the queue for Hiroshi Sano's cab, which she threatened to do when she shut her book with a snap and swanked over to him. He smiled his gold-toothed smile and bowed.

'Charlie,' she called out. The men winced but no one answered. They were looking at their cards and at each other, knowing what they had and working out the odds on what everyone else might have. I knew that if was just a bluff. It was a set-up. They were all waiting for Hiroshi Sano to leave, but not with Debbie.

'Charlie, I'm bored. I have to go home. Mr Sano and I can share a cab.'

I helped myself to more sandwiches and moved towards Hiroshi.

'Can I come too? I'm whacked,' I said. It was his lucky day, a fine example of Western womanhood on each arm. Charlie didn't turn around as he lifted his long bony hand in the air and clicked his fingers. Debbie's haughty face didn't comprehend the signal. I nudged her gently and she took the hint, walking over to him and standing restlessly by his shoulder. Charlie leaned back and whispered in her ear, his face hidden in her honey-blond hair. She stood up straight and sauntered back to where we were.

'You two go on. Charlie's going to drive me home in half an hour.'

She seemed pleased enough with whatever Charlie had suggested and I guessed that it hadn't been the promise of following Hiroshi and me to wherever we were going. He drank while I munched and the cab arrived in about a quarter of an hour. He told the cabbie to take him to the Intercontinental and I lied and said that I lived in Shepherd's Bush, which was further west and meant he would drop Hiroshi off first and I could see where. We both leaned back into the seats as the cab pulled away from the blacked-out Black Horse and Hiroshi put his hand on my bare leg.

'Hey, why don't you come to my hotel? We could have a few drinks.'

We stopped at a red light and I looked behind for a sign of Charlie and Pal. They were nowhere. I looked ahead, left his hand where it was.

'We could,' I said.

Hiroshi laughed, more relaxed now. He'd had a lucky escape and he was back where he had started, a million dollars to the good. He'd got the drams stashed somewhere and he'd walked into a den of lions and walked out without so much as a toothmark, his *kao* all freshened up and a few thou in his pocket. What does a man like that want when he's beaten his chest at his enemies? He wants a girl on his lap, that's what.

'How come Charlie calls you Al Sony, but Saito-san calls you Hiroshi Sano?' I said. He looked at me hard and then grinned slowly, like a fox.

'Forgive me, I didn't recognize you.'

'Don't tell me, we all look alike.'

'It's the dress. Saito-san's cleaner. Of course.'

'His cleaner?'

'You clean his house.'

'I do not clean his house.'

'I know that. You are his woman. The *sarariman*'s white woman. He just didn't want to introduce you to me.'

He laughed a lot when he said this, holding his sides because it was such a big joke. I didn't get it.

'Why not?' I said.

'He thinks I'm worse than pigeon's shit, that's why. Didn't you see his face when you bowed? I don't know how I kept a straight face.'

'You didn't.'

'That's right. I didn't. I made it worse for him, the conceited bastard.'

He was convulsing with laughter, his eyes all crinkled up and watery with the hilarity of it all. I couldn't raise so much as a smile, in fact my mouth was set firmly in a miserable pout as I listened to him all but wetting himself next to me, his hand still gripping my leg, his shirt sleeve pulled up to show the blue curl of a sabre.

'Japanese. You've got to understand how it is. See? He looks down on me. He doesn't want me to know he's got a white piece like you because that's what someone like *me* would have. Funny, eh? And he doesn't want you to go Jap on him because that's not what he wants from you. So what do you do? You introduce yourself and bow like a good wife back home. Beautiful. Beautiful. He slapped you about for it, didn't he? Quite right.'

I didn't answer him. I looked out through the rain-spattered glass at the downlit mannequins in the chain-store shop fronts along Oxford Street. I should have known better but it was so *hard* to know, to understand the feudal obsession with rank and status. I knew that Japanese women spoke an entirely different language from that of the Japanese man. Shinichro had said that I couldn't really learn the language from him without sounding as butch as a matron's dog. I knew these facts, and about the factions and the groups, but I didn't really *understand* because I saw the *tatemae*, not the *honne*, the superficial appearance, not the underlying truth.

'How come you and he know each other?' I said when Hiroshi stopped laughing.

'We do business together.'

'Chip business?'

'He's into components. I am into components.'

'Were they his drams you bet back in Vegas? His customers you let down?'

Hiroshi didn't answer. We were pulling up to the plush foyer of the Intercontinental and the doorman was stepping forward to open the door, an umbrella thoughtfully raised to shelter us from the rain. The door had barely opened when Hiroshi pushed me back and caught hold of the door handle to pull it shut. He craned his neck over me for a better look out of the cab's steamy window, his face greasy with sweat. I could feel the pressure of his fingers on my leg even though his hand was no longer there. He hung on to the door and rapped hard on the glass divider that separated the driver from us.

'Don't stop. Carry on. Don't stop. Move on, quickly,' he said. Turning to me, he said, 'Where do you live? Shepherd's what? Where?'

'Shepherd's Bush?' the cabbie said.

Hiroshi was looking behind agitatedly, his hand inside his jacket. He wasn't holding his heart, he was searching for a wallet, maybe, or a gun, and a gun it was, grey metal and snub nosed, its steel nostrils black as pig iron. Whoever Hiroshi had seen he was mightily afraid of, and I was beginning to feel that way myself.

'Where in Shepherd's Bush?' The driver was turning left past Marble Arch.

'Tell him,' Hiroshi said peering through the raindrops at Park Lane behind us.

'Can I get out here?' I said.

'Tell him.'

'Bow,' I said, calling out to the cabbie. 'Bow. Take us to Bow.' The old boy muttered under his breath that we should make our bloody minds up. I looked behind for any sign of the Three Musketeers we'd left behind in the Black Horse but wouldn't you know it? There was still no one there. We weren't the only ones looking behind us. The driver was looking in his mirror, at Sano and me, and he didn't like what he saw. We'd got as far as Holborn when he slammed on the brakes and told us both to get out. He got fifteen quid out of me and an argument, before leaving us in the backwash of wheel spray and puddle water as he put his foot hard down on the accelerator and took off down the road like Hiroshi was firing hot bullets at him.

'Saito. We'll go to Saito-san's apartment,' Hiroshi said.

'In Shepherd's Bush.'

'We can get another cab?'

'Or a night bus. Put that thing away. We'll get whatever comes first.'

It was one-thirty and I was exhausted. My legs were starting to tremble with fatigue but Hiroshi insisted that we start walking.

'Those guys at the foyer . . .' I said.

'Did you see more than one?'

'Maybe,' I lied. 'Who are they?'

Hiroshi didn't answer and kept on walking. The rain was coming down hard and the dirty water from the city skies was stinging my eyes. The little mac I'd brought with me wasn't up to the deluge. My shoulders and back were drenched and the rainwater was running down my legs in rivulets, dribbling around my ankles and soaking the leather of my silly slingbacks. Hiroshi's suit clung to his thin body like a wet paper bag but he hurried on, gripping my arm to make sure I kept up. I didn't want to go with him, to see Shinichro again. I was afraid because I was with Sano. I knew they had a deal, some sort of deal that involved the drams. Shinichro had to be the supplier, but who the hell was the customer, and if the guy in the foyer was, why was Hiroshi so afraid of him that he pulled a gun? He had the chips, didn't he? Pal had said so. Charlie had said so and Hiroshi *had* played like he knew there was nothing in the pot. I tried to think but my stomach had begun to ache, low down, like something was twisting around my pelvis and grinding into my back.

'I've got to stop and rest,' I said and hung back, leaning on a wall between two shops. Hiroshi looked about for a free cab on the empty road. There was nothing; a car trundled by but that was it, nothing.

'How far now?' he said.

'We're coming up to Marble Arch. It's miles. I can't go on. There's a phone that'll take cash, ring a minicab, any one, ring a minicab.'

'I have the address written down,' he said, but I knew it by heart, and the telephone number. I could have called Shinichro, told him where I was, and asked him to come and get me, but I didn't think he would. This was going to be bad enough, turning up with a man he didn't rate higher than pigeon shit and telling him that I knew he was a crook. The cab took twenty minutes and we sheltered in a doorway that was furnished by a damp discarded cardboard box, a shelter for someone who hadn't been able to make it back that night. The pain in my stomach was getting worse, the sinews girdling my belly tightened rhythmically like the skin of a drum and pain rumbled round my spine. I

69

doubled over sharply every other minute and Hiroshi stared at me, his face unpitying and resentful.

'What's the matter with you?'

'Something I ate. I'll be OK.'

I was, until the cab we were waiting for came edging along the kerb and flashed its lights. Hiroshi started out into the rain. I tried to follow but my legs buckled under me. I cried out, clutching at his wrist. I held tight but he bent my fingers back and pushed me off. I slipped and made a grab for his arm which was when he hit me, his hard fist sinking into my stomach, taking my breath away. Cradling my belly, I caught hold of the greasy window ledge and looked down to where the sudden heat was coming from, at the gush of warm liquid and bright red blood sluicing down my thighs and inside my knees, rushing down with the black rainwater and swirling around my ankles like twists of chiffon and silk. Big thick glutinous drops splattered on my sodden shoes and mixed with the dirt and trash that darkened the wet pavement. I looked up in disbelief and Hiroshi, staring at me in horror, turned and ran alone towards the car that was waiting for us. I saw the cabbie leaning towards his passenger door to catch sight of me, see what was going on, but Hiroshi slammed his hand against the wet metal and told him to go. I slid up against the shop window and then down again, very slowly, right down until my knees bent up to my chest and I was crouching on the spongy brown card. There seemed to be an inordinate amount of blood around my feet.

I remember the lights of another car, the voices in the rain and arms holding me. The Three Musketeers had finally come good for D'Artagnan.

Chapter Seven

I had to scream at them to take me home. They wanted to take me to hospital. I wanted to go home. 'Esther. Get Esther,' I told them and she came right away.

'I don't know,' she said when we were alone and she'd cleaned me up. 'I don't know. It's stopped but you need to see a doctor. You need a scan.'

'I don't feel any pain,' I said.

'Stay in bed. Stay in bed, at least a week, if you want to keep it.'

I got a call from Charlie at about midday.

'So you're OK, then? What the hell happened?'

'He hit me. That and a heavy period. What happened to you, more's to the point.'

'We followed you.'

'Not closely enough.'

'Granted. But we got as far as the Intercontinental.'

'You did?'

'Yeah.'

'Did you see what went down?'

'No. We saw the cab turning the corner.'

'Yes.'

'And we checked at reception.'

'Yes.'

'And no one had checked in. No Al Sony, anyway.'

'Seen anyone else there?'

'No. Just a couple of guys, Mediterranean types.'

'You mean tanned, dark hair and moustaches, hint of garlic, maybe?'

'Right. Did you see them?'

'No, Charlie. It was just a guess. We were in the fucking cab.'

Charlie breathed out slowly. 'Did he show you a good time?'

'I've had better.'

'No joke, eh?'

'No joke.'

'So what did you find out?'

'He's called Hiroshi Sano and he's got a gun.'

'Terrific.'

'The chips he got are kosher but they belong to someone else.'

'Yes, me.'

'Get real, Charlie. Pretend you never saw them. Be a real pro and just enjoy having won the game.'

'Flower, it's only just started getting interesting. How about lunch?'

'In about six months.'

'I'll call you Monday. I'll bring Pal, if I can get in touch.'

'How come he's still around?' I said.

'You, maybe?'

'Charlie, he's the sort of guy that sends you a postcard saying wish you were here and no forwarding address. Don't tell me he's holding out for your drams?'

'He says that Sony's got them and he wants to buy them.'

'Sano, his name's Hiroshi Sano.'

'George, he'll always be sweet little Al Sony to me.'

I lay in bed like they had told me to. Bed rest. Bed rest or you'll lose the baby, if you haven't already, Esther had said. I watched 'Kilroy', 'Neighbours' and 'Going for Gold' on the TV by day, and played *True Blue* at night to make myself feel worse. I told myself it was OK, but it wasn't. I hadn't lost the baby, but I felt guilty because I wished the little sac of cells had made the decision for me that night instead of hanging on, like a real survivor, and passing the buck right back. Once I'd had a drink, I could get some sleep. I could close my eyes and think about things for just one sloppy moment, before my brain disengaged itself. Think about Shinichro holding me, about never waking up and having to make up my mind about this. Esther had recommended a fortnight with my feet up, but I managed just two days. I was eating breakfast on my first morning up when Shinichro phoned and said he was coming round that evening and that I was to be in waiting for him.

Esther had done her best to keep the place tidy. She came in before and after her shift to see that I was still breathing, bring me some hot food, see if I could smile at her the once but if I couldn't that was OK too, she said, because sorrow is better than laughter, for by the sadness of the countenance the heart is made better. She left a fat, leathery Bible on the table so I could read it for myself but I didn't touch it, couldn't turn a single gauzy page, just in case I stumbled upon something about the wickedness of women. I dressed myself for Shinichro a full hour before he arrived and sat on the sofa watching the nine o'clock news, listening to old pineapple-face Noriega, up on drug trafficking charges, strutting his stuff before his old pal, the mighty USA. Some guy from the National Institute on Drug Abuse was saying that one million US citizens had tried crack and 24 million had used cocaine on at least one occasion. And who could blame them? Knock, knock, who's there?

He was smart and presentable as usual, his face smooth and his hair clean and shiny black. He looked around the place, at the unusual neatness of the cushions and the vase of summer flowers Esther had arranged to brighten the room.

'Can I get you anything? Tea, coffee, white wine, red wine, beer, scotch, gin? No herbal anything, I'm afraid.'

'Nothing, thank you.'

'Sit down, if you have the time. You look in a bit of a hurry.'

He didn't sit down, but I did, curling my feet underneath me and folding one arm across my chest the better to support the other arm that held a full glass of wine six inches from my face.

'I would be honoured if you would accept this,' he said. It was a white sealed envelope and I guessed what it contained. My face flushed red and my heart beat faster.

'It contains a gift.'

'What's it for?'

'For the abortion.'

I didn't answer right away. I picked up the controller and switched off the box so that there was silence in the room but for the music beating its rhythm in through the walls from someplace else.

'You don't have a problem with abortion, then, in Japan?'

'Not at all.'

'Oh, of course. I forgot. No Pill allowed back home, is there? Abortion is contraception.'

'Abortion is acceptable.'

'You don't have a problem about it, then, personally?'

'If you wish to have the baby then please forgive my presumption. I would be very pleased . . .'

'It is not something you have an opinion on, then?'

He didn't answer me. I stood up and placed my wine glass carefully on the low table in front of me, then I took the envelope from him. It was long, white and heavy as I held it in my hand. It probably weighed about the same as the little pink embryonic stub, who had caused me such pain. I shook the thick paper forward in my hand and, grasping its thick rounded edge, swung it back and drove it forward, striking him across the face with it like a club. I struck him hard, slowly and forcefully, once, twice, three times, four, and then jerked the leather belt of his trousers forward, sticking the envelope behind the waistband. I looked him in the face and decided that I had to lie to him, to everybody, for my kid's sake.

'Too late the hero, my love. The baby checked out. Didn't your friend Hiroshi Sano tell you when he called?'

'I don't understand.'

'Don't lie. Hiroshi Sano was the man at your house. I saw him at a poker game Friday night. We tried to get to your place after something went down at his hotel. He wouldn't get out of the cab he was so shit scared. We had to walk eventually, miles, in all that rain. He hit me, in the stomach. I lost a lot of blood. I lost the baby.'

Shinichro blinked a few times and stood absolutely still like someone watching a TV screen behind a shop window, seeing the action but not comprehending the words.

'It wasn't all bad, though. He was able to tell me what a fool I'd made of you and myself the other night.'

'I don't understand.'

'You told him I cleaned for you, to save your honourable face. He thought it was very funny. I am sorry I bowed to him, Shiny, really I am, but as you so rightly pointed out I'm just a *gaijin*, how could I understand? How could I comprehend the fiendish oriental mechanics that were cranking away underneath? Sure you won't have a drink?'

Shinichro turned and got himself a tumbler, pouring his own Scotch, a good three fingers' worth. I raised my glass but refrained from wishing him good health because he was already drinking. He took the envelope from his waistband with one hand and folded it roughly into the pocket of his loose trousers while he was still swallowing. I carried on talking, buzzing words at his head like a wasp, mixing truth and lies to hurt him the more.

'Still, I've paid, haven't I? I think it's quits. I embarrass you, you demean me, beat me, hurt me. I make love with someone who makes me feel good, but you had to sit in and spy on me. I lose a baby that I hadn't made up my mind whether I wanted or not and you come here wanting to pay me for it anyway. Good intentions, aren't we full of them? The thing is, Shiny, I *always* fuck up but *you*, you've only just started. You're mixing with the wrong sort. Me. Sano-san. You could have told me where he got the drams. Saved me going to Charlie's bank deposit box. All that shit about trade. You're creaming off the top, aren't you?'

Shinichro tipped the last drops of the Scotch down his throat, drew his hand back and threw the glass which smashed with splintering force against the wall. He held out his bloodied hand to stop me from coming near but I wasn't moving. I couldn't. I just had to stand and watch him in silence, with his face dipped down and the blood drip-dripping softly on to the drinks cabinet, making viscous pools of scarlet on the waxy surface of the wood. It was quiet, a minute's silence before he threw up his head and roared, his face contorted, arms stretched out, fists clenched, mouth open, like some enraged beast bellowing something alien, something foreign and frightening into the nothingness around him.

I picked the glass shards from his pitted face with a pair of steel tweezers, my hands shaking a little as I held his head to dig the little pieces out.

'Lucky you didn't catch one of these in your eye, you stupid, *stupid* bastard,' I said.

Shinichro grunted, possibly in agreement but more than likely as a signal for me to get on with it. By the time I'd finished, he looked as if he'd been pioneering a state-of-the-art Albanian razor. There was only one cut that looked as if it might require a stitch but Shinichro was content to let me hold a pad over it while he arched his neck and leant his head over the back of a kitchen chair, his hands resting on his thighs.

'Are you going to tell me the truth, Shinichro?' I said.

'About Sano?'

'Well, that'd be a start.'

'He is *eigoyasan*.'

'What does that mean?'

'It means he can speak English all right but he is no better than a fool.'

'He has a gun.'

'Because he is *yakuza*.'

'A criminal.'

'More than that, *yakuza*, a gangster in one of the three big criminal organizations in Japan. A man with no manners, no respect. A bad citizen.'

'And you?'

'I belong to NC Corporation, components division.'

'So how come he knows you? What's going on, Shinichro?'

He pushed me gently away to stop my clumsy dabbing at his face and rose to his feet. He offered me his seat before ambling into the next room and returning with the half-bottle of Scotch he'd started on an hour earlier. As he reached into the cupboard for two more tumblers I said, 'Are you sure?'

'I need a drink,' he said. 'For the pain.'

I knew exactly what he meant and watched as he poured two large golden shots into the glasses he'd put before us, filled a jug of water and broke a tray of ice cubes into it.

'Do you understand what *on* means, Georgina?' he said.

I kept hearing that word.

'You've told me before. Obligation, a debt, a debt of honour. Like *giri*,' I said.

'It is a debt, yes, but not like *giri*. *Giri* is "duty". I have *giri* to my name, *giri* to the world, a general duty. A man does me a favour in business, I incur *giri*. I will always be obligated to this man but I can live with this indebtedness because I know that some day I will be able to return the favour. *On* is much, much more. It is an obligation of loyalty to someone, an obligation which can perhaps be lessened but can never be repaid, never, not even by one tenth. In the West, you hear the expression "I do not owe anything to anyone, any man." No Japanese can say this. In Japan, we are indebted to everyone, to our ancestors, our

76

contempor . . . the people we live among . . . our society.'

'Honour thy father and thy mother.'

'Yes.'

'That's one of ours.'

'Interesting.'

'It got a bit diluted down the years, that's all.'

'I see. A pity.'

'Perhaps.'

He grunted and then said, 'So you understand *on* is a large debt to someone who has given you a large favour.'

'Such as?'

'Giving you life. Educating you. Guiding your career.'

'Your father and mother?'

'Yes, but also your teacher, maybe. Or your *bucho*.'

'Your manager?'

Shinichro grunted again, this time with a nod.

'My manager in Japan. I wear an *on* to him. He is my *on* man, you understand?' he said.

'That makes you *his* man.'

Shinichro didn't answer that. He drank a good bit of his Scotch instead. I took a slug of mine and topped up the glasses before I said, 'So what do you have to do?'

'I have to replace the drams Sano gambled away.'

'By stealing from your company? Don't you owe some loyalty to your company?'

'I am authorized to sell beyond the quota.'

I smiled, remembering how I had offended him when I had raised that very point.

'So you have *giri* to this man, to repay *on*, but what about right and wrong?'

No answer.

'What about right and wrong, Shinichro?'

He put down his glass and touched the bloody white pad that I had stuck to his face with irregular strips of sticking plaster.

'I will tell you a story, Georgina. A famous story from the eighteenth century, very popular in Japan, like your "Tales of Robin Hood" . . . "The Tale of the Forty-seven *Ronin*." *Ronin* is a *samurai* who has lost his master and these forty-seven were the army of the *daimyo*, a lord, Asano Maganori from Ako. Three

77

daimyo, including Lord Asano, were appointed by the shogun to receive an envoy from the emperor in Kyoto at the *shogun*'s court in Edo. All three were sent to another *daimyo*, Lord Kira, an expert in court etiquette, to learn the correct procedure for such an occasion. All but Lord Asano lavished gifts on Lord Kira. Lord Asano had not felt it necessary, but Lord Kira taunted him because of it, so much so that Lord Asano stabbed him. Lord Kira was not harmed too much but the *shogun* ordered Lord Asano to commit *seppuko*, and he, of course, obeyed. The forty-seven *ronin* were advised by their leader, Yoshio Oishi, to do nothing immediately. This they did, for one year, drinking and enjoying themselves, despised by all for their disloyalty, including their families. But, when the time was ripe, these *ronin* re-formed and attacked Lord Kira's castle, killing the *daimyo* and placing his head on Lord Asano's grave. The *shogun*, though he admired what they had done, ordered them to commit *seppuko*, which they did.'

'Unlike the Merry Men.'

'Hai.'

'So what are you saying? You're going to fulfil a *giri* to your *on* man no matter what the consequences?'

Shinichro blinked at me, apparently unmoved.

'OK. Let me see if I've got this right so far. Hiroshi Sano, alias Al Sony, loses a briefcase full of drams to Charlie East in Vegas. He got the chips from you. Right?'

No answer.

'Not you? Your *on* man, then. That's it, isn't it? That's the business you and he were discussing the other night.'

No answer.

'So he's so charged up that he lost them, he tries to get them, and his blessed *kao*, back the only way he knows how. He sets up a poker game, but ... in the *meantime* steals the things back.'

'Who says he stole them back?'

Shinichro was holding his glass rather more firmly.

'Who says Sano stole them back?' he said.

'Charlie. And Pal Kuthy.'

'The gangster who was here with you?'

'I don't think he's a gangster.'

'He had a gun. How do they know this? That he stole.'

'They reckon he wanted Charlie to lose face by having to with-

78

draw from the game because the chips had gone. Charlie didn't, so Sano came along anyway and played tight, like he didn't want to win anything back. He didn't need to, he knew they were stolen because he had them.'

'Do you think he has them?'

'I'm not sure now.'

'Why?'

'Because I reckon he had customers back at his hotel, and if he had the chips to deliver, why run?'

No answer.

'Unless he's playing both ends against the middle.'

Shinichro didn't understand.

'Jerking off the supplier and the buyer and keeping the million for himself.'

I looked up across at him and I could see myself reflected in the pool-black pupils of his dark eyes. Maybe he could see himself in mine, in the scorched blue of cornflowers. I covered my face for a moment with my hands.

'I am very sorry about the baby, Georgina,' he said.

'Sure,' I said, grasping the Scotch bottle. 'Have another drink and we can have a good cry together.'

He didn't cry, of course. He touched my hands and I cried, and when he'd finished his drink and gone I cried some more. I didn't cry for too long because there comes a time when it's all cried out and you're dry as dust. I got to drinking and thinking, not about the baby that might be, but about other things. About Shinichro's *on* man, and about the favours *he* owed to have to pull in one like this from Shinichro.

This time the Scotch and the wine didn't help me sleep. I was afraid of the night, of the sodium orange dark spread out against the London sky beyond the curtained blackness of my room. The sweat lay on my face like a dog's tongue and I kept my eyes open wide to watch for strange shadows, little hands creeping inward, shapes without mouths. I saw empty barrelled guns, and guns with bullets, bullets and babies. I wondered which one was for me as I lay upon my back and waited, dozing and alert to every click and shuffle until daylight edged like a cataract over the night and the clock radio roused me.

*

I called the Intercontinental Hotel straight away but reception couldn't get an answer from Hiroshi's room. I called Shinichro at work but he hadn't showed. I called the Intercontinental again just before I left the flat, and reception said that Mr Sano had left a message that he would be in between four and five. It was odd. I hadn't asked if I could meet him, just whether he was there. I imagined that I could be the last person he would want to see, then I remembered the gun and thought that it must give a person no end of confidence. I was still thinking about what I could say to him and whether I should even try as the train rumbled through the tunnel into Liverpool Street. My mind was wrestling with the problem as I wandered through tarpaulin tunnels and builders' debris towards the Broadgate complex. There was a band playing for the city folk who came there to sit in the sun and relax between deals. Charlie called out to me from somewhere in the sky.

'They skate here in the winter, you know,' Charlie said as we looked down on the circle of brick built in between the walkways. I didn't answer. I nodded down at Debbie's golden head bobbing through the crowd below us.

'Double booked, are we?' I said.

''Fraid so,' he said and called out to her. She looked up crossly, irritated that we were over here and she was over there.

'What's up with her?' I said.

'She doesn't like you.'

'I don't like her much either.'

'She thinks you lost her her big chance.'

'Big chance to do what?'

'Marry a millionaire, I suppose.'

'Marry? Charlie, you didn't. You didn't tell her you would, did you?'

'Course I did.'

'Did you mean it?'

'Why not?'

'Well, if you have to ask you're sunk, baby. Swimming with the fishes and that old trout in particular.'

Charlie stretched out his lanky arms to welcome his unsmiling fiancée.

'Have a care, George, you're talking about the woman I love,' he said under his breath.

We walked down to where another suited and shirtsleeved crowd had gathered, drinking gins and beers in the sunshine that streamed down between the cleft of the city blocks, rising up on either side of us like the cliffs of a Babylonian ziggurat. Debbie asked if didn't I think it all looked brutally derivative. She couldn't remember the name of the architect. I said it looked OK, what with the hanging gardens and the bar, and we said nothing more to each other until Charlie came dancing and hustling through, carrying our drinks easily in the long web of his fingers. Debbie had the spritzer, I had a bottle of Mexican beer, the flow of which was impeded by a dubious wedge of lemon, and Charlie had a foaming pint of Best. When we'd all taken a swallow of our respective poisons, Charlie wiped his lips on the back of Debbie's hand, and got an ungentle shove in the chest for being such an old romantic.

'OK,' I said. 'I have two theories.'

Both looked at me attentively, Debbie turning her cool Ray-Ban Wayfarers towards me and flicking at her hair.

'If Sano has got the chips, then he saw someone he didn't want knowing that at the hotel, because, as soon as we pulled into the foyer and he clapped eyes on these fellows, he made the cabbie drive on.'

'Where to?' said Debbie.

'Never mind that, what's the second theory?' said Charlie.

'Where to?' said Debbie.

'To my place in Bow, only the cab wouldn't take us,' I said.

'So where, then?'

'Nowhere. We walked. He caught a cab, I went home, eventually.'

'Why your place?'

My, she was persistent.

'I had no choice.'

'Why?'

'He had a gun. That's how scared he was. I can't tell you how scared I was.'

That satisfied her and they were silent until Charlie felt able to ask again.

'What's the second theory?'

'Sano *hasn't* got the drams. The guys waiting for him were the ones who've been expecting delivery since we were in Vegas.'

'Together,' Debbie said.

'What?'

'You and Charlie were in Vegas together.'

'Yes and no. We only met up on the way home, OK?' I looked at her, then at Charlie and wished that I had a very large fly swat handy. Charlie held up his hands for us to stop bitching.

'So if he hasn't got the drams, who has?' he said.

'How about the gentleman who said that he had?' his beautiful and charming fiancée replied. Charlie started to grin like a farm-boy and I realized then that Debbie was in fact holding the large fly swat that I had wanted to use earlier. The impact of her words stunned me like the flick of a sinewy wrist on the back of my head. Pal Kuthy. Why not?

'Funny how he was on the plane,' Charlie said.

'Yeah. Funny how he cosied up to you,' I said.

'And you,' he replied.

'Now, wait a minute. Don't start that again.'

'Have I said anything?'

'Let's think about this, then. If he *has* got the drams, why hasn't he gone? What's he hanging around for?' I said.

The two of them looked at me, smug, knowing looks in their eyes. I wasn't going to rise to the bait.

'Maybe those guys in the hotel have got tabs on everyone now. Maybe if Pal took off they would know he was the one who's got their delivery. Yes?' I said.

'I think we should find out a bit more about him ... don't you, Charlie?' said Debbie. She raised an eyebrow at him and then turned to look at me, her brown eyes wide and innocent.

'He seemed pretty keen on you, Georgina. I think *you* should find out more about him. You could do it easily, couldn't you, with your talents ... as a journalist. I mean, this is a great story for you, better than a picture caption, surely?'

I hated the way she was hogging that fly swat. I started to move away from the pair of them just to stop myself saying or doing anything that might spoil this pair's plans for a happy and fertile marriage but Charlie circled his long fingers around my wrist.

'So if Pal has the loot where does that leave sweet little Al?' he said.

Well ... it left him dead, didn't it?

Chapter Eight

I phoned Charlie that same afternoon from the Intercontinental, after the police had finished with me.

'Do you mean dead, as in drunk, tired or as in not breathing?' he said.

'Dead, as in Kennedy.'

'Shit. How do you know?'

'Police. They found him in his hotel room.'

'Tell me it was natural causes, George.'

'Sorry, Charlie.'

'How, then?'

'Well, let's put it this way, he had his Gucci shoes on but it wasn't any way I'd like to go.'

'Don't tell me.'

Which meant he really wanted me to.

'He was taking a bath.'

'So it was an accident, is that what you're saying?'

'Not quite. Someone had stuck a Braun electric in there with him.'

'So why didn't the stupid bastard try to get out?'

'His legs were broken.'

'Jesus Christ.'

He thought for a moment.

'I think I could have got out of a wired bath even with my legs broken.'

'Not even you could have got out with your fingers bust as well. He'd made a hell of an effort, and, before you ask, his mouth was taped up.'

'Jesus Christ.'

'There's more. Whoever did it stuck the appliance on a timer.'

'Set it?'

'Yes. Set it to switch on a few hours later. Left our Al there to think about it. Now what sort of a person does that, Charlie?'

He couldn't tell me but he could imagine. Someone meaner than a junk yard dog.

'Feeling good now, Charlie?'

'What do you think?'

'I don't know but I think I'm out of here. The police will probably give you a call to ask you some questions but as for me I've had enough.'

I'd had enough of him, of Debbie and of the police, who'd set me up with the meeting at the Intercontinental because they wanted to know how come I knew Hiroshi Sano. I'd told Charlie what I'd told them – that I was a journalist and that Hiroshi had bet some computer chips in a poker game and lost and hadn't they seen the story in the papers. I told them that Charlie had won the chips and had had them stolen, but I didn't tell them about Pal or his gun, or Shinichro. I didn't tell Charlie, either. They could find that out by themselves.

Six months earlier and a lead like this would have had the same effect on me as a T-bone on a starving dog. This time I found my appetite had gone. Instead of that insistent internal twitching that I was familiar with, the one that set my tongue licking around my teeth with lusty expectation, there was a deep, dark well of unease. I had no stomach for the fight. I couldn't see the point in it, of wanting to find out when I could sit back, close my eyes and stay out of it. I rang Richard and told him I was going to the country.

'You've missed Derby Day, dear. What's on?'

'Nothing. I'm leaving town. I need a break.'

'What about the story?'

'What story?'

'The Korean who bet his drams and lost.'

'Can't trace him.'

'That's funny.'

'Why?'

'I rang Charlie and he said the guy wanted to play him again to get them back but that he'd been turned over in the meantime.'

'He said that?'

'Yeah, I can run that as part of a bigger piece I've got in mind on chip thefts in general. Did you know that Compaq and Sun Microsystems have taken a hit on their fourth quarter because of it? Western Digital reckons it's been robbed of three million pounds' worth this year. Did you know that?'

'Well . . .'

'The local district attorney's office reckons that chip theft is running to between five and six point five million pounds a year.'

My heart felt as if it had almost stopped beating.

'You there?'

'Yes.'

'There's another thing. This business about quotas.'

'What?'

'I've got a contact who swears the legitimate chip manufacturers are pouring billions into the grey market by underquoting their yields.'

'You mean telling their customers the factories are yielding fifty per cent, and it's really seventy-five?'

'Spot on.'

'Twenty-five per cent sells at spot market prices instead of scheduled?'

'Very good, Georgina.'

'Great.'

'Maybe you *should* go to the country, George. Have a break.'

'I haven't been well.'

'You must have been absolutely ga-ga to miss that little lot. It's a story with legs.'

I put the phone down slowly, watched by Esther who was standing by the door, waiting. I was finished.

'You OK?' she said.

I nodded.

'Down below?'

Despite the ache like a graze in my belly, I nodded. Like all medical people, Esther spoke directionally. She said down below when she meant all the portals to your urino-genital tract. She asked if your bowels had moved or if you'd passed urine. She tried to make me feel better. She said that I should not be hasty in my spirit to be angry, for anger resteth in the bosom of fools. I told her that I *was* a fool and I *was* angry, God help me, but I didn't tell her that I was afraid. I was afraid of everyone now, of Shinichro and his *on* man, of Pal, who had a gun, of whoever had made Hiroshi run, even though he had a gun too, and of whoever it was who had broken his limbs and had made him wait to die.

'I'm going away for a couple of days,' I said.

'You need more than a couple of days. Go to your mother for a month. Have a rest. See a doctor. I'll look after this place, keep an eye out.'

Esther didn't understand. If I went to my mother's house I'd have to meet my father, and he always had a number of objections to my visits, not least of which was the sharing of his J&B Rare. It'd start off well, all hugs and kisses and big dinners but then the conversations would begin. He'd jab the sucky end of his yellow and cream meerschaum in my direction and start. This time, he'd remind me of the job that I didn't have any more before going back to the missed opportunity of a university career. He'd tell me to put my divorce behind me and all that messy business with the black man, Warren, and *Technology Week*. He'd tell me to start again, with a decent career. Anything but working with newspapers, why couldn't I try radio? The atmosphere would grow thick as lard and he'd relent a little, ask what I was doing with myself and never want to hear. Who could blame him? I didn't want to tell him, but he had to ask and because I had no suitable answers I would snap and snarl like a cornered mongoose. We'd rage at each other and then we wouldn't speak. My mother would stand and sigh in the kitchen. He always wanted things fixed, my father. He wanted them organized, written down and sorted. I was a great disappointment to him. I made a lot of mistakes, some more funny than bad, but he couldn't laugh at a mistake. To do that, you had to be able to admit to one. My sweet silly mother tried to keep us both happy. I'd been grateful to her for her defence as a child, loved her for it, but now it rankled. I wanted her to get up one day and whack the old man on the head with a newspaper, one that *she* wanted to read. I wanted her to reach forward and ruffle him up, to stop bending over backwards in search of a quiet life. I called them anyhow, but they weren't there. Then I remembered that they were away. I'd got a card from the Lakes.

It took four trains and three hours to get to my friend Delia's house in Hampshire. She'd been pleased to hear from me, surprised, but happy to get my call. She said she'd pick me up from the station and she arrived in a smart red BMW with two sun-speckled kids in the back.

'You look great,' she lied. 'Love the hair.' The hair had grown a bit since the last time I'd seen her and was curling around my ears in berry black twists. It was Delia who looked great. She had a light summery sun-bed tan and long golden hair that swirled about in the warm breeze. Her skin had a glow to it that signified wholesome food, low-fat spread, fruit juice and fresh air. Her children were just like her in smaller dimensions, clinging to her shyly as she introduced me. I stretched out my hand but they closed their eyes as if a touch from my dry palm would contaminate their pudgy little fingers. I took my hand back quickly, hoping they couldn't see that I had horrible secrets, terrible plans. They giggled and scampered under their mother's swirling skirts, holding their hands behind their backs like aeroplane wings, while Delia laughed indulgently and told them not to be silly.

David, her husband, worked in town and commuted to his office in Baker Street where he was the creative director of some advertising agency. The company had four ridiculous names that used to belong somewhere else in some other combination and David's was one of them. Money was no object now, if ever it had been to Delia. She used to be a copywriter. She'd done the 'Get Hard' campaign for Muscle Computers, which is how I met her. In those days she used to wear leather skirts the size of a gaucho's glove, a diamond in her nose, three in her ear and she drank like a fish. She had her own expansible expense account and whenever she met Warren, my dear old friend Warren, she used to pinch his bum and ask him if he had any coke. He thought she was OK, if a little loud, and she embarrassed him once by asking if he was screwing me, and if not why not. He wasn't, but he'd wanted to. I knew that now. Funny, how everyone seemed to notice but me.

I tried to talk but Delia was talking too much, swinging the car around the lanes too fast and every now and then looking behind and shouting at her children to keep them from fighting. When we got to her house, I stood in her enormous sunny kitchen, with its sleek grey German cabinets and household appliances, and moved from side to side as she whirred about chopping, slicing, rinsing and shouting, shouting and spanking, until it was tea-time and that was over and she could open the back door and loose the kids from the apron strings. They were like yo-yos. I hadn't done anything but drink a couple of cups of coffee but I grew weary as she clattered on, clearing up, loading the dishwasher, answering the telephone, writing things down on a board in the kitchen, until I had to sit down to avoid the giddy whirl of it all. She seemed only to have wiped her hands dry when the children were back again, asking for things, asking me things, like could I make sandcastles and what was that on my shirt? I read the little boy a book about dragons, while the little girl rolled Play-Doh into grey irregular balls, demanding constant praise for her efforts until Delia announced it was bathtime and the hectic to-ing and fro-ing started again. When the quiet came, it edged itself into the house like a blanket and Delia sighed and pointed to the drinks cabinet.

Her back garden spread out in a vast ellipse of green shaded by trees and honeysuckle. We sat out on the patio, in the cool stillness of it, in a swinging chair under a striped canopy and drank a little, and then a lot, of white wine.

'So where's David?' I said.

'Plays squash three nights a week.'

'So this is it?' I said.

'This is it,' she replied.

'How'd you like it?'

'How would *you* like it? It's shit.'

I drank a little more wine.

'You love the kids, though.'

'Yes, I love my kids.'

'And David?'

'Not as much as I used to.'

'Oh.'

'He had to have me, remember? Crazy about me. Still thinks he is. But he knows where I am now. I'm here, aren't I? It's settled. I'm home. Home alone, a housekeeper with attitude.'

She drank more wine this time, a big swallow of it, and we stared gloomily out at the garden that was still bright with evening sunlight, heavy with velvety roses, yellow and cream, the dark earth lightly covered with starry pinks.

'I'm pregnant, Delia,' I said. She turned and touched my hand, looking at me straight for the first time. 'I'm sorry.'

I nodded and the teardrops began to fall dutifully down the sides of my nose. They hadn't really needed to, I'd cried enough, frankly. I'd only told her about it to get it out of the way. If I'd been honest with myself, I didn't need to talk about it any more. The truth was, it was the lost story that was irritating the hell out of me. It was Richard putting one over on me, and me caving in like a duff soufflé. I thought Delia would understand about the baby, she'd be sympathetic and supportive and I could hide behind it, like a crocodile behind its smile.

'We've lost touch, haven't we? I thought you were still fooling around,' she said and added, more to herself than me, 'I was hoping you were, in fact.'

'I am. I was. It was an accident,' I said.

She put down her glass. 'You still live in Bow, in that flat, don't you?'

'No. The one upstairs. Warren's. It's nicer.'

'He was nice. His baby?'

'No.'

'You know whose it was, I presume?'

'Yes.'

'And?'

'Nothing doing.'

'So what are you going to do, keep it?'

'No. I don't know. Can I? I think I might like to.'

'Supported by whom? You can't have kids like that. You have them like *this*.'

She swung her hand around the garden and up at the house.

'Could you have done it by yourself?' I said.

'No, I couldn't. Oh, *now*, yes, just about. But not then. Now I know, I bloody know something about it, I know what's required and my kids aren't babies any more. Even so, it would be hard. David does *something*, after all. I've got him. It isn't all right when you've got no one. What the fuck do they call it? No extended family. Everyone thinks it's normal that Mum looks after her kids, but it's not normal anywhere else in the world. Everywhere else, everyone looks after the kids. That's what a family is. It isn't a man and a wife, two kids and a couple of babysitters and it certainly isn't a single woman stuck in a box in the sky. Who've you got, Georgina?'

'I told you, no one but me.'

'No one, and no one wants you with a kid, do they? They don't want you in any decent jobs or decent restaurants, that's for sure, or a bar. They don't want you out at night. They want you in McDonald's and supermarkets, and clinics, that's where they want you. How are you going to live?'

'That's pretty easy. I've a bank balance well in the black, and I can do freelance.'

'OK. Let's see. Do the work, if you can get someone half decent to look after your kid, then you stop and look after it. Never a break and bang goes your independence, your availability, your choice. I've lost my independence the easy way. Look at me. And because of me, David still has his. In fact, he's better off. He gets sex, sometimes, and someone to wash and iron his shirts. That's what really gets me. He's OK. He's got something else to think of. My whole way of thinking is no good to me now. I never do anything that needs it. You don't need a GCSE to do what I do and every bugger knows it.'

'You've got your kids.'

She laughed, bitterly at first and then fondly.

'Yeah. I've got my kids. A woman's compensation. I love them, really,' she said.

Christ, and I thought I had problems. It wasn't me who needed a trip to Hampshire to hide from danger but Delia who needed a trip to London to find it. She needed to cruise around for a bit, hang out, like only Delia could and people round these parts had never seen her do. She needed to go and see that she couldn't go back, that her life had changed so much that she wouldn't want to, but that maybe she could get halfway somewhere else. She grasped the bottle by the neck and poured the last of it into our glasses.

'What the hell,' she said. 'You can't compare motherhood to writing ads, can you? Working with those crazy people. It's out-rageous.'

She was right. It was. I knew now what she really wanted to talk about.

'I'm working on a great story,' I said.

Delia slapped her hand on my leg and turned to me, her eager eyes opened wide. I told her. I made it sound like everything could be in retrospect, a real wheeze, and the next day I made a call to Richard from her breakfast room.

'I lied to you about the Korean,' I said.

'George, you cow. I knew you were up to something,' he said.

I heard a door shut close by and listened for the shuffle of weary feet along the corridor. I opened my door before she rang the bell.

'So you're here,' she said, folding her arms and tapping her foot.

'That's how come I opened the door, Esther.'

'People've been knocking for you.'

'Who?'

'Chinaman, and a tall, good-looking one with a big moustache.'

'Come in.'

Esther said she'd used her key to check on the place while I'd been away, see if it was OK.

'There was a big man, too. Fat, you know. Nice face. Ask me, he looked like a policeman.'

'Straw-coloured hair?'

'That's him.'

D.I. Robert Falk. I closed my eyes and smiled.

'You know, Esther? Weeping may endureth the night but joy cometh in the bloody morning.'

I phoned him while Esther made some tea and observations on the Good Book. She called out that she'd left a few things in the fridge and that she had to go because she was on the late shift that night. Robert's phone wasn't answering and as Esther walked by she put her arms around my shoulders and squeezed. I heard his voice, soft, polite.

'Robert?' I said.

'Mrs Powers. I've been trying to contact you.'

'My neighbour told me.'

'I wondered if you'd be free for supper one night this week. There's a little Japanese restaurant . . .'

'Not Japanese, no. It upsets my stomach,' I said.

'Aah. Somewhere of your choice, then?'

'I'll think of somewhere but in the meantime could you help me out?'

He said he'd try, of course, but when I told him that I was on to a story about stolen drams he said that that wasn't his department. He tracked viruses and hackers, but not chip thieves. The insubstantial Met and City Company Fraud unit, Computer Section, was only interested in penetration or use of computers illegally, not in the theft of them or their itty bitty insides.

'I need some information,' I said.

'Do we have a date?'

'We have a date.'

'Names?'

'Hiroshi Sano, Pal Kuthy . . . and AO Electronix. How about a fish supper?'

'Excellent,' he said, and put the phone down.

I walked over to the desk in the corner of the living room. There were a few papers gathering dust in the in-tray and an old spiral notebook with the scribbled notes of my last story underlined with a thick pen. The computer had been used. I played a couple of games from time to time and checked into a couple of bulletin boards and an electronic mailbox for messages, but I hadn't written anything in a while. I turned over an old press release and wrote 'Components' at the top of the blank page and pulled my contact book out of the desk drawer. I made a list. In about half an hour I had fifteen telephone numbers, but it took two cigarettes before I could dial the first number and say, 'Hello, my name's Georgina Powers.' I wasn't used to it any more. I asked them all the same questions in the end. Had they ever delivered memory chips to Pal Kuthy's company. AO Electronix, and did the name Pal Kuthy mean anything? Only one had heard of AO Electronix, and had bought 256K drams from a Hungarian dealer on a regular basis. He couldn't recall any Pal Kuthy. I asked if it was legit and he said it was no big deal. Eastern Europe had excess capacity. He took stuff from a Soviet factory, too, working out of Zelonograd, Russia's own Silicon Valley, forty miles north of Moscow. Even though the market for 256K drams was shrinking, he could shift them at a great price because of the shortage in one-megabit drams. I'd heard of that, hadn't I? Manufacturers wanting to upgrade had to make do with what they could get, and the only US chipmaker manufacturing 256K chips had started charging prices in keeping with its monopoly, even to its regular customers. Everyone was looking to make a deal with anyone who could make one. Dollars, that's what Kuthy had said. Dollars. I was writing all this down when the front door creaked open wide.

'Get anything good, mama?' he said.

I tried to keep cool. I didn't know how long he'd been there or how much he'd heard.

'I'm working on a story. Did I leave the door open?'

'Your neighbour did.'

I wasn't sure. I didn't trust Pal, the man with the gun, the man who'd followed us from Vegas. He picked up my cigarettes and lit one, drawing the smoke in deep and blowing it out with a big smile.

'I get a kiss, yes?'

I stared at him. 'I don't think so.'

He kissed me anyway, bending his face over mine and pulling me into him with his arm around my waist. I thought his tongue would choke me while his hand squeezed and pumped at my breasts but I kept my eyes open, my mouth dull, and waited until his dark lashes flicked up and he drew back. It always works.

'No?' he said.

'No.'

He shrugged and sat down on my desk, lifting up my notebook and flicking through it.

'OK. Ask me. What do you want to know?'

'Where's your gun?' I said.

He lifted out his arm and I could see it in a sort of soft holster in the lining of his jacket.

'Why do you have one?'

'If you were in a position to buy a million dollars' worth of chips when every motherfucker out there wants them, wouldn't you?'

I shook my head. 'A certain type of person carries a gun,' I said.

Pal raised one balletic eyebrow and smiled, his wicked blue eyes sparkling with enjoyment.

'Yes? You know this?' he said.

'Yes. The type who knows how to use it,' I replied.

Pal pulled the gun out. It wasn't big but I supposed it could do the business. He put it playfully to his head pulling a desperate face but he didn't pull the trigger, he jerked his arm out straight and the cold muzzle pressed against my forehead, cool and hard.

I could see the gun, almost feel the cold metal penetrating the bone, but I was watching his arm bulging from its tucked-up sleeve, dark hairs twisting around, magnified in my sight. I focused as best I could on the primed muscle, waiting for the first twitch and the sound that I wouldn't hear. He didn't fire; he pushed and my head jerked back with the force. I grabbed the edge of my desk to keep upright while Pal tucked the gun back inside his jacket and said, 'There are a lot of strange people in this town.'

I was still holding on to the desk, my legs shaking. I thought I'd passed urine, as they say, but it was sweat, trickling down all over me. Delia should have seen me now.

'It's not fucking loaded, is it?' I said.

My words. Reminded me of a little book that a friend used to hang in his toilet. It was called *Famous Last Words* and it began with 'What happens when I press this . . .?' Indeed, I felt that was following in that glorious asinine tradition as Pal took the weapon out again. He stuck a hand into the lining of the other side of his jacket like a man looking for a credit card and pulled out something that looked like a metal tube, which he slipped like a sheath on the nose of the gun. He lifted a long finger to his pursed lips. Hush. Hush. I shouldn't make a sound. He beckoned me into the bedroom, walking backwards and smiling at me. I followed and lay down on the bed like he told me to. I even let him climb on top of me, stick his knees on my shoulders and put his hand on the side of my head so that my cheek was flat against the soft pillow, pressed down like a thumb in marshmallow. I saw the gun coming down out of the corner of my eye, and heard the zip, zip at the back of my head.

Chapter Nine

I wasn't dead but I didn't feel quite as alive as I should have done given that I was still breathing. I could hear it still, in my head, and I was panting like a birthing woman, not screaming, gasping like it was the first time I'd drawn breath, and my heart was jumping like a steam hammer. Pal dismounted, sat on the side of the bed and ran his hand up my leg.

'I'm not a bad guy,' he said.

'No. You're a real sweetheart.'

'You asked the question.'

'So you could have just said "Oh yes, it is", you know, in the way that guys like you know how to make people believe them.'

He shrugged.

'Give me a cigarette,' I said.

Pal reached into his magic jacket for a packet and tapped one out. He flicked me a light and gave me his hand so I could heave myself up off the bed, a real gentleman. My pillow had two neat holes in it like cigarette burns and the shock I had felt gave way to petty irritation. The white linen was almost new, not my choice, but new none the less. Pal followed me out of the room, still holding the gun.

'You heard about Sano?' I said, pouring myself a large gin and a little tonic and trying not to let the bottle tap too hard on the glass. I usually took Scotch for shock but the stock had yet to be replaced.

'Charlie told me.'

'You didn't know, then?'

Pal shook his head and said, 'Charlie thinks I should stick around. I'm not so sure.'

'Charlie – and Debbie – think you have the drams.'

He laughed.

'That you're just waiting around until things cool down, then you'll leave.'

'Sano had them, for sure. Whoever killed him has them now.'

'Didn't sound to me like the sort of death you get in a robbery. Sounded like a punishment. You know, *pour encourager les autres*.'

'That is why I carry this.'

He lifted the weapon. The obvious truth that the priority usage of a gun with a silencer wouldn't necessarily be defence was of no comfort and this was no time to contradict him. My hands were still shaking but I was doing all right, I could talk.

'You followed Charlie here, didn't you? From Vegas.'

Pal leaned back, resting his buttocks on the back of the sofa. He crossed his legs and folded his hairy arms. The gun was back in its pocket.

'No. I followed you, mama.'

'Liar.'

He shrugged, smiling again, always thinking things were funny.

'You think your man, you think Japan did it? The tough guy? You think he has the drams now?'

That raised the stakes. Pal had only met Shinichro once but he had said it. I hadn't wanted anyone to say that. I hadn't said it yet, not even to myself. I'd thought about it, and I'd shaken my head. Despite everything, he couldn't do such a thing, but I couldn't be sure. I'd lied to Shinichro about the baby, said that it had gone, but that was just an extra, it was the fact that Sano might be ripping him off, him and his *on* man, that would have hardened his heart. I tried to picture him as I knew him, like the photo on his business card, happy and smiling, a hard-working *sarariman*. I pictured him making love, moist shaded eyes looking down at me in the half-light, golden hands stroking my pale skin. I saw the man who brought me little presents of fruit, wrapped in fancy baskets, apologizing for the unworthiness of the gift. It couldn't have been him, it couldn't have been the man who loved me, or even the man who had hit me, who had thrown Pal to the ground and splintered a glass against the wall. Whoever had killed Sano was not warm, or peevish or raging; he had been cold enough to make Sano wait for it.

'Why would *he* have them, or want them?' I said.

Pal shrugged.

'Come on, let's go out. What do you want to do, eat, drink? I know you want to eat. Let's eat.'

He was smiling, of course, but not answering my question. He wasn't going to tell me how he made the connection between Sano and Shinichro. He was going to make *me* wait for it. I was afraid, and as Esther would have said, the fear of the Lord is the beginning of wisdom.

'I don't want to do anything with you.'

'Oh, mama, you know that's not true.'

'Don't call me mama.'

'No?'

'I'm not your mama.'

'You're going to be somebody's, no?'

'No. Not now.'

He got up and lifted my chin, gently turning it so he could look at my face.

'No? The other night? Sano?' he said.

'It wasn't meant to be. No big deal.'

He kept looking at me, right into my eyes, but I held my gaze until he took his fingers from my face and said, 'Let's go, eh? I want to eat.'

The garbage smell from the chute hung around the stairwell and the metallic lift reeked of stale urine tainted with disinfectant. Someone had sprayed the dull glinting walls with fast angular strokes of paint. The self-promoting signature said 'Ziggy' in fully colour and was so big that it dwarfed the dirty pictures and the misspelt crudities beneath it. Pal stood with his hands in his pockets, looking at the bright zigzag name and reading the smut. Every now and then he tipped his head from side to side to get a better perspective.

'With money, you could move from this place,' he said as the doors of the lift slid open. The sunlight shone down brightly on to the concrete steps that led from the gloom to the empty street. Pal slipped on his Zeiss shades and looked around.

'I have money,' I said.

'How much? A million?'

'Where do you want to go, Pal?' I said.

'To eat, I told you.'

'I don't.'

'Let's go anyway.'

He went to move but stopped and stayed where he was, looking around again like an animal sniffing the breeze, and then down at me. I wasn't moving either. His lips pouted forward for a moment and then spread out wide in a big smile.

'Come on,' he said.

There was a minicab firm just around the corner by a short line of steel-gridded shops. As we walked along the pavement I noticed a van move. It was dark grey with metallic rear windows and it cruised slowly along the road before passing us and turning the corner. I half expected its tinted electric windows to edge down and whatever terror it contained to point its steely eyes towards us. I stared at the van, watching its smooth progress along the road before it turned right with no indication. Pal kept walking, loose-limbed and easy, towards the corner where he stopped to cup his hands over a cigarette and light it, jacket swayed back, broad shoulders hunched, hips forward and wisps of his thinning hair catching in the light wind.

'See that?' I called.

He looked to the right where it had gone.

'Friends of yours?'

He smiled. 'I hope,' he said.

We took the fish and chips into Victoria Park. It was a nice day, hot enough for East End girls to be bare legged in short stone-washed denim and white high heels. Pushchairs were lined up by the pond like shopping trolleys and fat ducks collected around the toddlers for the stale white bread that they held in their little hands. Pal's gold-ringed fingers picked at the vinegary chips as he looked around and said, 'Very nice.'

'Very Santa Barbara, don't you think?'

'No, Balaton.'

'On a clear day you can see what's on the other side,' I said.

Pal laughed and licked the salt from his fingers.

'Why did you follow Charlie, Pal? What are you really here for?' I said.

'For what I say, the drams. I buy them from him, keep some for my company, resell the rest for dollars.'

'You ever bought anything from Al Sony?'

He swallowed some fish and shook his head.

'Did you know him?'

'I knew of him.'

'OK. So how long have you been dealing?'

'In drams?'

'Yes.'

'Years. Many years.'

'Sources?'

'For your story?'

I didn't answer.

'I tell you something, OK? I make computers. That's true. I also sell chips, some reverse engineered, some not, to the West, for dollars. First 64K, then 256K but no one megabit, not yet. That's it. That's me.'

'You play poker.'

'That's true.'

'So you bluff.'

'That's true.'

'To buy the drams from Charlie you'd be paying top dollar. I don't get it.'

'Not quite top dollar, but close. He's giving a good discount, if he ever gets them back.'

'But where's the resale value for you? Where's the profit there? It's not that much – for all this, to go to so much trouble.'

'The price is still going up, no? Pay dollars, sell for a few dollars more. I need dollars. Hungary needs dollars. You don't get democracy without dollars.'

'It's peaked.'

'In the West, maybe.'

Pal wiped his oily hands on a napkin. He folded it and rubbed it over his mouth, taking care to clean the edges of his fine moustache.

'This is a dangerous business,' he said. 'A man dies in his bath, in terrible pain. This man made a big mistake. He didn't deliver. He took *what was not his.*'

He tapped my leg when he said this, made sure I'd taken the point. I put what was left of my lunch on the bench. My appetite was not what it was. Pal leaned forward with his elbows on his thighs, looking at the rippling lake. There was a muscle twitching

99

on his jawline like he was chewing gum with his teeth clamped.

'You've got them, haven't you? You're setting me up,' I said.

'Say Sano did not have them. Let's think. It is more likely that you have them than me. You had a key.'

'What would I do with them?'

He laughed then.

'What I would do with them. Sell them. Why not? Your friend Charlie owes you big money, doesn't he?'

I was surprised that he should know that but I tried not to show it as Pal put his long fingers into the top pocket of his creased linen-look jacket and pulled out a white card with the picture of a Japanese businessman on the front and his name and title written on it in both English and Kanji.

'Or maybe give them back to Daddy?'

I took the card from his fingers and looked down at Shinichro's conscientious face. I knew I didn't have the damned drams. It was the only thing I was sure of. I was sure Shinichro didn't either but not one hundred per cent, now, not even fifty. If Pal had the drams, then he *was* setting me up, setting Shinichro up, too, for all I knew. We would have the horror that Sano had tried to avoid on our backs, while he took off from Heathrow with that smug grin on his face and a briefcase full of drams that he had got for free, who knows how. If he hadn't got the drams, why had he jumped to this conclusion about me? Because he'd picked up Shinichro's card from my dressing table? *He* was the one who had said that Sano had them. Sano had played a tight game to prove it, too. *I* knew that Shinichro had probably supplied Sano with drams, but how could Pal know? I had thought that Sano had stolen them back from Charlie and had been conning Shinichro for more, playing clever. Whoever had killed Sano had the drams. Had to have. That's what I told Pal.

'Then we'll have to find him, eh? Maybe he's still at the hotel. Conveniently, I have a room there. Let's go, it's getting hot out here,' he said.

He got up and I looked around to see the van again, the dark grey motor pulling past the main gate towards the mini-roundabout about one hundred yards away. Pal pushed his sunglasses up his nose and put his hand out for me. I took it. Once I

100

was standing, he held my arm out, as if he were displaying me, looking me up and down, smiling just a little.

'The little T-shirt and the tight black skirt, I like, but the workman's boots, ay yay ya.'

'Yeah, well, don't you think you need a medallion with that little ensemble?'

He looked down at himself. 'I have one, but people try to steal it,' he said.

'I'll bet.'

I was looking over his shoulder for the van as I spoke, but it had gone.

'I have to make a phone call,' I said.

'At the hotel,' he replied.

There was no way that I was going to get away.

The young man in reception at the Intercontinental didn't like the look of me. He didn't like the look of Pal either but at least Pal was paying the bill. I looked to him like the sort of professional girl who goes to a hotel room for the afternoon, and, as we all know, there are only two sorts who do that: whores and journalists. Pal spoke cheerfully to the young man before swinging the room key in his face and catching it, three inches from the boy's sniffy nose. He lowered his gaze before Pal's foxy smile and said, 'Lifts to the right, sir, madam.'

'I don't want to go upstairs. Please, Pal, I haven't got what you want,' I said.

'Upstairs we can shower, have a bath.'

I didn't want a bath. I could smell the salt and vinegar on my fingers, and taste the fish batter on my lips, but I didn't want a bath, not in the Intercontinental. He'd got me so far but here I could make a fuss.

'The police are all over this place,' I said.

'They were,' he replied. 'Not now.'

The bell rang and the lift doors opened.

'I have to make a phone call,' I said.

Pal raised an eyebrow.

'Work,' I said.

I made the call in a booth, watched by the disapproving eyes of the young man in reception. I should have put the phone down,

101

walked up to the geek and wiped the sneer off his baby face. I should have told him that Pal had a gun in his jacket and what did he think about that? And wasn't it about time they installed proper Jacuzzis in this crummy hotel instead of having to rely on Braun electrics? But I was in a hurry. I wanted to call Shinichro, call Robert, but while Pal was sitting down beside me I could only call Richard. It was press day and he was busy.

'I'm in the Intercontinental with a *contact*.'

'Oh yes?'

'Any messages?'

He mispronounced the name. 'Shinichro Saito, is that right?'

'What did he say?'

'He couldn't get you at home. Called this number off an old business card. Call him.'

'Where?'

'Said you had the number.'

'Richard . . .'

'Yes?'

'I'm in the Intercontinental.'

Pal was doubled over with laughter. When he finally stood up he had to rest his hand on my shoulder to support himself.

'Help,' he squeaked. 'Help. Help.'

He took my trembling arm just above the elbow and we walked towards the lift. As he swaggered across the marbled floor he clicked his fingers at the young man in reception and called out loud and clear: 'Some coffee, and cakes. Coffee and cakes for Mr Kuthy. 251.'

Anyone who advertised like that couldn't have murder in mind. Pal didn't want to kill or torture me. He wanted to tease me, he wanted to soap me all over and have sex with me. He wanted to feed me cakes and coffee and lick my fingers. It was time he wanted to kill.

'You bleed a little, eh?'

'Not much. It's OK,' I said, my arm over my eyes. Pal's moustache was tickling my stomach like a cat's tail.

'Like a virgin.'

'I wouldn't know. Tampax was my first.'

His tongue stopped. 'Did I hurt? You should have said.'

'No, you didn't, but you didn't ask.'

102

'You didn't say no. You said yes, yes, yes.'

'I never say no.'

Pal laughed, his hot breath on my thighs. 'Tough talk.'

'OK, put it this way, I never say no to a man with a gun.'

I felt nothing then but the sag of the bed as he pushed away from me. Peeking under my forearm I could see him striding across the room towards his jacket. I moved fast, jumping up and running naked for the door. I don't know what I thought I was doing. He caught me easily, slamming his hand over my mouth and pushing me against the papered wall. With the hand that held the gun, he muscled my arm upwards and pushed the gun into my hand.

'Take it,' he said.

I didn't, couldn't.

'Take it.'

Slowly, I wrapped my fingers around the cross-hatched pistol grip and he took the soft palm of his hand from my mouth and released me. The gun felt good, scary but good, about half a pound and hard. I swung my two hands together to hold it straight, pointing it right at him. He stood before me, naked, hairy-chested, unsmiling and I was shaking, pointing the gun at the man whose body I liked close to me and the bastard who had held me down and shot two bullets close enough to singe the hair on my head and ruin my linen.

'You have the gun,' he said.

'I want the silencer.'

I got it. He pushed it on, his blue eyes holding steady, looking at mine while he readied the gun. When I was tooled up he stepped back and held his arms out like a sacrifice.

'Well?' he said, crossing his heart. 'Try here.'

He tapped the centre of his forehead. 'What about here?'

He pointed to his groin. 'Not here? Really?'

'It's not fucking loaded, is it?'

He stepped forward quickly, pushing my hands to the side and down, and squeezed my fingers hard around the metal. There was a sound like someone opening a shaken can of Coke and the carpet ripped under the Chesterfield-style armchair near the window. He lifted my hand round again and stood close, so that I couldn't miss.

'Let's start again,' he said.

103

I swung round and hit him with the silencer. It caught him just under the eye, jerking his head to the side and grazing the skin. There was blood and some swelling. I wanted to hit him again but he held up his hand and shook his head. Smoothing back a few strands of hair, he indicated, very carefully, that he was going to walk towards the mirror, which he did, very slowly, and peered at his reflection, dabbing briskly at the damaged skin that had puckered up into a purplish red weal on his cheekbone. With a sigh of self-reproach, he bent over the minibar, opened the door and grabbed a can of grapefruit juice. Holding it to his face, he sat down in the armchair, his broad feet either side of the tear in the carpet.

I felt powerless with the weapon in my hand. I'd earthed my anger and fear and they had gone. Leaning back against the wall, I was back where we had begun, where he'd held me, stroked and nuzzled against me until I'd felt slightly drunk, and, closing my eyes with relief, had arched my neck towards his lips. I closed my eyes again and breathed deeply to steady the rapid pumping of my heart until I heard his feet padding towards me and felt his hand on my breast. I could smell his skin, warm and salty, feel his lips on me. My eyes flicked open and stared at his asymmetrical face, with its squeezed eye and its smile.

'Didn't I make you come? You fake it?'

'No. I only fake it when I'm bored.'

'I get it,' he said.

'You get what?'

'You want to be on top this time.'

'Right here will do just fine, Pal. Right here.'

The telephone rang in the room while I was showering. I turned the water off and dried myself, trying to listen to what was being said but Pal came in and told me anyway.

'I have to meet someone in about half an hour downstairs.'

'Does it interest me?'

'Of course, but the people who'll be there wouldn't want you there. They only want me to watch. We can sit in the bar.'

I wished I had a change of clothes for the bar instead of my Trouble T-shirt and DMs. Pal offered me a white shirt which I tied in front to make it look better. He said I looked great and

I believed him. Compliments were among the few sincere words the man uttered. He watched me slick on some lipstick.

'No trouble, OK? You sit nice and quiet,' he said.

'What am I going to see?'

'Some men doing business in a pretty lounge. That's all, but you sit nice and quiet.'

'Pal, why wouldn't I?'

'You're excitable.'

'Oh, you mean when someone sounds off a couple of slugs behind my head and then spooks me into going to his hotel room for an afternoon of orgasms? I'd say that makes me excitable. Men doing business in a pretty lounge, no.'

'How about a Japanese man doing business in a pretty lounge.'

I turned to face him. He was lighting up a cigarette, breathing smoke into space between us. He had a cool smile on his face, one that pushed into the swelling on his cheek and matched the hard look in his eyes.

'Break a man's legs. Break his fingers. Tape his mouth ... the old ways, say what you like but they work,' he said. He was leaning back on the bed, supported by his elbows, Shinichro's card in the same hand as the burning cigarette.

'Shinichro's coming here?'

'To do business, that's all.'

'You're not going to hurt him?'

'Me?'

'Anyone.'

'You care?'

'Of course I do.'

'What about me?'

I didn't answer. He repeated the question.

'What about me?'

'I don't think you're going to be hurt tonight. I don't think you ever get hurt.'

Pal tapped his cheek, tapped his heart with a fluttering hand and laughed. 'I think you could hurt me.'

Pal went downstairs half an hour before me and then called up to the room. There were a few people in the bar, a couple of guys drinking cocktails, a middle-aged couple at the far end, and, nearest Pal, a plump man, his feet tucked into the bar stool and a bowl of salted nuts to hand. Pal stood up, kissed me on the cheek and held the seat steady as I sat down. When the barman came over I ordered a Martini and refused one of Pal's cigarettes. We didn't talk much and I was turning the twizzle stick nervously in my icy glass when Pal put his hand on my leg. I had my back half turned to the bar to look out across the lounge, and I saw four men walk in. The two tanned Mediterranean types were taller than the Japanese, who were slighter too but just as businesslike. Pal turned my leg inwards so that I was sitting, like him, facing the bar, watching the action in the mirror. There was no handshaking. The two Japanese bowed, indicated to the seats and the other two sat down, adjusting the single buttons of their lightweight jackets, one feeling inside for something, checking everything was there. The two Japanese took their seats opposite, also adjusting their jackets and one feeling inside, showing the tattooed scroll under the Rolex on his golden wrist. They were talking to the waiter when Pal turned to me and said, 'Nice and quiet now.'

'OK. I can guess who the Japanese are. But what about the other guys?'

'Shinichro's customers.'

'Who are they?'

'What do they look like to you?'

'Spanish?'

'Colombian.'

I stuck the stick in my mouth and bit it.

'Now do you know what you're dealing with?' he said.

Chapter Ten

Any junkie will tell you that the beauty of a good hit is a break in the tension. There's a great whack of euphoria that sets your mind leaping and your heart palpitating until you can hear the mad cheers and see the sky thick with ticker-tape falling from open windows. Pal asked if I knew what I was dealing with. What he had in mind was world-class gangsterdom, drug barons and danger. What I had in mind was a world-class, front-page lead. Delia would understand. You spend weeks shuffling around with a hundred barely adequate little slogans and suddenly you come out with 'It's the real thing.' That was *it*. What was motherhood compared to that? Nothing. Believe me, I knew what she meant. I thought I'd kicked it, stuck out all these months thinking it didn't matter and that I was cool, take it or leave it, take a holiday, take a lover, live right. All I'd been doing was twisting that big elastic band inside to destruction. I craved release and here it was, and here I was, biting on a twizzle stick and hoping the buzzing in my head would clear so that I could speak, say something coherent. I was saved the worry by a movement in the foursome. One of the Japanese was talking into a mobile phone. He said something to his partner, who said something to the flat-faced, stockier Colombian, who repeated it to his handsome friend. Pal was watching the mirror like it was a movie.

'They're going,' he said.

The men stood up and walked together towards the white marble stairs and the foyer. Pal took my arm and we followed. I had started to think now. Either he was with them or he was with someone else who knew what they were up to. He was, therefore, with either the good guys or the bad guys. I wanted to look around for some good guys or at least the ones who kept Pal so well informed, but I didn't have time. The Japanese already had a car, as did the Colombians, sharp, chauffeur-driven Mercs, and they were leaving. I started forward but Pal held my arm and said we should have another drink.

Twenty minutes later he got a call and we took a cab to the Savoy. Pal settled back in his seat and smiled to himself.

'What's going on?' I said.

'Maybe Japan is trying to make a point.'

'No, what's going on?'

'Drams for coke, coke for drams. It's currency.'

'The coke or the drams?'

'The drams, of course. You can carry a million dollars' worth in a briefcase and no one is going to ask you why. Try carrying a million bucks. Try carrying two hundred kilos of wholesale cocaine.'

'So the Colombians have delivered where? Japan?'

'I think so, don't you?'

'And Sano was sent with the drams to Las Vegas where Colombians could sell them but he lost the lot to Charlie.'

'His bosses make the mistake of sending him alone. When do you ever see a Japanese doing business on his own, even if he can? Head office needs to know that one man is restraining the other. And that man needs to know he has a partner. They don't like to be alone, the Japanese. They go crazy with worry. They don't like to be the stranger in a strange land.'

It struck me that Esther would have said something like that, not Pal. I looked at his face for a clue but there was none, just that know-it-all smile.

'They took a risk on Sano, then,' I said.

'Curious, yes? Maybe because he was such a Yankee.'

'How come you know so much about the Japanese?'

'In my line of work you get around. Good story for you so far, eh?'

He spoke like a man giving a child a treat. I had a feeling it was in his gift, too, to give me that treat. We were stuck in traffic along the Strand and his fingers were squeezing my shoulder through the shirt. I'd sworn I'd never do this again – forget the little picture caption of Charlie, that was just a joke. I'd sworn I'd never chase a big story like this, not after the last one. That had been just the biggest story that I had ever hooked and it ended ignominiously on Max Winters' spike. It ended on everyone's spike. No one could run it. It was too damned embarrassing, too dangerous. I had to swallow my pride, DI Robert Falk had to too. But my good friend Warren Graham, the nice boy, the one who supplied the white linen, he got to keep his *and* all the money. The only profit I had made on my own I had handed over to Charlie. That's why I was here, coming down fast, because that damned Charlie owed me.

Pal wiped the mist from the window. 'Nervous?' He said.

'Like a baby walking on a rope bridge.'

'You want to dance later?'

'Have you danced in London recently?'

'No. I never have. I've danced in Régine's in Paris.'

'Wild. To what?'

'Disco. Michael Jackson.'

'What about Budapest?'

'It's been a while since I danced there.'

'Well, it's a little different here. If you're not playing House, you're nowhere.'

'Playing house?'

'Very high-tech. I think the Balearics are making a strong push this month. Think seriously sweaty and groovy. Remember those words: seriously and groovy. Dancing, but definitely no touching. You think you're touching everyone anyway once you get to trip.'

'LSD?'

'Ecstasy.'

'And the music in this House?'

'House *is* the music. Open house. Raves. Beats per minute. Bandanna. Smiley T-shirt.'

'I like James Brown. He's good to dance.'

'Oh, you can get *him*, sampled in a stolen ten-second soundbite, but not in his godfather of soul entirety.'

'Is there a slow number at the end? I want to dance close with you.'

'You don't get it, do you?'

'No. I feel very old.'

Pal was wiping the window again, looking out. I'd have said that he was about forty, sometimes he looked forty-two, sometimes thirty-eight. He was fit, no weight about the middle and no sag in the back. His hair was thinning but that didn't mean anything, there wasn't any grey. No grey on his dark silky moustache, either. His face was tanned and smooth but there were crow's-feet about his eyes, never mind the bruise, long laughter lines wrinkling his skin. He had all his own teeth.

'Have you ever killed a man, Pal?' I said, out of the blue.

'A man?'

'Anyone.'

'I wouldn't be here if I had not,' he said and turned to face me, a little smile beginning to twist the corners of his mouth again. I didn't hate him then. I couldn't, any more than one could the tiger more than the lamb. Fear – and desire – were the emotions, not hate, or love.

The taxi swung into the deep cul-de-sac that shelters the Savoy foyer from the street and the curious gaze of the *hoi polloi* that battles back and forth along it twenty yards away. Pal paid and, putting a hand on my back, directed me down to the lounge. The Latino/Nippon contingent were already seated and nibbling at their complimentary snack bowls but Shinichro was nowhere to be seen. Pal ordered me another Martini and a beer for himself and we settled back in the deep pink armchairs and waited. My man arrived ten minutes later.

If Shinichro caught sight of us, he didn't show it. He stood at the top of the little flight of steps, smartly dressed in a navy suit and sober tie, carrying a boxy black briefcase. He took a few seconds to look around the lounge and then walked briskly towards the foursome sitting on the far side. He bowed, not excessively deeply, and one of the Japanese extended his hand towards a seat.

'What happened to his face?' Pal said.

'An accident with some glass,' I replied. At that moment I couldn't have cared less what Pal saw or how he interpreted it. I was in awe of Shinichro, who had taken it upon himself to fulfil his *on*-man's bargain and deliver the goods to these men. I was proud of him and I wanted him to do it right, make no mistake and get the hell out of there. My eyes filled with unwelcome tears as I watched him and as I went to sip my drink I saw Pal watching me, not them. I wiped my palms on a napkin and took the drink.

'You want a picture?' he said.

'What?'

'For the story. You want a picture? We have just enough light.'

Pal was holding a slim metallic grey camera in his hand, about three inches long and an inch wide. He took the shot so quickly that anyone would have thought he was taking a pair of glasses from his face and tucking them into a case.

'You're full of little gadgets, aren't you?'

'Weighs two ounces. Good for little snaps while you are travelling around.'

'It's a Minox, I know that. What are you, a fucking spy now?'

'No one needs spies now. It's an open market for secrets. Look, your boyfriend's leaving.'

Shinichro was walking up the steps empty-handed and the flat-faced Colombian was pulling the briefcase off the table, showing a good deal of gold bracelet as he did so.

'You're very cool, you know that?' Pal said.

'I've done big stories before.'

'You like the look of these guys?'

'The ones over there?'

'Uhuh.'

'Not really. I prefer the more sensitive type.'

'Like Saito-san.'

'He's sensitive, yes.'

'He's *sensible*, not sensitive.'

'What are you getting at?'

'I ask if you like the look of these men.'

'I said no.'

'But you take risks.'

'You know I do.'

'It's lucky you are with me. If these men knew who you were and what you did they'd want to finish you.'

'Look, I've done nothing. You set all this up. You wanted me to find out. You can't give a kid an apple and then punish it for taking it.'

'I could give you to these men. They'd break your legs first and your arms after.'

'You're right, I'm lucky to be with you.'

It was the closest I'd got to seeing Pal lose his temper. I'd thought he had meant the story but he hadn't, he was getting at me about something else. We sat in silence until the dark-suited Japanese left. The tall, handsome Colombian got out of his seat and followed them. Five minutes later he was back to check in with his friend, who nodded, buttoned his jacket and stood up. The two men turned and looked over to where we were. I wished I had somewhere to hide but Pal looked right back at them, his arm resting on my shoulders.

'You want to eat now?' he said, turning to me.

After a quiet, sullen supper, Pal took me home in a cab and left with it. He said he had business to attend to. We didn't kiss, we waited in the cab for a couple of minutes in silence. The cabbie opened the dividing glass but Pal shut it again. The meter was running so the man had no beef.

'When can I have that picture?' I said.

'Needs specialist development.'

'I've got contacts in the photographic trade.'

'I'll get it developed. I have pictures I want to keep on here.'

'I don't understand, Pal. I don't understand what you're here for.'

'I told you. I followed you.'

'Cut it.'

'I came to buy the drams.'

'And that's what you're going to do now?'

'That's what I'm going to do.'

I couldn't sleep. I had to write things down. I'd just seen a million dollars' worth of one-megabit drams change hands. The representative of a major Japanese chip seller had handed goods over to two Colombian drug traffickers under the watchful eye of two representatives of Japanese organized crime. If I was nice to Pal he'd let me have the picture. It was a story that made your hands shake but it was one that you had to get right. Richard Munroe had a contact who reckoned the Japanese were underestimating their yields. I knew they were for sure. My man Shinichro was, because his firm wanted to cash in on the spot price. Like all the others, his firm had contracts for scheduled delivery to its customers. If his firm couldn't meet these because of stated low yields, exacerbated by politically inspired export monitoring, those customers would just have to buy at the spot price, wouldn't they? If drams were going out the side door, some of the profit coming in by that route would have to be reinvested into something else. It couldn't all show up in the profit and loss account, if the firm had already stated its yields. Someone at NC Corporation had taken the initiative and invested in a few bags of toot.

I thought that maybe I should call Shinichro, find out how he was. I wondered if he'd seen me sitting on a pink sofa, sipping cocktails with Pal. So what? We couldn't break each other's hearts any more so what did it matter if we stepped on each other's toes? I decided not to call. If he had anything to say, he could call me. I called Charlie instead, but Debbie answered the phone. She told me it was late and Charlie was asleep. I told her to please wake him but he was already grabbing the receiver from her hand.

'Missed me?' I said.

'I was a bit worried, tell you the truth. How'd it go with Pal?'

'Well, I spent a lot of time with him but I'm still not sure how it went.'

'Yeah. He's like that. What do you reckon? Has he got them?'

'I don't know. He's a dealer, all right; he might have your million now, but then again he might not. He asked me a lot of questions that gave me the idea that he still thought *I* had them.'

'All blow.'

'I think so. Let's say that he hasn't got them, let's say he's chasing around just like us.'

'So what?'

'Well, there's good news and bad news.'

'Oh God, give it to me.'

'The good news is that whoever Sano had to deliver to has got what they wanted. The delivery could have been your drams, but then again it might not have been.'

'That's good? Well, it's not bad. We've got a chance.'

'The bad news is that you haven't got a chance even if they are your drams.'

'Why?'

'Because the Medellin Cartel didn't make the deal with you.'

There was silence at the end of the phone. Charlie took so long to answer that I had to ask if he was still there.

'How do you know it's them?' he said.

'I know I'm assuming a lot – they're Colombian, they're into drugs but they could be the Bogotá Rotarians.'

'Shit.'

'Anyway, I found out that drams are one way they like getting paid nowadays.'

Charlie went very quiet again. I think he was reappraising his hand in the light of new information. His voice was businesslike when he spoke.

'How do you know this?' he said.

'I saw it go down.'

'So who made the delivery?'

'Couple of Japanese wide boys,' I lied.

'What about Kuthy?'

'He's looking to make a deal, so he says. Could have made it, could be at Heathrow right now.'

Charlie took a deep breath. 'So I'm down a million.'

'Yeah, so what, eh?'

'You know what's the worst?' he said.

'Don't tell me. Losing the game?'

'Absolutely. Losing.'

'I'm sorry about the story, Charlie, and your picture in the paper. It caused more trouble than I thought it would.'

'Teach me to mind my manners, won't it?'

I waited for a bit and then I said, 'It's not all bad.'

'No?'

'No.'

'What's the up side?'

'I'm going to let you pay in instalments.'

'Pay what?'

'The fifty thousand you owe me.'

I was still laughing when I called Richard. It was getting late but there was music in the background when he answered the telephone, something classical, and a lot of fumbling and muttering.

'What's up?' I said when he finally grunted 'Hello.'

'I'm wallpapering.'

'Right. The new house. I was over your way yesterday. Vicky Park.'

'Should've popped in.'

'I was with a contact.'

'In Vicky Park?'

'The story's shaping up well. I wanted to know how things were doing at your end.'

'What about?'

'The five to six-point-five million pounds' worth of chip theft on the West Coast.'

'Oh, that.'

'Oh, that? Come on, Richard.'

'What do you want to know?'

'I want to know if anyone got any further than the bald fact that there has been five to six-point-five million pounds' worth of computer theft on the West Coast.'

'Ah.'

'Maybe you've got a contact there who could speak to me, or have you tied it up?'

'Yes, we have, actually.'

'Which one?'

'Yes, we have tied it up.'

'Oh.'

'We'll be running it.'

'Richard. It's me. Give a little. We're supposed to be working together.'

'Georgina, it's a good story. I'm doing it for *Technology Week*.'

'You're there already?'

'*Datamatics* kicked me out soon as I resigned.'

'And?'

'Max said no way.'

'No way you can work with me.'

'That's right. I'm sorry.'

'You run that story this week and you are going to look a prize prat by the next.'

'How so?'

'Because I've cracked it, that's why.'

'So why ring me at this time of night for information?'

'It's called teamwork, Richard.'

'I call it desperation, Georgina.'

'Richard, that wallpaper brush you've got in your hand.'

'Yes?'

'Has it got a nice long handle?'

'Goodnight, Georgina.'

I called international directory enquiries straight away and got the number of the Santa Clara Police department and the district attorney's office of Santa Clara County in Silicon Valley. I got the numbers of a couple of chip manufacturers and personal computer manufacturers from my contact book. I planned to put a few questions that'd make these guys say what Richard had and then

I was going to screw him – give the lot to *Datamatics* – and a national. He could go jump and take that coprophagous old fox Max Winters with him. It would be late afternoon on the West Coast so I had plenty of time.

After a couple of minutes I got through to a very personable lieutenant who came right out and told me the worst. He said that they had just completed an investigation which had led to the arrest of thirty-five current and former employees of a major personal computer manufacturer.

'Our officers here confiscated upwards of seventy-five thousand dollars' worth of computer memory chips. It's just the latest in a long line. We took in a number of assembly line workers in a chip fabrication plant for doing the same thing, ripping off drams from their employers,' he said.

'It's nothing new, though, this chip theft?' I replied.

'No, there's nothing new in that. What's new is that we're getting guys kicking the front doors down and going in armed now.'

'Because of the prices.'

'Because of the prices, and because of the cocaine cartels.'

I bit my tongue while the lieutenant went on to explain that the recent drug laundering laws in the US had forced the banks to report all major cash transactions and the cartels were now looking for ways of getting paid other than in cash.

'The cartels are involved, for sure. At the lowest levels we've got workers selling chips they've taken out of the fabs for coke. At the highest level we've got big deals being paid for in stolen drams because the cartels want anything but cash, something that's easily concealed and internationally negotiable. Computer chips are perfect. No way you can tell if they're stolen, even the ones we buy undercover we can never prove whether they are or not, and you can fit a million bucks' worth into a briefcase,' he said.

Didn't I know it? The only problem was that Richard damned well did too, only he'd found out the easy way.

Chapter Eleven

I had a letter from Delia enclosing a Mothercare catalogue for the summer season and a little book on pregnancy from the Health Education Council. It had colourful diagrams. There was a cheerful note inside telling me how wonderful it was to see me and that the kids liked me a lot. I had been sick as a dog and missed my doctor's appointment that morning. The cocktail of Martinis, human chorionic gonadotrophin and assorted active hormones was a vicious one and my body was trembling with the aftermath. Frankly, I wanted to crawl into a corner and die. I wanted to jump out and kill someone, too. Richard Munroe would do for starters, then Max Winters, Pal Kuthy, Shinichro Saito, and finally myself. Delia's sense of humour made her an also ran.

I stood in my kitchen and flicked through the catalogue, mentally reeling at the design permutations of a little white collar and floral print. I discovered what a layette was, how much it cost and that breast-feeding mothers could wear bras with zip-up cups and sixty hooks and eyes for ease of use and milk-absorbing breastshields. I noted the primary colours of motherhood were pastels – pink, blue, yellow and white – and the material was cotton/polyester or unbreakable plastic. There was nothing in black Lycra or cheap silk. The Health Education booklet was for vitamins and a good diet, and against alcohol and cigarettes. Most drugs were out, too, including, more crucially that morning, aspirin. Stomach heaving and head aching, I poured the bubbling glass of Alka-Seltzer into the kitchen sink and gazed out of the window. The egg and I were not compatible. The only positive thing I could think of that it had contributed to my lifestyle had been an increased sex drive, and, Lord knows, I could've done without that, the trouble it got me into.

There were two tower blocks directly in front of the tenement in which I lived and beyond them I could see the local primary school; a squat sprawling collection of sub-utilitarian sixties' low rise and Portakabins staked out behind a high wire fence. In the corner of a wide piece of tarmac, to the side of the buildings, were some large rubber tyres swinging from ropes and a metal slide. There was a patch of green behind the flats but I couldn't see it from my window, just the car park with its old hub caps scattered around like bottle tops. My flat had no balcony, either, just a long open corridor leading to ten variegated front doors, at least five bolts apiece on the inside. No animals but dogs, lots of dogs, and no children, not in my block. Couples and singles lived here because families refused to come. I thought of Delia's country garden green with trees and flowers, of my parents' house by the sea and of holidays on the island, girls and boys running down the cliffs to the sea with stocking nets on sticks and a fresh wind blowing in from the west. The egg would like that. It would like curling its tiny toes into the pale damp sand and dipping into pools for shrimps and crabs, white and transparent as rice paper. It would like scraping seaweed from granite rocks with its busy little fingers and slopping it into a bright red bucket that brimmed with salt water, clear as teardrops. It wouldn't like it here, living up in the dirty sky above the dusty streets. We'd have to move, but to do that I'd have to use Warren's money, the little windfall that had come my way when he had left in such haste, his fingers sticky with the filthy lucre. I hated him, almost as much as he had loved me, far far too much to take it. It was bad enough that I had to live here in his old flat with all the pretty, pretty things he'd bought for me. There was no choice, I had to live somewhere but I wouldn't take his dirty cash. Charlie would have to pay me, that was all. He had to.

I was contemplating this, and the possibility of *Datamatics*, or anyone, buying what I had and running it before *Technology Week* did, when I saw the dark grey van down below. It was parked so that the back windows were facing the flats. I stared down for a moment and then stepped back, intimidated by the glinting eyeless glass. If I got the number, maybe I could find out whose van it was. Robert Falk would find out for me. But it would mean stepping forward again, putting my face to the window to see, and I was afraid to do it.

I decided to dress myself and look again in ten minutes. I pulled on a white cut-away T-shirt and baggy denims, cinching them around my waist with a heavy leather belt, relieved that it still felt comfortable in its usual notch. The nausea was fading and I was hungry, for hot new bread that smelled of yeast, and cold fresh butter and cheese. I pulled at the curtains in my bedroom and looked down at the car park which stretched around the corner. One burnt-out saloon and an old blue Mini were on this side, but I couldn't see the van from there. I had to go back to the kitchen and look. I ran some water into the kettle and glanced out. The van was still there but I couldn't make out the number. I'd asked Pal if they were friends of his and he had said 'I hope', but the question was: were his friends my friends too? I left the kitchen, went to the phone and dialled Robert Falk's number. I dialled and waited, and as I waited for him to answer I changed my mind, replacing the receiver very slowly. It was quiet in the flat. I could hear a vacuum cleaner droning upstairs and smell curry being prepared for lunch. These were little clues about someone's life, a decent, homely, life.

I left clues. I left my lover's business card on my dressing table and empty wine bottles in the kitchen. I left pregnancy test kits on the window ledge and my contact book in my desk. I played *True Blue* on my record player and talked on the telephone, to everybody. There was no such thing as privacy with the clues to my life that I sprayed about, like crumbs from a dry biscuit. If I ran to the bathroom and turned on the taps, what good would it do? That was for the movies. All the surplus noise could be filtered out until you were cut out like a silhouette, pared down to the essential truth, the *honne*. Tiny microphone-transmitters can be planted anywhere. They send out microwave signals to a receiver, anywhere. They can be turned off and on by remote control, or by light, or heat, or pressure, or by voice. They can store data and wait in silence to transmit later. They can be powered by the plumbing system, by the water running over them and that very water can conduct the sound for miles. They can be wired into anything that will conduct electricity. If I had an electric typewriter they could pick out each key that I tapped. Switch on my computer and someone outside could read the radio waves, see what I wrote. Laser beams could reach up to a window and read my breath, see its vibrations, and build them into sound. Turn off the sound, and they could build a picture of a face at the window, of bodies on the bed. I had no privacy. I was spread out for inspection like a white rat in a lab.

I let the kettle boil and made myself some tea. I would have liked coffee but it had started to leave a bitter, metallic taste in my mouth, like the cigarettes I yearned for. I switched on my computer and wrote the story so far before calling *Datamatics* to see if they were interested. A friend of mine called Jenny Davies took the call.

'You've heard about Richard?' she said.

'Yup.'

'Has he got this?'

'This is an exclusive, Jenny,' I said.

'How exclusive?'

'I'm offering to a daily, that's it.'

'We'll be pushing it to get it in tomorrow. We've put the front page to bed.'

'It won't hold. I'm selling it today.'

She bought it. *Technology Week* and *Datamatics* hit the streets on the same day and I would have given anything to see Max and Richard get their personal issues. It would serve them right. I thought about the van outside and waited for a moment, holding the receiver to my ear and pushing a pencil through my fingers on to a notepad.

'There's something else,' I said, and I told her.

'You saw it?' she said.

'I was invited.'

'Let's see. What've you got? Name of a components manager of a major Japanese corporation, two unknown Japanese mafia men and some unknown Colombians.'

'Right.'

'The manager confirmed his company underestimated their yields? That's the one we should follow up.'

'Not the bit about chips delivered in payment for cocaine in the Savoy.'

'Of course, but you haven't got enough, Georgina.'

'I might have a picture.'

'If you get that, great. The drugs squad would be interested and you should get a line from them. You have to get something from

120

the components manager too, if only a denial. We'll be very interested if you nail that down. As it is, no.'

I knew that. Now everyone did. The broadcast theory of personal security hadn't worked for Charlie, but maybe it would for me. Just to be sure, I had to tell Robert Falk. I'd call him, but not on this phone.

His banana fingers squeezed the thick cut of lemon over the buttered sole on my plate.

'I hope you don't mind my saying so but you're looking . . . tired, Mrs Powers. Late nights?' he said.

'I'm pregnant,' I replied. His hand drew swiftly back from my plate and pushed the steel frame of his glasses back up to the broad bridge of his nose. I popped a salty chip into my mouth.

'Don't worry, I'm assured that it's not catching,' I said, munching out the words with my mouth full. His pale eyes cast around for his napkin, his cheeks as pink as langoustine. I found his discomfiture surprising because I'd always reckoned him to be unshakable, like a St Bernard in an avalanche, any avalanche. He calmed himself, methodically tucking the spruce white linen back under his chin before reaching forward to pour some Mexican beer into my glass. His large hands were steady enough and, having completed this task, he felt able to look at me again across the table.

'It's not his,' I said.

'Whose?'

'Warren's. It's not his, if that's what you're thinking.'

'That would be impossible, wouldn't it?'

'On every count.'

'You haven't seen him, then? Recently, I mean, Mrs Powers.'

'I think you'd know before me, wouldn't you, Robert?'

He smiled a little and began to bone his fish, expertly separating the flesh into fillets. I looked down at my plate and pushed it towards him. He stopped working on his own and began slicing at my portion until the fish's white backbone lay arched on the side next to four plump buttery ovals of cleaned meat. He pushed the plate gently back towards me.

'The father's Japanese,' I said.

'The dead man?'

'You found out, then?'

'Hiroshi Sano. You asked me. I checked.'

'Anything more?'

'Came in from Vegas. Looked like a gang murder. Body covered in tattoos so it's likely. He's Japanese mafia.'

'Yakuza.'

'Mrs Powers, please, you weren't involved with this man, were you? It's not him?'

His voice showed sincere concern, something I had always been able to take from him. It was touching.

'Hiroshi Sano lost a million dollars' worth of drams in a poker game to my friend Charlie East. Remember Charlie? He was a bit player last time but not this time. Sano came to London to get them back but before he could they disappeared from Charlie's deposit box after someone turned over his flat and got the key and number. I'm sure Sano was supposed to deliver those chips to someone else originally. I think that's why they killed him,' I said.

'Do you know who "they" are?'

'All I know it that he was supposed to deliver for someone, to someone. His bosses are Japanese, their customers are Colombian. I think one or the other murdered him.'

'Drams for drugs and, eventually, dollars? That's very interesting, Mrs Powers. I see you haven't lost your touch.'

He was right. I hadn't lost my touch for trouble, over here and over there, inside and out. I didn't want to tell him about Shinichro, that he was in the frame, that he could have killed Hiroshi for any number of things: possibly for love, certainly for money, and undoubtedly because of sheer bloody obligation. I didn't want to tell him that Pal Kuthy could have killed him too, easily. He could have killed him and taken the drams, watched Shinichro replace them in the lounge of the Savoy, knowing he had Sano's million dollars' worth for free and Shinichro's million dollars' worth changing hands that he could now buy. He was on easy street especially since he had someone watching every move that everyone was making. I wanted Robert to find out who it was.

'What about Pal Kuthy?' I said.

'I'm still working on it.'

'What does that mean?'

'Mrs Powers, how well do you know *this* man?'

'He followed Charlie from Las Vegas. Said he wanted to buy the drams.'

122

'He didn't follow *you*, then? From Las Vegas?'

'No. Why should he?' I said. I stopped eating for a moment and watched him drink from his glass, the half-pint like a thimble in his big hands and his ruby-red lips wet and shiny.

'I've done a story on it,' I said.

'I know. I saw it in *Datamatics*. Something very similar ran in *Technology Week*. You could give me a little more background, Mrs Powers,' he replied.

There is no point in asking another human being if you can trust them. The only person who can tell you is yourself. I trusted Robert Falk, even when he was hiding things from me. I told him everything except the bit about Shinichro. He didn't need to know about him.

'I'll see what I can do,' he said when I had finished. 'Meanwhile, you think the guy with the gun, this Kuthy, has gone?'

'I think he's made the Colombians an offer for the drams and if they took it he'll have gone for sure. He'll have left town with – what's the price now, fifty-five dollars? – more than two million dollars' worth of drams, half of which he got for nothing. What would you do?'

He wiped his last fried potato around his empty plate and slotted it delicately into his mouth, leaning back to flip the napkin over on to his lips. He leaned one massive arm forward to pour more beer into our empty glasses.

'What I would do is another matter. You have to ask what he would do.'

'I'm not sure. Even after the deal, he still made out he thought I had the stolen drams, that I had something to do with it.'

He lifted his glass and tapped it against mine.

'Your very good health, Mrs Powers.'

He took me home and I let him see me to the door. He watched me open it, step in and switch on the light. His eyes glanced cautiously around the room.

'Will you be moving from here?' he said.

'No.'

'What about the father?'

'You mean will he be moving in? No.'

'What will happen when you have to stop work? You will, you know.'

123

'I'll manage.'

'Well, you've got enough money. You should be OK.'

'I've never touched any of it.'

'Our mutual friend left it for you. It was traded fair and square. Use it.'

'I don't need his money.'

He watched me walk over to my answering machine with its red light flashing. I had a couple of messages, one from Richard Munroe telling me that I was going to die and another from Delia.

'Answer the phone. Answer it, you bitch. Oh, fuck it,' she said. I looked over at Robert, who was pushing his glasses up his pudgy nose.

'Friends of yours?' he said.

'The best,' I replied.

Delia called me again from her car phone, said that I should meet her where we usually met. There were three places where we usually met but she cut me off when I began to list them. I waited and she called again.

'Shut up and listen. Remember the City Golf Club?'

'Yes.'

'Not there.'

'Remember Kettner's Champagne Bar?'

'Not there?'

'No, not there. I'll be at the other place in half an hour.'

It was raining and I'd be pushing it to get to Dean Street in just half an hour. She sounded angry, and I felt sick again. As I turned the corner into the wind, I saw the grey van pass me by, its red rear lights blurring in the drizzle. It hadn't been around for a couple of days now, not since I'd made the call to *Datamatics*, not since I'd last seen Pal. I stepped quickly into the minicab office and told the man to take me to Bow Road. I needed the next station, Mile End, because my stop was on the Central Line, but I reckoned that if whoever was in the van was to follow me they'd have a harder job if I took London Transport, the indirect route. If I'd gone one station up to Mile End and if they were local, they'd know I had a choice between the District or the Central, more than likely the latter because if I'd wanted the District, I'd have made the cab stop at Bow Road, the earlier station and the one nearer to my home.

The train came before anyone joined me on the platform, so I changed at Mile End anyway. It took longer than half an hour but Delia was waiting, tucked behind a corner table in the Crown and Two. Since she didn't smile and didn't offer, I bought myself a drink, an iced lemonade with a slice, and sat down in front of her. She could hardly speak for the rage in her.

'How dare you?' she said.

I was taken aback by the blast.

'What've I done?'

'How dare you put me and my kids in danger?'

'What?'

'You come down to my place and we're in it, aren't we? In it with you.'

'I don't know what you're talking about. In what?'

'What did you have in that fucking bag?'

'My bag? A change of underwear, change of clothes, toothbrush and some book on virtual reality that I didn't have time to read.'

'Crap. You were running from someone, weren't you? It's something to do with that bloody story.'

'What are you talking about?'

'Did you leave anything behind? Hide something?'

'I don't know . . .'

'You bitch.'

She shoved the palm of her hand against her forehead to keep control. Her long-nailed fingers scraped at her blonde hair, her gold and diamond rings sparkling in the gloomy light. I asked her again what was going on and she looked at me with resentment, her eyes ready for angry tears.

'This guy came to see me, day before yesterday. He said he wanted to see you. I thought he was, you know, your boyfriend. He made out he was, anyway. I explained that you'd been and gone. We had this, sort of, conversation. If you could call it that. You know the sort of conversation you think is all right but the more it goes on the more you know it isn't.'

'What did this guy look like?' I said.

'Are you kidding?'

'What did he look like?'

'Tall, dark, good looking, hair thinning and a big moustache. He had an accent, like a German, maybe a Dutchman.'

'Hungarian.'

'You *do* know him.'

'He's not my boyfriend.'

'I don't give a fuck what he is to you. He scared me, George. He came after me and scared me.'

I believed her. Pal could scare, go from nerve to nerve with a diabolic grin, and Delia was a sensible woman. Despite the wild times we had had, she wasn't one to take tremendous risks, which is why she had married David, of course. She needed a certain level of excitement and stimulation, but she preferred what was outrageous for that. Physical danger was not something she was drawn to. She was definitely a material girl, but she was not one of the world's bungee jumpers.

'What did he say?' I said.

'Nothing.'

'What was he after, then?'

'I don't know. You tell me. You know.'

'Come on, Delia . . .'

'He came in and asked where you were. He said a friend had said that you were staying with me. I told him you had left. He asked if you were OK. That's how it started. We talked. I said I thought you'd need some support, for the baby, and he went along with it all. Then he asked about some things you might have left with me, that you might have left them because no one would find them, but they would. I said I didn't know what he was talking about, of course. I mean I didn't. I don't. There were always ways to find things, he said, and he smiled, the evil bastard smiled. The kids were there and he started to play with them, grabbing them by their heads, roughing up their hair, pulling them to him. He didn't do anything that hurt them, they were having a good time, but it was creepy. I didn't want him to touch them. He had his hands on their heads, kept grabbing their heads so that his fingers gripped them, then he held them still. It was nothing, now I'm saying it, but I felt something was wrong. I didn't know what to do. I was afraid. He hadn't done anything but smile and I was afraid. I told him I didn't know what you had in your bag, that you hadn't brought anything. I told him I didn't know what he was talking about and you know what he did?'

Delia didn't wait for me to answer, she started picking at her

126

long nails. Maybe he'd showed her the gun, like he'd showed me. I'd lied about the baby to him, to Shinichro, to protect myself, to protect it. He knew that I'd lied now and maybe not just about one thing either. He thought I still had something of his but I couldn't think what. He had the drams, didn't he? We were both in trouble and Delia was telling me how much.

'I had a knife on the drainer and he picked it up with this melon I had ready to wash by the sink. He picked that up with one hand. Weighed it, lifted it up, sniffed it, licked it. Licked it. He said he really needed to know if you'd left anything with me for safe keeping. I said no, I didn't know what he was talking about. He said that the melon was a good size, good and ripe. He said it smelled good and held it up, right in front of my face, and sliced it, split the skin, cut it all around until the rind peeled off and all you could see was a ball of green flesh in his hand. No one cuts melon like that, do they?'

'No,' I said.

'You don't walk into someone's house and do that, do you? You don't just cut someone else's melon, do you?'

'No, you don't.'

'And if you do, you cut it in half, scoop out the seeds and all that shit, don't you? That's the normal way.'

I didn't reply.

'He just cut the skin off until it was this round dripping mess in his hand, and you know what he said?'

I shook my head, my mouth was dry.

'He said it was about the size of a kid's head.'

Delia was looking at me for an answer but I couldn't. It took a while for me to say, 'Did you call the police?'

'No, I bloody didn't. I thought about it, but I didn't. What could I say, and what the hell would they do? Could they really protect my kids?'

'Where are they?' I said and then changed my mind. 'Don't tell me.'

'Don't worry, I won't. They're somewhere safe.'

'What about David?'

'George, who is this man? What does he want?'

'I don't know. I don't know what he wants. All I know is that he thinks he's one of the good guys.'

Chapter Twelve

I told her to go home. I said that I would go and talk to Pal, that nothing would happen to her children, that I had the answer to whatever he wanted. Delia was OK about it. I wouldn't have said she was reassured, exactly, because she said her kids were staying where they were for a while.

'What about David?' I asked again.

'I told him I was leaving him,' she said.

'And he believed you?'

'Yes. We haven't been getting on too well lately. I thought "what the hell, say it", so I didn't have to tell him about your charming friend that way. You never know, some good might come of it.'

'You think so?'

'Yes, but I don't think for him.'

David wasn't getting off lightly and neither was I. She stuck her finger in my face and warned me one more time that I had better go see this Pal and say the right things to him because, so help her, she only cared about her kids and if anything happened to them, anything at all, then my life wouldn't be worth dog meat. She was fiercer than I thought she could be. I had thought that motherhood had mellowed her, softened her up, but I had been as mistaken as the Mothercare catalogue. All that city business chic had been an act. All that pastel and plastic was, too. Delia sticking it to me, to David and to Pal, if she had to, that was the real thing. I watched her walk away from me, striding purposefully down the busy street, angry but clear minded while I stood on the damp pavement, dithering, trying to make a decision that would come good. I could go home and wait, see if my nerves could stand it. Or I could take courage and try the hotel. No reason for him to use a different one, was there? Go right there and ask him.

What do you want? Tell me. What do you want? I'd make a point
of going to reception. Make a big deal of it, make sure they
understood who I wanted to speak to. If I had to go to his room,
I could ask them to give me a call after about five minutes. *What
do you want? Tell me. What do you want?* I'd ask him to his face.
That's what I'd do. The truth was I was afraid to do that, and I
was afraid to go home, where the walls were thin as skin. A voice
called out to me as I stepped off the kerb.

'Hey, Georgina. Hey, I want to talk to you.'

I stepped back from the spinning wheels of a cycle messenger
and looked around. Richard was walking out of a snooker hall by
Meard Street. I started to walk backwards away from him, waving
and shouting back, 'Not now,' but he hurried through the traffic
and up the road to catch up with me.

'Look, I'm not sorry,' I said. 'And I'm busy right now.'

'You made me look a complete dickhead. My first week and I
run the same story as the paper I've just left. You didn't have to
do that,' he said.

'You dumped me.'

'Hellfire, Georgina . . .'

'I'll see you, Richard.'

'I told Max it was his fault.'

I stopped and looked round at him.

'And lived? I'm impressed. Really,' I said and set off again. He
hurried to keep up.

'I said you were working on something that we could use. You
are, aren't you? I got that impression last time we spoke.'

I wanted a cigarette, yearned for one without disgust for the
first time in ages. The need for one made me feel jumpy, and I'd
read that stress affects a foetus too. So I took the short-term view
for both of us. I didn't look at Richard, I started across the road
towards a newsagent's. He followed me like a faithful dog, stood
by my side while I paid for twenty Bensons and a cheap lighter.
Silently, he followed me outside and watched me rip the cellophane off the pack. I took one drag and blew a satisfying plume
into the sky. It tasted great, like fresh leaf tea on a sunny Sunday
morning, bacon and eggs and the papers.

'*Datamatics* wants it if I can get a picture. I owe them,' I said.

'I want it.'

'I feel sorry for you if you're relying on me.'

'Come on, we're mates, George. Max won't be a problem.'

I inhaled and exhaled. Christ, I wished Max was my biggest problem. I could handle that hard-faced cripple. It was the able-bodied man with a paralysing smile, the one who could squeeze little skulls like they were ripe fruit, who I wasn't sure I could.

'I'll think about it. OK?'

I wanted to get away, walk somewhere, anywhere, alone, just so I could think about what I should do about Pal, but Richard stood there waiting. He wanted to know if everything was really all right and he wasn't moving until my face showed it. I smiled brightly and said, 'How's the wallpaper?'

'Why don't you come and look?'

'Now?'

'It's Friday afternoon, why not? How about a late lunch?'

I went with him. It was a cop-out but so what? Given the choices I had before me it was like a condemned man choosing to eat first before he went down and if the grey men came to my cell door offering a last supper Richard would be first choice for chef. He cooked like Floyd, only sober.

The back of his terraced house looked down on the Grand Union Canal and the front across Victoria Park. It was a handsome property that needed a bit of work doing to it and Richard was just the man for it if the kitchen was anything to go by. He'd wrecked whatever had been inside and installed a magnificent double oven against one wall and shelves and well-stocked wine rack against another.

'Red or white?' he said.

'Beer, if you've a cold one,' I replied, coming in from the hall. The place had three bedrooms and a large lounge overlooking the park. He opened the fridge, which, compared to mine, looked like the stacked hold of an Australian cargo ship, and took out a couple of cans. He beckoned to me, and I followed him over to some cardboard boxes filled with crockery and cutlery towards a hole in the far outside wall that was shielded by plastic sheeting. He lifted it up and we ducked outside on to a flat roof and into the sunshine. There was a rough little garden below us that stretched down to the slick still water.

'I paid fifty-five. By the time I've done it up, eighty-five, ninety, the way the market's moving. There's an old lady in the flat downstairs. She has the garden. I'm going to turn this bit outside into a patio, french windows there.'

'Very nice for Pimm's at six,' I said, 'but the municipal architecture ruins the ambience, somewhat, don't you think?'

Across the canal a huge structure, one of three planted four-square among the little terraces, stood grimly against the clouds, decked with gaily coloured strings of washing like bunting caught on a guard's grey uniform. Richard looked down at me as if I'd spat in his soup.

'I suppose you could moor a boat down the end there,' I said, trying to sound more positive.

'I've thought about that. Couple of beers, and off I go, no worries. No bloody traffic anyway. Peckish?' he said and stepped inside again to rummage in a cardboard box by the sink. There was a personal computer parked on the kitchen table, cables strung out the back to a plug in the wall.

'For recipes?' I said.

He aimed a gentle kick at me.

'Homework,' he said.

'Where's the modem?'

He pointed to a box under the table.

'Are you on-line to *Technology Week* yet?'

He rolled his eyes upwards.

'Come on. It's a great story, Richard. It could be yours. I just need a little help, like right now.'

He supped at his beer for a moment and pulled out a chair to sit down, but I elbowed him out of the way.

'Go fix lunch, lovey. I can manage here,' I said.

I could have asked Richard for his password, but he was too busy mashing garlic and chopping parsley to be troubled, so I tried my old one. It should have been wiped as soon as I'd come off the payroll, but these things tend to get forgotten. I got straight into the paper's network. Lucky for Max it was me and not someone like my erstwhile mate Warren. He'd have been all over the system, poking and peeking around, riding it like a stolen fastback through an inner city estate. I hadn't got his skill, or his sense of duty, that is, to test a system to destruction. I wasn't interested in the challenge because it was there, all I wanted was a little information posted in the public domain. I tapped in the code for

Technology Week's back issues and the name of the company I needed to know about: AO Electronix.

I admit I was surprised when the name came up, highlighted from the rest of the close text in a little white oblong. I'd always assumed Pal was lying about his business, but here it was in a four-year-old story, a small unaccredited news item concerning a Bristol businessman by the name of Alan Finn. Finn had received a six-month jail sentence, suspended for two years, after he was found guilty of evading export laws. Over a period of two years he'd sold £28,000 worth of semiconductor manufacturing equipment to AO Electronix, a Hungarian digital watchmaker. In passing sentence, the judge accepted the fact that the equipment was intended for making watches but noted that British Aerospace was said to use the same equipment for the manufacture of missile circuitry and that high technology could be used in the Eastern bloc for purposes other than military. You don't say.

'You ought to get into property, y'know,' Richard called out from his post at the cooker. I was reading the next story. It wasn't that different, two years on, 1986.

'I'm OK where I am, overlooking people like you and your inner city patios,' I said.

'You wish. Nothing so nice to overlook and aspire to where you are. Few wrecked cars and some dog shit.'

'Don't exaggerate. Anyway, I don't have aspirations,' I said.

'It's an investment.'

Again there was no by-line. This time the tale was of a German national, Helmut Schumann, fined £10,000 and sent down for two years at Knightsbridge Crown Court after he was convicted of exporting Digital Equipment PDP 11s, worth several million pounds, to – there it was, highlighted on the screen – AO Electronix, a digital watch manufacturer based in Budapest. The ruse was typical. Schumann completed false user certificates for Customs and Excise, shipping the equipment to Bangkok in Thailand where it was then despatched disguised as 'air-conditioners' to Hungary. The court heard that the final destination for these computers was the Soviet Union. A rich smell of meat and tomatoes being turned in softly frying onions and garlic began to fill the air. I waited, holding my breath, expecting the rich smell to affect my stomach, but there was no change. Richard was still talking about bricks and mortar.

'Look, it makes sense. Why pay rent to someone when for the same outlay you can own your own home? Got what you want yet?'

'Is Textline on the network yet?' I said.

'I think so. Punch it in, see what you get.'

I got Textline and its library of national newspapers. This time I didn't bother with the company name. I typed the name 'Pal Kuthy' and waited. The search revealed one mention, in a three-year-old story this time, a large exposé, courtesy of the *Sunday Times*. Richard was stirring the pot and warming to his subject.

'I mean, look at me. Single man. The taxman does me no favours. Bloody no way. This way I get mortgage tax relief, subsidized housing, basically, and help with something that I will eventually make a profit on. I can get a ninety-five per cent mortgage, three times my salary just like that.'

'I thought two and a half times was the recommended level.'

'No one bothers about that. Anyway, I included expenses.'

'Max's? Whoa there. Bet that impressed the hell out of them.'

'*Datamatics*, actually, but who's checking? They're too busy pulling the punters in and trying to make them form an orderly queue.'

The tale began atmospherically. Six huge trailer trucks operated by a Hungarian trucking company based in Budapest arriving at a loading bay in Munich in the dead of night. The freight labels were addressed to Klimatechnik Kft in Hungary. Once loaded, the trucks journeyed to the quiet frontier town of Helmstedt, and on, unchallenged, into East Germany. Meanwhile eight containers, up to ten tons apiece, were travelling on a Swedish freighter from Hamburg, to Helsingborg in Sweden, all the while tracked by US Customs, and friends. Under some pressure from Washington, the reluctant Swedish Government impounded the whole load. When opened, the containers revealed innocuous mislabelled shipping crates packed with strategic electronics equipment. It was destined, so the investigators maintained, for the Soviet Union. The computers had originally been purchased in New York and transported to South Africa, where they were re-exported and re-imported, before departing in cargo ships to three destinations in Germany and, finally, to Sweden.

'I'm not saying you could afford to buy round here ... and being freelance you'd have to show at least a couple of years' earnings,' he said. I leaned back on the kitchen chair and stared at the screen.

'I could, actually.'

'What?'

'I could afford to buy round here.'

'Oh.'

'I wouldn't have to show earnings. I'd pay cash.'

Richard walked over with two more cans of beer and sat down at the table. He didn't say anything while he watched me read the rest of the feature. It was an interesting piece. The customs and security personnel working on the case were convinced that these components were destined to become a state-of-the-art semiconductor fabrication unit in Zelenograd, north of Moscow; a whole factory for making computer chips was being shipped there in crates from the West. There was more than one man in the frame. Four conspirators, two Germans, one Swiss and a South African had been charged and sentenced to lengthy terms in prison, but one other man, thought to be Hungarian and variously known as Pal Szentey, 'Budapest Jo', Joseft Kadar, and Pal Kuthy, was notable in that he had never been caught. He was indicted in his absence on export charges in both the USA and Germany and was last seen boarding a plane in London for Amsterdam. He was being actively sought by the West German intelligence service, Bundesnachrichtendienst, our own MI6 and the US Central Intelligence Agency. Unfortunately, the limitations of database technology precluded the service offering me a picture.

'Cash, eh?' Richard said. I came to and looked over at him.

'Cash,' I replied.

'So why don't you?' he said.

'I told you. I'm OK where I am.'

'A hard-to-let in Bow?'

'I am, and better off. Money in the bank, earning interest – see how it's gone up just recently? – and no responsibility. Take my advice. Sell up as soon as you've fixed this place up. It's all going to go pear-shaped pretty soon.'

'Oh yeah?' Richard scoffed at my prediction and quaffed a good measure of his beer. I shut down the machine.

'Yeah. Esther, my next door neighbour told me,' I said.

'And she knows about these things, does she? What does she do, take in Lawson's washing?'

'She's tapped into a higher authority than that.'

'Thatcher?'

'Higher, Richard, if you can believe there is one. Said something along the lines of not beggaring yourself at a banquet upon borrowing. In other words ...'

'I know. In other words, there is no such thing as a free lunch,' he said, pointedly handing me my jacket. 'Think about it.'

He made me hang the jacket up and I thought of Delia as I did so. She was right. I had run away to her and brought trouble with me like a virus. Now it was Richard I was infecting with my presence. I had nowhere to go that was safe, and no one could possibly know I was there. I asked if I could use his phone and called Esther; she was sleepy, muttering something about night duty.

'Go to the kitchen. Look down at the car park. See if there's a grey van there.'

The receiver clattered on to the table and I heard Esther padding away from me, flat footed in her slippers. There was silence for a couple of minutes and then the sound of her heavy footfall coming back to me.

'No. I can't see nothing,' she said.

'Can you remember seeing one like it driving about?'

'No.'

'Have you seen anyone at my door?'

'Like who? Men, you mean?'

'Tall guy with a moustache.'

'Oh, I've seen him.'

'Today?'

'Not today. Yesterday? Are you all right?'

'Sure. I'm staying with a friend for a while.'

Richard overheard. 'You're what?' he said.

'See if I like the area. I might want to invest, you know.' I gave Richard the thumbs-up.

'Are you thinking of moving?' she said.

'Just a thought.'

She told me to be careful and I said of course, wasn't I always? Richard began setting the table and I quickly dialled Robert Falk's number and asked if he had anything for me.

'I'm having a little difficulty with this one, Mrs Powers,' he said.

'Why?'

'Let's say there has been a certain amount of resistance. The drugs squad were all over the Sano business, now they're on hold.'

'OK, what about the other guy?'

'I know what he was, Mrs Powers, that's all.'

'I think I do too. Thing is, what is he now?'

'The problem is it's not my department, Mrs Powers. It's way off.' He paused, breathing deeply, and in his gentle resonant voice said, 'You shouldn't be doing this, Mrs Powers, in your condition. Take it easy. It's only a story, it's not really worth the aggravation. We know that much, don't we? You and me. Better than most.'

'But it's never only a story, is it, Robert? Anyway, I can't leave it, it's got closer than that.'

Robert went very quiet. I could almost see him pushing his steel glasses up his nose while he bought time.

'Who is he? Please, you must know more than me. What have you got?' I said.

He didn't reply.

'He's a spy, isn't he?'

'Possibly, Mrs Powers, he may have been. The problem is, as you rightly point out, what is he now, who are his friends and, more importantly, how dangerous will it be to find out?'

I told him I wouldn't be home for a while and gave him Richard's number, while Richard threw a cloth over the computer and beckoned to me to sit at my place. I said goodbye to Robert. The plate before me was wide and warm and piled high with steaming coils of pasta, but as Richard's reddish-brown arm stretched out towards me with a ladle full of hot bolognaise sauce I realized, with regret, that I was no longer very hungry. I did my best.

'Too much oregano, huh?' he said, glancing at my half-full dish and wiping a crust of white bread around his empty one.

'Richard, it's perfect, it's just . . .'

'You're too tense to eat.'

'You noticed.'

'I listened. I can read letters upside down too. You're not the only reporter in this room, y'know.'

I didn't answer him, just toyed with spaghetti and tried not to look up.

'Is he a spy?' he said. I still wouldn't answer him. He stood up and pulled my dish towards his.

136

'Well, feel free to use the facilities, George, but this story'd better be a good one, and it had better be mine.'

While Richard washed up I called Shinichro at work. He was civil enough, first refusing and then, at my insistence, agreeing to meet me that evening. I rang Esther again too.

'I'm trying to get some sleep, girl,' she said.

'It's important, Esther. I owe you for ever, I know.'

'OK, shoot.'

'You've still got my keys.'

'Uhuh.'

'Go into the flat; don't sing, anything. Dead quiet, OK? Get me some clothes, enough for a few days, and something nice, the black dress, and some shoes, the lace-up boots with the heels, and, oh yes, the toothbrush. In my desk by the computer, my contact book.'

'Contact book?'

'My address book.'

'One of them Filofax things?'

'No, it's like a little hardback exercise book.'

'OK. You going away or something?'

'Staying out of sight, with a friend. OK?'

'You hiding from *him*?'

'Something like that. Don't use a suitcase, put the lot in that big laundry bag. I don't want it to look like I'm leaving.'

'That red bag? It's full. Always full.'

'Empty it . . . and take it with my stuff to the launderette, the one in Quebec Street. I'll meet you there in half an hour.'

'Why all this cloak and dagger stuff?'

'He watches me, follows me about. I've got to get away for a few days. I need time to think.'

'OK. But you kids ought to learn to talk about things.'

Shinichro met me halfway in the Piazza in Covent Garden. It was a hot, sunny evening and the square was crowded with tourists come to shop for expensive knick-knacks and watch street entertainers juggle and moonwalk. The cafés and pubs were packed with theatre-goers and office workers celebrating the end of another week's graft. Shinichro was standing on the corner of Floral Street, holding a plastic bag in which he had placed a neatly folded copy of the late edition of the *Evening Standard*. He nodded

137

to me when I arrived, his face still scabbed and scarred.

'You look very nice,' he said.

'You too, in spite of . . . you know.' I pointed to his face. 'How's work?'

He didn't reply. Work had obviously not been too wonderful recently.

'Let's have a drink,' I said.

We stepped into a busy pub opposite and Shinichro insisted on first shout. It took an age and he returned looking a little more ruffled and disgusted than when he had left. He still couldn't get used to a crowd of us, touching us, breathing in our odours and hearing our savage language.

'I saw you at the Savoy,' I said while he recovered, taking his first long swallow of cold lager. He didn't react, much. He blinked, took his time, wiped away the slight froth from his sweet lips with the back of his hand.

'I saw you too, with your new boyfriend, the gangster.'

'You were good. Cool, the way you handed over that stuff.'

'I'm glad you enjoyed the show.'

'I wanted to ask you . . .'

His eyes narrowed a little.

'I wanted to ask you if those drams you handed over were the ones that Charlie won.'

He didn't reply right away. He looked steadily at me for at least thirty seconds and said, 'No,' and took another drink. I had to ask him right out.

'Did you get them from Hiroshi Sano?' I said.

'No.'

'They were brand new, then.'

'From our warehouse in Harrow. Is this important?'

'There was something special about that first batch, Shiny.'

'In what way?'

'I don't know.'

'Who does know?'

'Pal.'

'Your friend.' The words came out marinated in acid.

'He treated me little worse than you did . . . better,' I said. Shinichro looked away.

'He wanted to buy Charlie's drams right from the beginning,

you see, the ones Charlie won in Las Vegas. When they went missing he hung around. He thought I'd taken them at first. I convinced him that I hadn't, at least I thought I had, and he switched the blame to Hiroshi Sano. I told you what I thought Sano might be up to. I didn't know whether or not Pal had killed him, to tell you the truth. Then I thought, maybe he had and he was setting us up, you and me, because *he* had taken the drams from Sano and he knew someone somewhere had to make good the deal – you, for instance. And you did make the deal with them. Then he told me he was going to make the Colombians an offer for those chips. I thought he was going to walk with two million. I was wrong. He didn't walk. The fact is, he thought you'd been scared into handing the drams over, the original ones, not new ones, replacement ones. That I'd stolen them all the while, that I'd given them to you, that we were in it together.'

'He thought I was afraid? Why should I be afraid?'

'I'd be afraid if I thought whoever killed Sano was after me, but that's not exactly the point, is it?'

'I was not afraid. Not of him, nor the *yakuza*. In any case, *yakuza* have no cause to harm me. Sano, yes. Me, no.'

My skin goosepimpled with sudden relief. Shinichro hadn't murdered anyone, but more importantly for me, and for Delia, neither had Pal. I gave Shinichro my drink to hold while I dug some cigarettes out of my bag. He watched me light up and then handed back the glass. The threads of smoke lingered about our heads and I wondered if he still cared enough to disapprove.

'They did it?' I said, and then, almost to myself, 'Not Pal.'

'I presume for Sano's abject failure in completing his set task. I was instructed simply to replace the shipment. I met my obligation.'

'Nothing special about the drams from Harrow?'

He shook his head and neither of us spoke for a while. I smoked my cigarette while he supped his drink and looked irritably around at the crowd. The thought occurred to me that I should tell him about the baby, tell him that I'd lied because I wanted to protect it. I wondered what he'd say if I told him that I had thought that *he* might have killed Hiroshi Sano. He finished his beer, turned to me and said, 'I think you will find that maybe they were special only to this man. The gangster you like so much.'

'You mean not to the *yakuza*?'

He nodded, jerking his head.

'Or to the Colombians?'

He jerked his head again and said, 'Just to this man. Your good friend, Pal.'

Shinichro wouldn't stay for another drink, not even for old times' sake and when he left I went to the call box to tell Richard that I was on my way. It wasn't late and it was Friday night. Richard wasn't home. As I replaced the receiver and dug in my handbag for a cigarette someone grabbed my wrist and held it tight, and a voice said, 'Little mama shouldn't smoke, should she?'

Pal twisted my hand palm-side up and pressed his mouth against it, his dark moustache smoothing down my skin like the face of a nuzzling cat.

'How did you find me?' I said, my face flushed and the sweat starting under my arms. That I got my cigarette out of the pack and lit it was imperative, but he was still holding my hand and hurting the flesh on my wrist with his thick rings. While I strained to get away from his tightening grip, he felt in a side pocket for a packet of his own. He pulled a cigarette out of the soft pack with his teeth and, with his free hand, placed it carefully between my lips and lit it with his golden lighter.

'Let me go,' I said.

Pal looked around the crowded pub, whose customers stood shoulder to shoulder inside and outside on the pavement in the fading light. He looked at me and started to smile sympathetically.

'You're going to scream?'

'I could.'

'Lot of people here who would help you, I think.'

'That's right.'

'They'd be too late.'

I stared at him. He looked pleased with himself and he was right. There wasn't much point in making a fuss for nothing.

'Aren't you going to kiss me?' he said.

'See the guy over there?'

Pal looked over his shoulder to a group of likely lads in rolled-up shirt-sleeves; two were standing up leaning on the bar and three were sitting on bar stools.

'Which one?' he said.

'Any one. The one with the loudest tie.'

'So?'

'I'd rather kiss his arse.'

The look on Pal's face didn't change much but the playful light in his eyes disappeared to be replaced by an ominous glitter, like moonlight on gunmetal.

'I want the drams. Charlie's drams, not your little man's,' he said.

'I haven't got them, I told you. You're to leave me, and my friends, alone,' I replied.

Pal looked away with a sigh and a smile. Here was a man who knew what unpleasant task he had to do next because he had had to do it time and time before to awkward little people like me. He turned back with the weary resignation of one who was used to donning the gloves and putting things right but just wished that folk wouldn't screw up so in the first place. Resting one hand gently on my stomach, he stroked it back and forth. I shivered at his touch, my mouth and throat thick with panic.

'It doesn't show so much, does it? Not even in this nice dress,' he said, his hand circling the precious space between my hips, his fingers pulling at the tight black material that clung to me. 'I'd like to take it off, you know, make love to you like before, milk those little mama breasts a little. I didn't hurt you, did I?'

'No,' I said, conscious of the chattering noise around us, of the people who were laughing and not paying any attention. How easy it would be for him to hurt me now, kill me even, without anyone noticing. He bent down over me and whispered in my ear like a lover.

'Even though I could have. You know I could have,' he said. I stamped the cigarette into the floor with some irritation and said, 'Look. You can do what you like but it'd all be for nothing. I haven't got what you want. You saw Shinichro hand over the stuff. I saw him do it. You want drams? You know the guys to ask.'

The discreet blow travelled a very short distance but the impact to my stomach was severe. I doubled over with the shock and shouted with pain, so that Pal had to support me and fend off the concern of well-wishers at one and the same time. He took the part of the worried father, calling for assistance to bundle me into a cab and loudly telling all, while I choked, that he thought I was miscarrying. The cabbie wasn't keen. He said we should call an ambulance but Pal and the crowd that followed us out of the pub persuaded him that he had a moral duty. As we pulled away, my face pressed in agony against the window, I saw Shinichro standing on the pavement, holding his plastic bag and his newspaper, a ragged look of despair on his face.

I squeezed my eyes shut and listened to the cabbie asking Pal if I was OK, if I was going to be sick, if I was bleeding or anything messy like that. Pal reassured him but the cabbie didn't stop whining until he had to brake suddenly and swerve to avoid something in the road.

'Crazy bastard. Did you see that, mate? Bloody drugs, or what?' He wrestled with the steering wheel to get the cab back on track and there was a hard bump against the side. The driver put almost his whole body out of the window to roar at the culprit, who had dropped back behind us. Pal hauled me away from the door, slamming me back into the seat, and the cabbie tried to drive on, crazy with rage, bobbing his head in and out of the window, in for reassurance and out to abuse.

'See him? Fucking bastard. What the bloody hell does he think he's doing? Effing chink. No, mate. Piss off, I said.'

I looked dreamily across Pal's shoulder and I could see Shinichro running down the middle of the road by the side of the cab, waving his arms and screaming at the top of his voice in Japanese. The traffic was slow and cars had begun to honk, hoot and flash their headlights. People thronging the pavements were beginning to stop and stare at the show he was making of himself. When the cab stopped at some lights, Shinichro ducked out of sight only to reappear again on the pavement, clutching at the handle of my door and swinging it open. The cabbie braked hard, apoplectic with rage. As the man fumbled for his door handle, I saw Pal's hand move inside his jacket. I called out a warning but Shinichro had already grasped my arm and was pulling me out of the vehicle. If Pal was going to shoot, I was going to get it in the back. I felt like wetting myself. As my feet hit the ground, my legs buckled and Pal stumbled over me as he struggled to follow us. Shinichro took his chance and planted his knee with some force underneath Pal's dipping chin.

I remember being dragged past so many people, Shinichro pulling and pushing through, holding me up, making me hurry away down little streets and turnings until he could hail a cab of his own.

'Is she all right?' I heard the new cabbie say.

Shinichro held me tight and replied, 'Too much to drink, matey. That's all. Don't worry. She's all right with me.'

Chapter Thirteen

I could hear them arguing from where I was inside the bathroom. Not a loud shouting match the like of which I might have favoured but a fast hard yammering between the two of them. I didn't understand what they were saying but I didn't have to. I knew it was about me. The small chic young woman who had opened the door to us had shown it in her face and who could blame her? It was Friday night and she had been waiting for Shinichro for a couple of hours at least.

She'd had the decency to call a doctor but I wouldn't come out of the bathroom, her black and white bathroom, with its huge mirror above the sink, lit all around with naked lightbulbs the better to do your make-up by. The intense, stabbing cramps had stopped and I felt bruised and dazed, hurt on the inside, and on the outside, hurting everywhere. I could take an aspirin now for that pain, the easy, physical pain, but what was going to take away the deep, dull ache that tightened my throat when I wanted to speak? I hadn't expected it, not that pain, the inner gnawing that made me want to howl like a chained dog, let it out into the silvered darkness of night before the pale, sad face of the moon. I wanted to crumble to dust; dry, desiccated dust that spills through fingers as it is sprinkled on freshly turned earth. I'd grown used to the child, it was part of me. I had decided but I didn't know I had decided until now and I had only myself to blame. I should have built a cocoon for us, a shelter, a nest. I should have run away, stayed away from all that trouble like I'd sworn I would after the last time when all that was hurt was my pride. It was the best excuse I'd ever had to start again and now it was all used up.

The surprise came when the doctor said he was sure there was no baby, but there had been. The fact was when Pal hit me there was nothing much left, no little thing alive for him to hurt. I remembered that night in the rain. It was Hiroshi – good old Al – who had been more to blame than Pal; I understood that now, but he hadn't meant to kill my baby. Pal's intention was clear, but none of it mattered because it was all my fault. I'd lost the baby the night of the poker game. It had been washed away. I'd lied to Shinichro out of pride and to Pal out of fear, but I'd been telling the truth without knowing it, like a fool.

Shinichro was calling my name through the door but I wouldn't answer. I stared at the chrome-bright towel rail and wished I had something soft to hold, something to hug, something childish and small. I reached out and took the towel that hung neatly from it instead, held its thick, rose pink, high quality cotton to me, breathing in the rich expensive perfume of the woman who had let us in.

'Where is she?' I said in the morning. My lips were parched and my voice dry and thin as old paper. Shinichro rested the scented tea on a delicate black table by the side of the bed above me, and then squatted down to answer me.

'With friends.'

'Did you sleep up there all night?'

I pointed to the white futon folded on its wooden slats. He nodded, kicking the air mattress on which I rested with a bare foot.

'How was this?'

'Fine.'

I couldn't remember much, which was probably just as well.

'Who is she?' I said.

'Her name is Hanae. She works for an advertising agency dealing with my company's account.'

'I said, who is she, Shiny?'

He took his time replying, and who could blame him?

'My fiancée,' he said.

I beckoned for the tea and he placed it on the floor beside me. Great. There I was lying on the floor of the woman's bedroom, having driven her from her home when she was expecting a fun evening out, maybe a whole weekend, with her boyfriend, whom she finds out had also been my boyfriend, and more. I'd spent half the night in her toilet and availed myself of her doctor. It was not a good start as a first impression but it spoke volumes for her Oriental sense of duty.

'Does she know who I am? Or am I still your cleaner nowadays?' I said.

'She knows.'

'God.'

'She has known all the time.'

'Oh, Jesus.'

Shinichro sat down cross-legged on the floor beside me as I lay back and covered my face. He pulled at my arm, I pulled it back. I could hear his voice just fine. He didn't need to see my face.

'She came to London first. I followed. But things were not the same. I didn't understand at first what it could be, until I met you. I went with you to understand.'

'Another bloody experiment. God, you're inhuman. Try using an anaesthetic on your victim next time . . .'

'At first, Georgina . . . then, of course, I began to care for you, despite your unpredictability.'

'No trouble with that.'

'Pardon?'

'Unpredictability.'

'Oh.'

I took his arm and lifted myself round so that I could sip the weak tea while it was hot. I looked around the room. It was sparsely furnished in the minimalist style that was the rage in such times of plenty. Nothing was out of place. Fresh flowers bloomed in a tasteful white vase above a low chest of drawers in matt black wood, upon which rested a large oblong mirror. This arrangement served as a dressing table for my absent hostess and it was remarkably free of dust and unfashionable clutter.

'What happened when you discovered that she's nothing like me?'

'I did not expect her to be like you, or you like her. She had changed imperceptibly, almost imperceptibly. I wanted to know how.'

'Very good,' I said.

'Good? I don't understand.'

'Imperceptibly.'

'Imperceptibly? You think so?' he replied, smiling.

'Yes. Very good.'

'Not bad, I think.'

We laughed at this. It hurt after a while. I couldn't keep it up but he stroked my arm when it showed, making my tears start again at his gentleness, his terrible, faithless gentleness. I was scared to let myself go, scared of losing myself completely to grief and despair. I pressed my lips together until they hurt.

'OK. Tell me what this imperceptible change was that you had to find in spades in me to prove she'd been contaminated by us Westerners,' I said.

He slapped his knee with the ball of his hand and shook his head. 'There you go again. Always misunderstanding. No, rather, misinterpreting.'

'Explain, then.'

'She was not so serious about things.'

'Not serious about you?'

'Not me. About herself, her job, what she was here for. It shocked me, to tell you the truth.'

'Yes. And you certainly shocked her back, didn't you?'

It was about time I got my cigarettes out of the bag. I could smoke now, when I liked and as much, without the tiniest twinge of conscience. I was free of responsibility. I looked at the cigarette and remembered when they'd started to taste good again. Remarkable thing, biology.

'She knew. She told me. Find a white girl and see that I'm not so bad, she said. She told me that she had loosened up. Those were her words. Japanese are too anxious to please, she said, to put on a good public face and do the proper thing. Loosened up, yes, that's what she said.'

I pointed to a dressing gown hanging on the back of the door, something sumptuous in rose-pink towelling. Shinichro brought it and helped me on with it.

'Where are we?' I said.

'Notting Hill.'

'I have to think where I can go that's safe. I have to phone my friend, Richard. I was supposed to be with him last night,' I said. I felt his hands stop. 'You can't go back to your place either,' I said.

Shinichro turned me around and smoothed his hands down the collar of the gown. His hooded eyes glistened as they looked into mine. I could see my face in them.

147

'I was so jealous,' he said. 'I have done you great harm. It was all my fault. Forgive me.'

'Thank you, anyway.'

'For what?'

'For making a public show of yourself for a good stretch of Long Acre.'

'I took him by surprise, eh? Very good ambush.'

'I'll say.'

'Like Pearl Harbor, yes?'

It would have seemed churlish at that point to remind him of the ultimate consequence of that famous raid, that the ultimate consequence of all our vain actions is chaos. I kissed his cheek instead and went for a shower.

When I'd finished and cleaned up after me like I had never done before, just to prove that I was no savage, Shinichro was waiting for me in the large kitchen-diner. He had made some toast and poured us some juice. He looked up to see me standing meekly by the door holding my clothes.

'I can't wear this dress...' I said. He got up from the table and walked with me into her bedroom to rifle through her wardrobe.

'I can't wear her clothes.'

'If it is of necessity then you must, but I think you are much too tall. I have some things here, if you don't mind.' The navy sweatshirt he found for me was baggy, which is never a problem, and the jeans were too big. I had to borrow a belt from Hanae's high-quality collection.

'Does Hanae smoke?' I said, sitting down to breakfast at her black trestle table. Shinichro buttered my toast.

'No.'

I drank some juice. She bloody wouldn't, would she?

'Are you all right?' he said. My hands were shaking and I felt hot and feverish. The tiredness that I had felt was being replaced by weakness and this was no time for it. I had to tell Shinichro who we were hiding from. He seemed not to be listening as I explained what was in the newspaper articles held in *Technology Week*'s database but he was, of course, intently.

'He is a smuggler, then, an adventurer,' he said when I had finished.

'Oh, he's that all right, and a spy of some sort, or at least he used to be. Sounds so old fashioned now, doesn't it? Spy. Spook.'

'If you work for computer company, no.'

'No, I suppose not. Cold War warriors may be out, but trade war warriors are in.'

'Of course, but they were never out. They are one and the same. What else is there but trade and land? What else is there?'

'Look, I'm a journalist. I don't have opinions on that kind of thing. He's got connections, and friends. Here we are running about the town because he knows where we are, and where we've been. I've had a grey van following me all week. I'd swear my flat's been bugged, and my neighbour's, more than likely. He knows where you live. He knew where we were going to meet. He knew exactly when you were going to turn up and that you'd switched the deal to the Savoy. And no one's picked him up. What's the price on drams now?'

'Steady. They will start to fall after the Games.'

'Why?'

'There is always a big boom in consumer electronics every four years. This year has special circumstances, which, you will remember, we discussed ... at length, but I think the market will look again at prices after Seoul.'

'So why's he here? Why isn't he off selling what he's got?'

Shinichro rubbed his nose and leaned back in his chair, lifting his arms and clasping his hands behind his head. He closed his eyes for a moment and then spoke.

'If these drams have been pre-sold, then all he must do is deliver them. That is no problem. However, what if he knew these Colombians? Maybe he sells for them and gets rid of their money.'

It was more than possible. More possible than the idea of Pal the businessman walking around with a million dollars cash to buy chips for his company. That had to be why he was in Las Vegas. The Colombians must have been there waiting for a delivery from Hiroshi Sano, and Pal, the man with all the right connections, was the one who was going to sell the drams and get the dollars for them, and put the money in some numbered account in Budapest. The secrecy laws there were better than those of Switzerland with all those top communists diverting revolutionary funds to their own accounts for the rainy season. Pal'd offered to buy the drams from Charlie even though he was in no position to do so. He just wanted his hands on that briefcase and once Charlie had shown him who knows what would have happened? The point Shinichro was making was maybe he didn't have the dollars. He had to sell those chips to get them. Shinichro was right.

'OK. But you replaced those chips. Fine. Pal gets on with his job. But he didn't, did he? He wants the original batch, like you said, and he's getting a hell of a lot of help trying to find them. That's what I'm trying to say. Who are his friends here? The articles said he was a wanted man, that MI6 wanted him,' I said.

'MI6?'

'Intelligence. Our spies. Like the CIA.'

'Of course. I misunderstood. Maybe they do not wish to catch him any more. Maybe they do a deal. Maybe they are helping him now, working together. You see, there is always *tatemae* and *honne*, everywhere. And *kurumaku*.'

'What's that?'

'In Kabuki theatre it is the black curtain that covers the people who work behind the scenes.'

How the world had changed. In times of turmoil a man has more in common with his enemy than with his brother, provided they're in the same business. We were in real trouble if our lot were involved. I recognized that much. I'd been this way before when Max had spiked that story and Robert Falk and I had felt it, like nails in our hands. Maybe this was what Robert had meant by 'a certain resistance'. It was his little warning. Perspiration had started bubbling on my face. I could feel it slicking down between my breasts. If I stood up, I knew my legs would not hold me. Where could I go if Hanae came home? I couldn't run for the life of me. Shinichro looked across at me and said nothing until he had poured me some tea. He spoke again when I had finished the cup.

'Did you see the chips?' he said.

'Charlie showed me them in packs.'

'Forgive me. It could be that they were not drams. You see, only a very experienced person could tell what these chips were. They could have been anything, microprocessors – maybe very valuable – memory, but of what sort? There are many different kinds. Or counterfeit chips, perhaps, with false documents of certification and part numbers that do not exist. They are very common.'

'In that case why would you have to replace them?' I said quickly. 'If they weren't drams from your *on*-man.'

'Hai. You're right,' he replied. 'Mmm. You're right.'

'You did give them drams, didn't you?'

He looked silently at me, a firm expression on his face.

'I have to ask,' I said.

'I did. The very best in stock,' he replied.

I watched him eating. There was a change in him, too, an almost imperceptible one, like the one he had seen in Hanae. He must have learned that there are no immutable rules that could and should be applied, just appropriate ones, or in some situations no bloody rules at all. He'd loosened up, all right, he'd relaxed in this strange, hostile place even if he didn't like the smell. I liked the look of his face even more, the full lips and strong bones, the yellow sheen to the pale skin. I imagined him as a young boy, as a baby, chubby, with eyes as dark as olives and hair as black as crow feathers. It was a sweet, warm, nostalgic picture until the edges started to burn away. He did not feel any grief, any pain, as I did. He had brought me money for an abortion when my child was already dead. He wasn't to know, I said to myself, breathing deeply to calm the roaring pulse that beat in my wrists and temples, but I couldn't forgive him, or myself. I started to shake and Shinichro came to me and held me tight.

Hanae called a little later and he spoke to her for a long while as I lay in bed.

'We can stay here for the weekend. You sleep now,' he said and I did.

On Monday morning, Shinichro got up early and dressed in a smart but sober striped suit. He obviously spent a good deal of time at Hanae's. I had washed my dress and dried it, folded it into a plastic carrier bag. Shinichro's sweatshirt and jeans looked all right, baggy but OK. It was the black canvas Widow Twanky lace-ups that gave the whole look its surreal charm. I looked at myself in Hanae's mirror, angled stylishly on its slim stainless steel legs, and thought that I couldn't walk the streets like that. People would start tossing coins at me. I'd brave it and go home. There were worse things than death. Flares, for instance, and those shoes with those jeans. But as I stood there I changed my mind. If I could risk that, I could risk going into *Technology Week* to see Max Winters.

'What are you going to do?' Shinichro said.

'I'm going to see my old boss. What about you?' I replied.

'I'm going to work.'

'Business as usual?'

'For you too, it seems.'

'How do I look?'

'You should have more rest.'

'Not my face. This lot.'

I got no reply.

Richard was holding a news conference as I walked in and he kept going despite the looks I was getting from the band of reporters, most of whom knew me, who were gathered around him. Max didn't look up until I said 'Hello.'

Max had lost a little more of his thick reddish hair so that the blue veins on his pale skin seemed more prominent, like tattooed snakes curling down to his temples. You could feel sympathy for someone as unsociable as he if you thought for a moment that it was because of the terrible accident that had snapped his back, crushed his legs and confined him to a wheelchair. It wasn't. Max had always been a mean son of a bitch. Everyone who knew him before said so, even his business partner, Ray, who knew him better than anyone. No one ever felt pity for Max, not even at first. He didn't know how to talk to people. He communicated with his employees via the internal telephone or E-mail. A face to face was not to be recommended. When he was angry he shouted and when he was pleased he said nothing. Richard had obviously taken over his weekly briefing sessions, which had never been more than short monologues to an uncomfortable reluctant audience. I noticed, however, that Richard kept the team within earshot.

'Can I have a word, Max?' I said.

'I hear you're working for us,' he replied. The smoke from his thin pungent cigar drifted up into my face as his fingers tapped on the keyboard of his computer terminal.

'Richard wanted the story.'

He didn't comment further. I stood there watching him smoke and key words into the machine with his pale, calloused fingers. The silent minutes passed by and then I understood. He wasn't going to say anything. I had come to see him. It was for me to

152

make the first belly-crawling move. We were in the here and now; what was past was past.

'I looked up some back issues.'

'On Textline?'

'Yes.'

'Our line?'

'Yes.'

'How'd you get in?'

'Richard,' I said. He'd probably check whether my password was current and whether I'd used it, but then again he might not. Meantime, I was going to lie. He'd expect that.

'There were a couple of stories on exports to denied parties. I pulled up one that was connected, in the *Sunday Times*,' I said.

'Dates?' he said and I gave them to him. He carried on typing and the minutes went by.

'I haven't got all day,' he said and looked up, one eye brown, the other flecked with green. To my annoyance, my face flushed, burning my cheeks and giving him the satisfaction of knowing he'd scored a direct hit.

'I wondered if you remembered them?' I said.

'I do.'

'Well?'

'What do you want to know?'

'Who wrote them?'

Max smiled at this point, an incident so rare and unnerving that I should have called the news team over to record it for posterity. He took a deep draught of his cigar and blew the blue-brown smoke slowly out of the side of his mouth.

'Which ones?' he said.

'Come on, Max.'

I was surprised at myself. Not at my irritation, that was justified, at my irrationality. The old ginger tom could eat me alive. Fortunately, he seemed in an unlikely good mood. He looked away from his keyboard and drew a press release from the top of a deck of grey, plastic trays. He penned a couple of lines on it and placed it on top of his screen before taking another and working through it in the same way as if I wasn't there. He carried on with this repetitive task before tackling the *Wall Street Journal* for any suitable leads. It was when he had the broadsheet open wide in

153

front of his face, clipped between his fingers like it was hung out to dry, that he spoke.

'I'll think you'll find that the person who did the stories for us helped the *Sunday Times* team too. Under a pseudonym, because he was freelancing without permission. He called himself Dominic Charles for them, but for us he was, of course, plain old Charlie East. You know, the investment wizard – the one who owes you fifty thousand pounds.'

Max didn't drop the paper to see the look on my face. He didn't need to. He'd got everything he wanted even if he wasn't going to get a story from me. I wasn't interested in writing it any more anyway. I had been damned, an outcast with the devil that was Charlie East. I didn't stop to talk to Richard as I made my way past the compacted paper debris of Max's smoky cabled office. Charlie East. Back there in Las Vegas, a lifetime away for some, but I remembered what he'd said. 'Georgina, I'm hot.' And he hadn't been talking about the degrees Celsius burning up that desert town.

Chapter Fourteen

I bumped into Shinichro on the way out.

'I have a day off,' he said.

'You've got the sack, haven't you?'

'Sack?'

'Dismissal. Tin tack. Sack.'

'Ah ... also the push? No, of course not. I am in a very good situation at work, an improved situation.'

He stood patiently in front of me on the pavement as I snapped open my bag for my cigarettes. I could see from his face that he did still disapprove, but I lit up anyway.

'Now is not the time,' I said.

'As you wish.'

'I'm busy today, Shiny.'

'I will accompany you, if you don't mind.'

I got a feeling he wasn't asking but telling. I started to walk down Old Compton Street towards Cambridge Circus and he kept pace beside me. The sun was bright and the smell of freshly ground coffee and chocolate croissants drifted past us with the dank smell of diesel. The traffic was busy but light, and the motorcycle messengers stayed off the pavements.

'I need to phone Charlie East. Remember Charlie?'

'I know of him. We have not been introduced,' Shinichro replied, opening his briefcase and resting it on his bulky thigh. He handed me a mobile.

'Press this and then this, then the number,' he said, pointing his finger as I stared at the calculator works. Charlie's voice snapped on the line when the service connected but it softened when he realized it was me.

'Hello there, flower,' he said.

'We need to talk . . .'

'Can't now. I'm so busy . . .'

'. . . in about twenty minutes.'

'I'm at work, George.'

'It's about Pal Kuthy . . .'

'He still around?'

'. . . and Dominic Charles, and a story he wrote about the afore-mentioned. Twenty minutes, Charlie boy.'

I could hear him pull his mouth away from the phone and curse, curse, curse.

'An hour, give me an hour. Shit. No. Two, give me two. We've got a leak on the budget deficit. Lunch. Let's have lunch.'

'Twenty minutes, in reception.'

Shinichro cleared his nose as I handed him back his phone.

'I wish you wouldn't do that,' I said.

The smart lady in the sharp Armani-style suit gave us two visitors' passes and let us sit and wait, in subdued lighting, on two wide low-backed armchairs directly in front of her, but at least twenty-five feet away across a brown carpeted floor. She deferred to Shinichro even though I did the talking. He was dressed for the part and he had a nice business card, which he presented in that polite, efficient way of his, with a little bow of his head like a full stop at the end of a perfectly constructed sentence. He was the sort of visitor who could be expected at a city stockbrokers: smart, neat and businesslike. Some hollow-eyed individual with no formal identification, wearing oversized jeans, weird boots and carrying a change of clothes in a plastic Seven–Eleven bag, just didn't cut it.

'Call him again, if you would,' I told her after twenty minutes had expired. She did as I asked. I watched her nod as she listened. When she put the receiver down, she said, 'Mr East will be another ten minutes at least.'

'Where's the toilet, please?'

I knew where it was because I'd been here with Charlie before, but the receptionist directed me as I had wanted her to. Once I'd got through the doors I took a couple of right turns and found the stairs. Charlie was on the fourth floor. His workstation was tucked in behind some shelves stuffed with ringbinders and refer-ence books. The noisy open-plan office was jam-packed with wall-to-wall screens, a dealer at each one, market makers in a roomier space at the far end. Charlie sat with five other slave analysts in a recess intended for three filing cabinets at the most. His desk was awash with paper held down by three telephones, two of which were lit up and ringing. His owners were pulling at his leash. They wanted an edge and they wanted him to give it to them. Charlie was holding his head trying to hear himself think and I had to tap his shoulder to get his attention. When he saw me he kicked at his desk and shot his chair into the back of an analyst behind him. He dragged his bony fingers through his hair and grasped tufts of it in frustration. It wasn't how you'd expect a cool poker dude to react and I realized then that Charlie was as much a cool poker dude as Ronald Reagan was Top Gun.

'No. George. I can't talk. Not now. Can't you see—'

'OK. I'll talk,' I said. He didn't answer, he just stared.

'You knew he was after those drams, didn't you?'

No answer.

'Charlie?'

'What the fuck are you *wearing*?'

He looked around, embarrassed, hoping everyone else was too busy to notice. They were. I was Cellophane. I could have been naked and no one would have noticed. The really cool poker dudes were trading.

'You knew who he was in Vegas, didn't you?'

'I knew all right. I knew he wanted those fucking drams, too.'

'You set me up.'

Charlie's ungainly jaw dropped. He looked confused, but I knew better. He was never confused. He was either winning or losing. I nodded at him. 'You did.'

Charlie stood up and edged his lanky frame behind me, his arm stretched out, half pushing, half directing me.

'Can we step outside for a moment, flower?' he said.

As we walked through the office the level of noise began to rise and Charlie looked behind him. Red boxy text appeared on the television screen that hung in a corner by the low ceiling. The interest rate was now 9.5 per cent, the highest it had been all year. The noise became a subdued roar. Someone called out to him but Charlie pushed hard at the door, bundling me through it. The door swung back and shut with a soft pop like the top loosening on a vacuum flask. The noise disappeared like a genie in a bottle and it was quiet. Charlie turned to me, poking his finger in my face.

'Now look. I don't need this shit from you,' was all he had time to say because within that single moment he was biting into his bottom lip to staunch a rush of searing pain. Shinichro, who had been standing unseen in the shadow of the stairwell, had stepped smartly forward. He had firmly grasped the offending digit and bent it back and down. Charlie's long frame buckled at the joints, twisting in an effort to conduct his agony elsewhere, anywhere but where it was. Shinichro wasn't a tall man but at one point Charlie was looking up at him.

'Charlie. This is a friend of mine. He hasn't got a lot of time,' I said.

'He says he hasn't got them,' I said as we burst out into the sunlight. Shinichro walked briskly by my side.

'You believe him?'

'I believe him.'

'Why?'

'He looks like he's lost a million dollars.'

'Forgive me. He looks like a man whose finger was giving him great deal of pain.'

'You didn't have to hurt him like that. You hung on all the while he was talking.'

I stopped and turned to face him. He was perspiring a little with the heat and the pace. The fitter you are the quicker you sweat. I hardly managed to glow, just to gasp a little while he was breathing easily. I didn't say anything. I looked to the right down the busy City Road, waiting for our time to cross and take a turn towards Liverpool Street. Every building within our field of vision seemed to be wrapped in tarpaulin or scaffolding. When was it all going to slow up? When were we going to see the end, the point of this tumultuous activity, just stand back and take a look at what was being done? I stopped again before Broadgate.

'Where are we going?' he said.

'I don't know. I'm thinking. Why?'

'Why do I think he has them?'

'Why did you have to hurt him?'

'He had something to tell us.'

'So what? What is this cruelty thing? Is it genetic or what?'

'Are you going to mention the war?'

'No. Of course not. I'm sorry. But why did you do it?'

'Because of Las Vegas. OK?'

I started walking again, lighting a cigarette as I went.

'You've got a nerve,' I said.

I needed a drink. There was a pub on the corner and I walked in. I didn't care if Shinichro followed but he did. It was quiet inside and cool. He tried to pay but I pushed his hand away.

'Did you sleep together?' he said, sitting down on a tall bar stool next to me.

'It's none of your business.'

'You shared a room.'

'How do you know?'

'I called the hotel.'

'They told you?'

'It was a business call.'

I sighed and took a long swallow of gin and tonic. 'I've shared a room with him more times than I care to remember, but not his bed. And the only time I saw him in Vegas was on our way out of the place. Where do you get off, sleeping with two women and checking up on me?' I said.

'Get off?'

'You know what I damned well mean.'

He drank a little beer and fiddled with a place mat. I felt dizzy with the first hit of alcohol and the nicotine, my head and my belly ached. My feet were killing me in those ridiculous shoes. There was no new information from Charlie except that he had known Pal Kuthy, recognized him from photos he'd seen on the *Sunday Times* assignment and, yes, he knew he was dangerous and, no, he didn't have the drams all along and, yes, that's what he thought they were, drams. Shinichro hadn't said a thing but he'd held on to that finger of Charlie's for far longer than he needed to, making him step painfully along the corridor until we found a quiet spot to talk. Shinichro had taken his little revenge, and for nothing. He sat next to me in silence sliding the beer mat through his fingers over and over again.

'That's why you hit me, isn't it?' I said, but he didn't answer. I

159

bought the next round and paid for it while we sat at the bar together, drinking in silence. I don't know what he was thinking, but I was wondering where we could go next that would be safe. There was nowhere left. He paid for the next round and when we'd finished that I said, 'Oh, to hell with it, Shiny. We have to go somewhere. Your place or mine?'

'I think we should go back to Charlie, Georgina. He is not telling you the truth.'

Charlie's office was sandwiched down a narrow road off the dusty City Road and Shinichro and I had one more drink before walking the quarter of a mile back there. As we turned into the street, Charlie and Pal were pushing themselves out of the revolving door and into the sunlight. We moved back, pressing ourselves against a shadowy wall, and waited. The two looked like they were talking out a deal. Every now and then Charlie held out his hands. He looked at his watch a couple of times, too, and ran his hand through his hair. Pal spent a lot of time smoothing his fingers over his thick moustache, jacket back, hand on hip. It could have been any old hustle until I saw his hand reach back around his waistband. Shinichro squeezed my arm to silence and steady me as Pal pulled out something heavy and metallic. Charlie saw it, sticking his arms out like he was in a position to negotiate, like he was reasoning with some clubhouse hothead whose drink he'd spilled. He was smiling in appeasement, his grin spread like a chimpanzee's chuckle. Pal was smiling, too, but like he always did, for no particular reason other than that he was happy in his work. He touched Charlie's shoulder once with the metal cosh and Shinichro started to pull me back round the corner. I shrugged him away and shouted. Pal looked towards us. They both looked, Charlie raising his arm and Pal swinging his down so that the heavy cosh connected with Charlie's knee, one blow, then another, then another. Pal's arm arching up and scything down like a peasant cutting corn. Charlie's legs collapsed and he went down, screeching like a tom cat with his tail in a trap, and Pal looked at him and then over at us, that big friendly 'aw shucks' smirk on his face.

'Hey, Japan!' he shouted.

Shinichro stood quiet and still, gripping my arm as Charlie's hysterical screams nailed us to the floor. A couple of men came out of a building behind Pal. They stopped when they saw Charlie and hurried by, the pair of them talking, looking back a couple of times and then forward at us. They crossed the road, out of the firing line and went about their business. Pal kicked Charlie on the thigh and called out to us again. I couldn't hear him for the traffic in the street behind us and the sound of hammers thumping into concrete. I could hear Charlie's cries and see Pal's mouth moving and then it stopped. He stuck the cosh back into his waistband and backed down the street before turning and walking out of sight. We walked towards Charlie and stood over him, looking down at his contorted face, pale-lipped with pain.

'Phone an ambulance. Phone Debbie. I think he's broken my fucking leg,' he cried, gripping Shinichro's jacket as he squatted down beside him. Shinichro felt along Charlie's angled shin up to his knee.

'How is your finger?' he said and the hope in Charlie's wild eyes faded.

Charlie couldn't bend his unnaturally angled leg straight, wouldn't, it hurt too much. Shinichro kept telling him, 'It is not broken. Straighten it,' but Charlie wouldn't. He curled up like a squawling child and gripped his damaged knee with his bony fingers. I wanted to call an ambulance but Shinichro told me to wait and I watched while he ringed his hand around Charlie's ankle. I said nothing. My mouth was dry. I felt a little disorientated, empty in my stomach. Charlie looked at me and at Shinichro for pity, his pale face grey as old wash water. Shinichro looked at him but he spoke to me.

'I think Charlie boy should tell you where the drams are, Georgina,' he said.

'Shinichro, please . . .' I said. Charlie rapidly got the idea and began to scream. Shinichro pointed a finger at the swelling joint.

'His leg is not broken but the ligaments, possible the ligaments, have snapped,' he said and Charlie whimpered, 'Please. I don't know. I don't. I don't.'

'What he must do is this.'

With a quick movement of two hands, one above the knee and one on the ankle, he snapped the bended leg straight like someone tugging a stiff door shut. The effect on Charlie was electrifying.

161

His eyes opened wide and his dumb mouth gaped like a hole in the ground. Shinichro stood up and Charlie collapsed backwards, gasping and panting, the palms of his hands pressing into his eyes as if he were trying to push them into his head.

'You see, if the ligaments are broken, the bones, the tibia and fibia, strike the back of the knee. There is nothing to hold. It is a typical sporting injury. Very common when the foot is placed flat and the body twists away . . . and it is very painful. Straightening the leg brings everything back into position, as you can see. However, bending the leg back . . .'

Shinichro squatted down again and gripped Charlie's ankle tightly again until the man's voice cracked with desperation and he began to beg.

'No. Please. Please. I don't know. God help me. I don't fucking know where they are.'

'Shiny . . .' I said, my voice cracking with false authority. He didn't appear to hear. He held the ankle tightly, keeping it pinned to the ground and not allowing any movement in the stiff and now grotesquely ballooned leg, though Charlie was edging the rest of his body along the ground. Shinichro gazed at Charlie for a couple of stony moments until suddenly Charlie began talking really fast.

'I knew about him. I did. I said I did. I did. I'm sorry. The drams were stolen. They were stolen. Honest to God.'

Shinichro looked up at me and nodded.

'Call the ambulance, Georgina,' he said.

'Would you have done it?' I said when he sat down in my kitchen.

'I don't understand.'

'Bent his leg back again?'

Shinichro didn't answer that question.

'I think you have other things to worry about.'

I looked out of the window. The van wasn't there but I still felt that our words were leaking out of the flat like water from a mesh bucket.

'This gangster. He thinks one of you has what he wants,' he said.

'He thinks you might, too.'

'Perhaps. But he does not believe the chips were stolen by anybody else.'

'At random.'

'At random, yes.'

There was a girl down below playing in the sunshine with a little white terrier. It seemed to have springs in its legs that bounced it from the ground and up to something the girl was holding in her hand. There was no telling if she had anything or not but she teased him with her fingers anyway, her high plaited ponytail flicking about her brown neck, the beads in her hair as bright as Smarties. The dog jumped and yapped around her, and its pink tongue lolled about its grinning mouth. I came away from the warm window.

'What would you do if he came here?' I asked.

Shinichro smiled to himself. 'I would offer him a solution, of course.'

'Somehow, I don't think that would make the slightest difference to him, do you?'

He shrugged.

'So what did you have in mind?' I said.

He didn't answer but he smiled, crinkling up his half-moon eyes and showing his even teeth.

'Aren't you afraid?' My voice betrayed a little frustration. He was impenetrable when he was like this, like a box that would open only when you pushed the correct pieces of wood this way and that. I had to ask him the right question and then he would give me the right answer.

'I think your friend will give us all a little time now. To think about our position.'

I walked past him into the front room and took the sweatshirt off. I was hungry. I wanted a shower and a rest. On the way to the bathroom I caught sight of a quarter-bottle of Scotch that stood glinting golden brown on the sideboard. It was nearly six o'clock but the sun still shone brightly outside. It didn't seem right to drink Scotch in the light of day, but I wanted to. I wanted to curl up on my bed with it, swig from it and suck from it until the drips ran down my chin and I could lie back drunk and feel the room spin out of sight. Shinichro's soft voice behind me made me turn. He gazed at me for a moment, his drooping lids heavy over his dark eyes, and, taking care with each word, said, 'Lie down. I'll bring you some ice, in a glass.'

We could have made love, I suppose, if I'd felt up to it, but not

163

like we used to. It was different now. Then, we had looked at each other as exotics. Of course, I enjoyed his company and he enjoyed mine but we never really had to prove how much. We were too busy using each other, inching over each other's foreign skin, marvelling at the potency of our differences, at the thrill of the mismatch in our little theatre of miscegenation. How foolish we had been to believe that there would be no consequences, that he might care and I conceive, and that it might hurt so much to lose everything. I left the bottle of Scotch on the sidetable by my bed with the tumbler of melting ice cubes while Shinichro lay beside me and stroked my hand. He got up more than once to look out of the bedroom window, wandering into the kitchen to check that one too. My mind was looking through windows, too, for something it had missed. Poker players had a saying that financial traders understood very well. There is always a fool in any game, and if you don't know who the fool is, then it's you. I'd be damned if it was going to be me, not again.

'I must call Hanae,' Shinichro said.

'No, don't.'

His face tensed.

'Not from here. You can't phone her from here. They're listening.'

The words were hardly out of my mouth when the telephone rang.

Charlie was calling from St Bart's, the old City Hospital by Smithfield's meat market. I picked up the extension in my bedroom.

'How are we?' I said.

'I'm in agony, what's with you?'

'I've got a pain. In my neck.'

'That fucking gorilla get you too? What is he, the ex-MC of "Endurance"?'

'Actually, the pain in the neck started in Vegas . . .' I said.

'Look, Georgina . . .'

That was it. The sarcasm disappeared. He had given up, and the sheepish tone in his voice told me. I was talking to the fool, and he was about to show himself.

'When's visiting hour?' I said quickly.

'Seven.'

164

'Ward?'

'Five.'

'Let's talk then.'

'Don't bring him.'

'He was just doing a bit of first aid, Charlie.'

'Yeah ... and the bridge over the River Kwai was a road improvement project. Who is he?'

'Oh, he does for me. You know, around the house.'

'Yeah? Well, I think every home should have one, George. I really do.'

Chapter Fifteen

Shinichro said he would accompany me and wouldn't take no for an answer. I took some paracetamol for the headache and the bruises and phoned Robert Falk before we left. He wasn't much help.

'If there has been an assault then you must report it,' he said.

'I'm telling you.'

'It's not my department.'

'I know, but . . .'

'Look, why don't you phone when you can give something to *me*.'

'Right.'

'Where are you now? Are you OK?'

'Home. I'm all right. I'm going to see Charlie.'

'Where is he?'

I hesitated for a moment and then remembered that Charlie had phoned me. Anyone listening on the echoing line would know where he was.

'Bart's. I've got to go now.'

'Mrs Powers . . .'

'Yes?'

'Do be careful.'

'Yeah, thanks.'

For nothing. I put down the receiver and looked at it.

'No good?' said Shinichro, smoothing back his wet black hair that filled the air with the scent of jojoba. I shook my head.

'Not his department.'

'He is a policeman?'

'Computer fraud, any threat to computer security, that sort of thing.'

There was an explanation. Robert could have just been cautious about speaking to me over the phone. Maybe he didn't want to look like he was taking sides, getting involved. There was another explanation, of course. That he really didn't want to get involved this time, that he wanted a quiet life for a change. It was possible, but very, very disappointing. I glanced at myself in the mirror. I looked tired and pale. Maybe some lipstick and a ton of bronzer dust . . .

'You look nice,' said Shinichro.

'I look like death,' I said.

Debbie looked up briefly as we walked in and then continued reading the glossy magazine that she had bought to while away the hour set aside to comfort Charlie. She looked as sour and as sulky as ever but despite her distress she had managed to slip into her *Out of Africa* ensemble that only spared her watching public the pith helmet. Charlie's sickly face was junkie grey and bubbles of saliva clung to the corners of his dry mouth. His leg, stiff with white plaster, was raised slightly to ease the swelling. He opened his puffy eyes to acknowledge my 'Hello' but said nothing. I pulled up a chair to sit down and Shinichro stood beside me, sturdy legs apart, hands clasped behind his back. Charlie raised his eyes to him and a heavy hand.

'Before you ask, you bastard . . . the finger's fine,' he said. Shinichro gave a tiny courteous bow and Charlie licked his dry lips before speaking again in a voice cracking with weariness and pain.

'Done my kneecap and my ligaments. I'll be in plaster for weeks . . . months.'

'You're lucky he didn't shoot you,' I said.

'I wish he had.'

'That bad?'

'What do you think? The guy rearranged my kneecap to face the other way. Clip clop. That's me walking down the fucking street.'

'I'm serious. He could have shot you. He's got a gun.'

'George, he's a pro. He's got tools and methods for every job. A regular plumber. He's not going to shoot me.'

'Because you've got what he wants, right?'

'No. I told you . . . and I told him . . . and him.' He glanced at

Shinichro and lay back in the bed, his sepulchral arms by his sides. The lids of his eyes squeezed in for a couple of moments as if to block out the pain. When he had recovered a little he gazed wearily at me. There were green grapes on his locker and Charlie waved his arm at them.

'Want some? Take some. She brought them. I won't eat them. A ciggie. That's what I want,' he said and Debbie ignored his less than affectionate reference to her except to say, 'You can't have one in here,' without lifting her head. They must have had a row.

'You knew who he was from the start. Why the hell didn't you tell the police?' I whispered.

'He was going to buy the drams off me, OK?'

'But you could have sold them to anyone.'

'Not with him around. He was on my back. I'd have made the deal and dumped him then.'

'I don't think. He'd have dumped you, more like. Did you really think he was going to pay for the things? You should have turned him in as soon as you could. You could have told me, at least. It would have saved me a lot of grief.'

Charlie grew more agitated as our conversation progressed and tried to lift himself up to make another point but the pain was too much. He slumped backwards with a suffering sigh into the heap of white bar-coded pillows behind him. Debbie was not unduly troubled by the altercation or Charlie's obvious discomfort. She read her magazine while Charlie clutched his fingers around his leg as if he could somehow soothe away the soreness that gnawed at his bones under the thick white cast. His voice trembled as he spoke.

'Well, I didn't, did I? What would you have done, anyway? Written another fucking story with a picture of me in a six-foot box? I thought when someone took the things that would be it. He'd go. Go look for some more.'

I sat back in my chair and folded my arms.

'What do you want to tell us, Charlie? That you really haven't got them? I believe you. You'd have told him at the first crack he took at your knee, wouldn't you?'

Charlie looked defiant. 'No way.'

'The finger?'

'The finger, definitely. I can't stand physical pain, you know that.'

168

Debbie cleared her throat. Charlie glanced warily at her and then nodded at the silent Shinichro.

'Doesn't say much, does he? What's his name?' he said.

'Shinichro Saito. He's a friend.'

Shinichro nodded slightly but did not hand over his card this time.

'He thinks you've definitely got them,' I said.

'What's it to him?'

'Oh, nothing much. Sano's cost his company two million dollars to date, that's all. I think he'd like at least a million back.'

With some effort, Charlie leaned forward to challenge us, his face flushing with the struggle.

'I won those things fair and square.'

'I thought the money didn't matter. I thought you said that to win was the important thing, or isn't that good enough for you now?'

'Don't be fucking silly. A million? Easy to say when you've got it, not when you've lost it. Anyway, the game didn't stop there. It's still on, isn't it?'

'What did you bring us here for, Charlie?'

He jabbed a thumb at Debbie. 'Ask her.'

Debbie didn't even look up.

'Debbie?' I said. No reply. She chewed her lips a bit, getting lipstick on her big teeth like she always did.

'Tell them,' Charlie commanded but she ignored him, lazily flicking over a couple more pages of her magazine and wriggling her bottom into a more comfortable position on the vinyl armchair. Charlie stared at her as if his will could move her before turning, defeated, to me.

'She's had them all along.'

My face flushed red. I could feel the blush on my neck, the rush of boiling anger rising to my cheeks. Charlie carried on talking, explaining the obvious.

'Debbie checked the box number I gave her. She turned over my place, got the key, the other number, faked my signature and took the drams. She's still got them.'

'How come?'

No answer, and no movement from Debbie.

Imagine how she'd felt. I'd got the right one, the one with the million-dollar drams, she got the one with the love snaps in it. I'm

169

sure it must have occurred to Charlie that she might want to go and feast her eyes on a million. Take it, maybe. Of course he did, that's why he'd given me the right key. He trusted me more than he trusted her. He knew her, after all he slept with her on a regular basis and made love to her in unorthodox positions in numerous unsuitable venues. He knew what a vain, jealous, avaricious person she was and he loved her, far too much to trust her, because that would have been far too onerous a burden for her to bear. He might have expected her to open the box but he expected her to be volcanically and vengefully angry when she did, forcing him to soothe her in the time-honoured way that he'd learned so well. He really didn't expect her to be so . . . so damned cunning.

'How long have you known?' I said.

'A while.'

'I see. Everyone would think they were stolen but you two had them all along. You just had to wait for the pack to push off home.'

'Right.'

'Just a pity Pal's so persistent, so experienced in these matters, you know, in lies and deceit.'

I arched my neck to the side to try and get into her line of vision.

'Lucky they didn't steal the photos? Oh, well done,' I stage-whispered to her face. Her eyes flicked up to deliver a quick contemptuous glance before returning to the magazine. Christ, he had really screwed up this time. The last time, I'd only lost a little money and he'd only lost his job. This time I'd lost a lot more, I would never know how much. He had been the fool in the game all along. The fool that I'd thought I was for a time, and I'd thought she was for ever. Charlie was the sucker and Debbie had been holding the best hand all along, and what's more she'd played it. I tried to keep my voice calm and it was thick with emotion.

'Let me get this right, Charlie. My friend here is out of pocket a couple of million . . . a man has been murdered . . . you have been crippled . . . my friend and her family have been terrorized, I have had a . . . been thumped about, threatened, bugged, watched, followed and bullied because Pal Kuthy thought I might have these things, or at least know where they were, and all along this horse's twat has been sitting on them?'

170

There was silence for a moment until Debbie muttered into the shiny bright pages of her magazine.

'At least you got a good screw out of it,' she said.

'Not with this soft job,' I said, pointing at Charlie and leaning over his leg to get my face nearer hers and my hands nearer her moisturized, made-up throat. Charlie shrieked and Shinichro half pulled me back towards my seat. She looked at me, her face crimson now, her slightly buck teeth showing through her red pepper lips as she spat out the words.

'Not in Vegas, then?'

'Not while I was awake, bloody hell no.'

'Ladies . . .'

Shinichro's voice was firm and reasonable. Debbie looked sharply at him and picked up her magazine once more, straightening and smoothing it. She wasn't reading now, couldn't. She looked ready to rip it apart. Charlie, whose mortified face was a mash of pain and embarrassment, pushed desperately at me to ease my weight off his leg. I sat back in my chair, fuming. Shinichro pulled the curtains between us and the bed next door with a little bow and a smile to the occupant and his shocked but curious visitors. He directed his remarks to Charlie.

'Excuse me, but there is no problem now. Your fiancée can return the drams to this gangster.'

'If he thinks I'm going to bloody well hand over a million dollars just like that . . .'

Shinichro ignored Debbie's shrill but not unreasonable opinion and continued to speak to who was wearing the trousers, or at least half a pyjama.

'Then what would be your intention?'

'I'm going to sell them,' Debbie replied, but Shinichro, though he heard, kept talking to Charlie, who was listening hard.

'These drams were part of a shipment from my company which were to be delivered by Hiroshi Sano to certain valued customers. My company has already replaced the chips. What we must ask ourselves is why then is this man, this gangster who attacked you, so anxious to find the originals?'

There was no reply from either of them. Charlie eyeballed Debbie who continued to glower down at her magazine and then he said, 'That's why I asked you to come. Can you explain?'

171

'Perhaps . . .' Shinichro continued in relatively untroubled English, 'the dies are not what you suppose they are. Perhaps some of the dies, maybe all of the dies, are of interest only to this . . . gangster.'

'Well, your company would know . . .' Charlie said.

'No, sorry. As far as my company is concerned, only one-megabit drams were despatched with Sano.'

'Worth one million dollars which Charlie won and I've got now,' said Debbie.

'Worth one million dollars for now. Not always. I repeat. The chips have been replaced. So. I repeat. There must be something else that this gangster wants. It may be delivered with them. If you try to sell them, whoever buys them will no doubt inspect the goods and if all is not as it seems your customer might not buy. Worse still, what if some of this secret product is more valuable than one-megabit drams?'

Debbie did not reply to this right away. For the first time, she looked for guidance from Charlie but his blank face told her nothing. She looked to Shinichro and shrugged coolly. She had a good hand but was she still going to play it right? Shinichro was appealing, quite rightly, to a key emotion: slavering, eye-bulging greed, but Debbie wasn't biting.

'I'll take my chances,' she said.

Shinichro stood silently for a moment, considering her reply, though he still did not appear to acknowledge her part in the discussion. She was right to think that he could be bluffing, and to be cool about it too. Shinichro spoke again to Charlie, who was taking on the wooden appearance of a ventriloquist's dummy without moving his lips.

'At present only we know you have these drams.'

'And that's two too many. I told you, Charlie. Why you had to tell her . . .'

'Excuse me. This gangster thinks any one of us might have them. We are all in danger from this man, for now. We' – he indicated himself and me – 'would be out of danger and you' – he gestured to Charlie and then Debbie – 'would be in great difficulty if this gangster knew that you had the chips. More, if he has . . . employers, and *they* knew.'

Charlie lay back in his bed, his face a blank. He was thinking.

He was wondering whether Shinichro was still bluffing or whether this was the type of man who would do what he said. Charlie had had some experience that proved the latter. If Shinichro or I told Pal Kuthy that Debbie had the drams, it was over, he'd never get his winnings back, probably never walk again, never mind limp. At the moment there was still everything to play for, but what kind of hand did this smartass Jap have? Had Charlie accounted for everything?

'If you will allow me. I could examine the product for you and assess its value,' Shinichro said.

'You must think we were born—' Debbie began but her little whine of protest was interrupted by Charlie finally telling her to shut it. She shot him a poisonous blowdart of a look and volleyed a final weighty cannonball into the argument before settling down to her value-for-money periodical.

'Just remember. I've got the bloody things and no one else and I told you not to bloody tell *her*,' she said.

Charlie had wanted to tell us because he was less frightened of us than he was of Pal and he thought that there might be safety in numbers and maybe we would cut a deal, though I noted he hadn't mentioned that yet. The price of the drams was going to drop in the next few months, every newspaper was saying so. The money was important now he had it. It was a million dollars, for God's sake. He wasn't a pro, he was an amateur, and it was beginning to show. His health was suddenly important too, now that he had come to understand that he was not immortal. It was a tough decision and here he was flat on his back, helpless as an upturned bug, surrounded by friends and loved ones, all there to help him make that important life and death decision. They wanted the money. He wanted the money. It was his. He'd won it fair and square. Now the bitch had it, and she'd share it, since she was willing to forgive him, but only at a price. He'd have to share his life with her more than likely, and on her terms from now on, if she didn't get them both killed. It was one thing to say you'd marry a sweet-lipped, creamy-skinned girl when you had your hands on your wallet, but when she had, right from the start, that put a whole different complexion on things. And who *was* this slimeball Jap musclehead who was offering to take the drams off their hands and look them over? Charlie's eyes gave him away when he looked at us. He was thinking, 'Who was he really?, What was he to George?, and What was in it for them?'

'If your friend here could bring a suitcase to the hospital, with fresh clothes, perhaps, and the drams, of course, Georgina and I could visit you and take them away. Once we can find out what they are, we will understand better your position.'

'*Our* position,' I said, standing up and taking Shinichro's arm, while smiling broadly and sincerely at the morose couple sitting silently opposite.

'I must go home now,' Shinichro said, patting my shoulder.

'I don't want to, anyway how safe is it?' I said.

'Don't be afraid.'

'I'm not really, not any more. If he found me I'd just tell him, wouldn't I? I'm not a fool. I'd tell him where to look. Let her take a decision on how brave she can be.'

'I'll call a cab for you.'

'No. You go. I want another drink.'

'I don't want to leave you alone.'

'Hey. I'm used to it. Anyway, you haven't called Hanae yet.'

'No. I'll call her on the way.'

'Thank her for me.'

'Yes.'

'There'll be trouble?'

'Some.'

He didn't move from the bar stool. He took one of my cigarettes and lit it, flicking the filter with his thumb as smoke poured from his flat nose. There was no cough this time or even a stifling of one. I caught the barman's eye with a fiver and ordered two more beers. Shinichro let me pour them.

'From your conversation with this policeman, do you think the gangster is protected?' he said.

'He's not a gangster, Shinichro. A gangster has a gang, a mob, an organization, a team. Nobody says gangster any more, anyway.'

'What is he, then?'

'For a start, his name's Pal Kuthy, sometimes.'

'I don't want to speak his name.'

'I know, just like I don't really want to speak hers.'

Shinichro crushed the long cigarette in an ashtray.

'He was better than me, yes?'

What a bloody question. What a bloody question it was, made all the more pathetic because it was just the one that I wanted to ask him. Was she better than me? Was she? Did her hips move like mine and did her lips? Was there some passion they shared that moved him more than fresh cigarettes and heady perfume on wet white skin? Did he like leather and laces on her feet so he could draw his hand up animal hide to human flesh, narrow ankle to soft thigh, and did he laugh with her like he did with me, or used to? Poor Shinichro had watched his rival through an open door, had seen and wondered if it was more than he had ever had. In the scale of things around us, it shouldn't have been important but somehow it was. It was most important.

'I can't remember,' I said. 'It was too long ago.'

I wasn't going to ask the question. The beer was going to my head but I wasn't going to ask. I'd assumed I'd been used. I had no argument with it at the time but I didn't know then.

'You cannot remember me?' he said.

'Him. I can't remember him.'

I lied because as soon as we spoke of it I could. How could I forget? I just couldn't compare. They'd both entered and each had tapped a different, dark, but equally rich, fantastic seam. I couldn't explain that to him, and if I did the next question would have been to choose, and when Shinichro had given a life and Pal had offered death, why should I hesitate? I leaned over, kissed Shinichro softly on the lips and looked into the black half-moons of his watery eyes.

'I remember you very well,' he said and kissed me back, first on the lips, the side of my mouth and then on the palms of my hands. I thought of Pal's lips, of his thick brushing moustache, of his hands, of his warm musky body and his crazy crooked smile. He was protected. Shinichro was right. Nothing had happened to him or could. The man was one of the good guys. He'd said so. He'd been given a chance to get in and get out but Debbie had created an unpredictable delay. I just hoped that protection didn't stretch to letting him kill someone and to that end I hoped everyone was watching now. There was a slight cough and a large shape stood beside us. Shinichro lifted his head and stared blankly at the man in the steel-rimmed glasses.

'Shinichro,' I said, 'this is Detective Inspector Robert Falk.'

Shinichro grinned broadly to disguise his revulsion as the big man grasped his limp, reluctant hand in a banana-fingered grip and shook it firmly before turning to me.

'I've been following you about, I'm sorry to say. You're on your own. It's all right.'

I bought him a beer. We waited while he took a long thirsty quaff from the golden pint and wiped the froth from his rosy lips.

'Can you talk now?' I said.

'Mrs Powers, like it or not those drams have to go back to Pal Kuthy and no one gets hurt. That's the word. Now, who's got them?' he said, looking first at me and then at Shinichro, who stared blankly back while discreetly wiping his right palm down the side of his trouser leg. I shrugged.

'Robert, we've all been at the sticky end of this for too long. I haven't got the drams. Shinichro here hasn't and neither has Charlie. They've gone. Don't you think it's possible that it's all down to the spooks division and Kuthy should give up and get out of town? How much of a licence has he got, for God's sake?'

Robert shoved his glasses up his nose. The public bar was warm and he was sweating a little.

'He's inside.'

'What?'

'He's been nicked for assault but I'm telling you now if there's no evidence, no witnesses, he'll be out tomorrow, tonight, even.'

'There's Charlie.'

Robert shook his head. I lit a cigarette, blew the smoke up into the air.

'There's me. I saw what he did to Charlie. I know what he did to me . . .'

'No, Mrs Powers.'

He stared at me and repeated the word slowly and certainly. 'No.'

'Whose side are you on, Robert?' I said.

'Law and order.'

'And justice.'

'Fortunately, that's not my business.'

'Great.'

'I told you, Mrs Powers. When you have something for me, call me. You have to call me straight away.'

Shinichro stepped down from the bar stool.

'Excuse me. I have to leave now. I will see you tomorrow, Georgina. Inspector Falk,' he said, bowing a little to the policeman before leaning across to kiss my cheek. He picked up his briefcase and left, the big man's cold eyes watching him go before turning to me.

'Is he taking the piss, or what?' he said and I had to admit in Shiny's defence that Robert's surname could be a real problem.

Chapter Sixteen

The handover was relatively simple. Debbie arrived with Charlie's black Samsonite weekend holdall. She left her flat on the Finchley Road in her long batik sarong, black T-shirt set off delightfully with a large, conspicuous, semicircular black straw bag carried elegantly over her shoulder. She went to Charlie's flat in Chalk Farm, as instructed, and got some things for him: a dressing gown, toothbrush, toiletries, a couple of books and his Super Mario. She emptied the drams from her bag into Charlie's holdall and took a cab to the hospital. I arrived a little later, followed twenty minutes afterwards by Shinichro, who came straight from work, carrying a briefcase. It was warm enough for the shorts and T-shirt that I was wearing, and the canvas duffle bag I had over my shoulder wasn't too big to be suspicious. It looked as regular a fashion item as Debbie's designer basket. Debbie pulled the curtains around the beds this time, not all the way round, just enough to look as if we wanted a little privacy from the visitors on each side. She unzipped Charlie's black holdall and slipped a sweatshirt on to his stomach. His hand felt inside the folds and stopped there.

'What's up?' I said.

'I'm holding them,' he replied.

'Why?'

'Just in case I never see them again.'

'Charlie, we're going to take a look. If they're just a million dollars' worth of bog standard drams then you can have them back and make your own mind up whether you and Pal can cut a deal. So long as you tell him we're not part of it.'

'I don't see why you trust her all of a sudden,' Debbie snapped.

'Debbie, I owe her fifty thousand pounds. Why should she trust

178

me?' he replied in exasperation and I gazed sympathetically at him while Debbie pinched her plush lips together at this fresh evidence of our mutual intimacy. We all sat down this time, and after about twenty minutes talking to Charlie about his leg and whether he'd be able to play pro football again, Shinichro and I got up to leave. This was too much for Debbie. According to the plan, Shinichro and I were to leave together. He was to drop me off at the *Technology Week* offices where I would meet Richard on the pretext of following up a story, and Shinichro would make his way to his company's headquarters in Harrow to check the chips. I said nothing to them about any story I might really be writing. As far as Charlie and Debbie were concerned, Richard had some things of mine at his house. After inspecting the chips, Shinichro would then return to his office in the West End. Debbie's role was to sit at Charlie's bedside dutifully holding his hand for at least an hour. She was having none of it.

'You're not leaving with those,' she said.

'Debbie, we agreed . . .' Charlie pleaded.

'I don't trust her, or him. We know all about her and what do we know about him? That's a million dollars there.'

'Keep your voice down . . .'

'I wouldn't be surprised if that Pal Kuthy and her—'

I protested at this point but Shinichro grasped my arm, saying, 'Let her come. Why should she not take some of the risk?' Debbie's eyes narrowed in an expression of caution.

'Yes,' I said. 'Everyone else has so far, why not you?'

'It's a trick. I'm not a fool,' she said.

'Sit down, Debbie, for Chrissakes,' Charlie said.

'I won't.'

So she came with us, striding out on one side of Shinichro and me on the other; poor Shinichro, like sushi in a white slice sandwich. I said goodbye outside the hospital, more than a little worried for him. He was going to go to work, but with Debbie in tow. It didn't look right. To anyone who was watching, it looked all wrong.

Half an hour later I was talking to Richard in the offices of *Technology Week*.

'Going swimming?' he said.

'I haven't got that many clothes at my place.'

179

'What happened to you Friday night?'

'Old boyfriend.'

'So what's new?'

'You know, you're beginning to get a bit thin on top,' I said, peering at the top of his head. He dragged a hand through his light brown curly hair and frowned.

'I meant what's new about the story.'

'Oh . . .'

I should have apologized but we were interrupted by a young reporter on the City desk before I could. She'd picked up something on the wire. It was getting busy now as the paper rattled its way towards press day. The fog of cigarette smoke was beginning to rise in the room like smog over the city. There were more people talking on the phone, wedging the receiver between chin and shoulder and hunching earnestly over notebooks instead of leaning back and laughing, feet in the in-tray, flicking ash on the floor. Richard seemed to have settled in well. He looked comfortable and must have felt it to stick his TV/radio on top of his terminal to make sure he didn't miss the first Test against the West Indies. He tapped the side of the set to settle the picture of the vacant tea-time scene at Trent Bridge and turned back to me.

'What have you got?' he said.

'It is him, Pal Kuthy or Budapest Joe or whatever – a high-tech smuggler of the old school moving rapidly into further education. He's in town looking for one million dollars' worth of drams. He thought Charlie still had them, Charlie said he didn't and he's in hospital.'

Richard raised an eyebrow.

'Damaged kneecap and ligaments. Kuthy didn't believe him.'

Both eyebrows this time.

'Well, at least he didn't have them blown off,' I said and Richard pursed his lips as if he could feel the pain.

'Like that, is it?'

'It is.'

Richard stood closer to me and spoke softly in my ear.

'Look, George. Are you going to be able to write this one?'

'You mean is Max going to be able to print it?'

'Whatever.'

'It's not like the last time, Richard. Not quite. Can I do some work here today?'

Richard offered me his seat and walked over to the City desk. I had nothing to do, really. I had no desire to write a story, certainly not for Max and his rag, not even for my mate Richard. I had to wait a while, waste some time in relative safety before I could give Shinichro a call, and in any case I had nowhere that I wanted to go and I was tired. The last few days, few weeks, were beginning to wear me. I should have gone to Disneyland. If I'd gone to Disneyland instead of Vegas, Charlie would have been up to his neck in the same mess but I wouldn't have been wallowing around in it with him. I might have met Hiroshi Sano, but not Pal Kuthy. I need never have known either of them if I'd gone to Disneyland like I'd wanted to. I would still have been pregnant. I could have had the baby. At least I could have made the choice. Now I'd never know. I'd keep thinking about it and I'd never be able to drink it away to the point where I could slap myself and say I'd made my own decision. I always made my own decisions, for better or for worse. For worse, mostly, but, hell, they were mine. I fought myself for them. I'd slung my husband out, hadn't I? That was a great and righteous decision. And what about Warren? Righteous. The pair of them, crooks they were, thundering great crooks with counterfeit kisses. I had dumped them both, but I hadn't dumped my baby. I would have had my baby. I would have had it if I hadn't gone to Vegas and now I wanted to die for the loss of it. My mind was in that dark place that existed somewhere between hell and earth.

Wait a minute. Charlie owed me £50,000. He'd have given me that damned key anyway. I'd been locked in from the start. I never had a choice. I never had a choice from the moment the dealer had dealt the cards in that desert town. I stared at the screen with its patient white command and little cursor trembling in anticipation. I did nothing at all for a long time and then I hit one key to shut it down.

'Finished?' said Richard, tapping the TV set above the terminal, a sheaf of press releases in his hand.

'Yes,' I said.

I hoisted the duffel bag over my shoulder and waited. He patted in his pocket for a spare key to his house and gave it to me with a warning.

'Lock the place up, and be careful,' he said and as I walked out I looked back to see him patting his hand over the thinner parts of his hair and comforted myself that I hadn't mentioned the little bit of weight gain around his waist. I tried to think of a compliment that I could pay him one day and I was walking out the swing doors when someone shouted my name. I had a call. Instinctively, I looked over at Max, who was watching under a trail of cigar smoke like a ginger cat blinking through an evening bonfire. It was just like old times. I took it at Richard's desk. It was Debbie. Her shrill voice frayed full of threads. She was not happy.

'He's disappeared,' she said.

'Well, you weren't supposed to tag along, were you?'

'He said he was going to Harrow.'

'That's right.'

'So why didn't he take the Bakerloo? He lost me at Piccadilly.'

'Where are you?'

'In Harrow.'

'Where?'

'At NC headquarters.'

'And he's not there?'

'No.'

Oh, I thought to myself. I'd waited too.

'I thought he got on the train before me,' she said.

'His office isn't at Harrow. It's in the West End.'

'So why did he say he was coming here?'

'Look, he just didn't want you along. He didn't want you at his place of work.'

'Balls.'

Indeed. Debbie was thinking what I was thinking, that Shinichro had walked with her million: her million, Charlie's million, Sano's million – his million.

'I'll call his office,' I said.

'You bitch. You planned this, didn't you? Well, you won't win. Charlie won those chips. They're ours.'

'Debbie, I didn't plan anything. Don't panic. He just didn't want you along. Don't do anything stupid.'

I was talking to myself. She'd gone. There was nothing to do but call Shinichro's office even though I knew he wouldn't be there. As soon as I put the phone down from the fruitless call, Debbie was back on the line.

'Remember how your friend tried to put the frighteners on us?'

'He was just trying to make you see sense, Debbie.'

'He was trying to scare us. By threatening to tell Pal that I had the chips.'

'He wasn't serious.'

'Well, I am.'

'Don't, Debbie.'

'Don't nothing. It's done. I called the hotel. Pal knows who has them now. He's going to get them and when he does I'll have them back.'

'How?'

'I'm going to the police. I'm going to say he stole them. I've still got the list with every single number. I can prove that they're ours.'

'Charlie's,' I said.

'Ours.'

'Stay safe, Debbie,' I said, and I meant it. There was surely no reason why I shouldn't be now. Charlie was safe and so was I – as safe as anyone could be who'd just folded their cards. As for Shinichro and Debbie, they had just raised the stakes, and doubt and disappointment settled in my mind like snow in a sunlit valley.

It was nearly five o'clock when the messenger arrived, helmeted and crinkled in thick crusty leather, with a package for me. Richard made some remark about making myself at home as I signed for it and ripped open the Jiffy bag. Inside were two packs of unidentified chips – four thousand little squares of mysterious miniaturized circuitry. There was a note from Shinichro, saying 'Keep these.' I had been given my instructions, and they appeared simple enough. I stepped out on to Old Compton Street with the curious chips in my duffel bag and bought an *Evening Standard* to read on the way home and in my doctor's surgery. I'd decided to see my doctor, see what she said, get the once over just to be sure, and anyone watching would think I wasn't in any hurry to go anywhere. I stood on the street corner and flicked through the paper to the back through the thick property supplement to the City pages where the interest rates were flagged at 9.5 per cent and rising. Richard now had mounting debt and I had a little extra to come on the cash I had sitting in the bank. I vowed from then on to make all my financial decisions based on biblical proverbs. Two short pieces on the continuing chip crisis caught my eye. Two US firms were having a spat: one, whose share prices had taken a three-million-dollar hit because of delayed new product, was accusing the other of using its monopoly position in drams to hike up the prices. These outfits were both as American as franchised fruit pies, but they weren't on the same side. No way. The lesson was buy and sell on the world market and pray you never became a customer. It looked like the US/Japan trade pact was just about to blow. I laughed to myself. Debbie had just a bit more time to take advantage of her investment, if she ever got it back. The front-page lead was the latest in the continuing saga of Peter Wright's MI5 reminiscences in his book *Spycatcher*. The man had had his day, for sure, bugging and burgling his way across London at the State's behest and they wouldn't even give him a decent pension. Times had and hadn't changed. Pal was too young for a pension and I don't suppose redundancy amounted to much in the spook business. So what could a poor boy do but put his silenced gun up for hire?

The down-page page-one filler on the Gulf War raised the suspicion that Saddam Hussein was using chemical weapons against the human wave attacks from Iran. Inside was a feature on George Dukakis, Democrat nominee, and how it was cool to be small and uncharismatic yet want to be President, dare to be. No one was going to admit that he had no chance because he was Greek. I was glad I had no news value. No one owed me a living, no one thought I had what was theirs. I didn't have a mortgage or a business loan, I had no real estate, no borders to defend, nothing to prove, no thirst for power, no desire to be seriously, groovily, rolling-in-it rich, no dependants. If I could just look after myself for a while, make some good decisions for once, I'd be OK. Damn it, I'd get to Disneyland.

I was the last one in for the Well Woman Clinic that day. If I'd known it was on, I wouldn't have gone. I wanted a single shot not rapid fire. The Clinic's no-nonsense nurse told me what I already knew, what Esther told me all the time: that my diet could be more balanced, that my blood pressure was fine, that fifteen glasses, or their equivalent, of wine per week was excessive (I couldn't tell her the truth), especially for a woman, that smoking was affecting my lung capacity and more, and that I should give up, that I wasn't remotely overweight but I could do with more exercise, that my breasts had no lumps, but that I should have a smear and had I thought of an IUD? I said that if it was anything like UDI it would be nothing but trouble. She saved it for the doctor to tell me that I wasn't pregnant any more, the doctor's words pummelling my heart like it was fresh news. She patted my hand and told me that one in six pregnancies ended in miscarriage and seventy-five per cent in the first trimester, before she filled in a card so that I could have a scan at the local hospital. By the time I got home to my flat, I wanted to get right on with balancing that diet the nurse had suggested with some of those excessive glasses of wine. The fridge contained one open packet of bacon that was losing its pink sheen to a creeping sclerotic brown, a can of tuna that I no longer fancied and a paltry selection of salad products so impoverished they looked almost organic. The lettuce had started to slime but the cucumber and tomatoes had kept and there was some edible cheese, and one bottle of white wine standing proud next to a dubious carton of milk.

'Why do you bother?' I said to myself. 'Greta Garbo kept a single orchid in her fridge, that's all. The woman was honest. She liked take-aways. A nice Australian Chardonnay and a pizza would have done her just fine. I could sit opposite an orchid and talk to it all night with a bottle of this . . .'

I hauled the cork out of the bottle, delighting in its feisty 'pop' as it came out of the neck, and rummaged in a drawerful of plastic bags for the pizza menu. I poured myself a large goblet of wine and as I leaned on the counter to read the selection I looked up out of the kitchen window to catch a glimpse of the sky shredding orange clouds into the blue and saw the van with its metallic windows tawny peach in the evening sun. It annoyed me more than frightened me. I felt like sliding up the cranky sash and yelling down at it, 'Just the fucking orchid and me tonight, all right?' but my senses silenced me. I began to feel something closer than the van, to hear a silence wanting to break. I could smell smoke, the poisonous but delicious aroma of duty-free Marlboro drifting in over my head. He was there at the door, smiling as I turned around, his eyes twinkling softly with amusement.

'I like the shorts, very much,' he said.

I stood for a moment, still and chilled like a fresh trout in aspic.

I was afraid of him because the smile didn't mean friendship, if it ever had. I lifted the wine and he shook his head. Not for him, not now. I took a swallow and held the glass tight to me, my arm across my body. I thought that I would never have to see him again, never have to judge the true extent of my hatred for him. The shock to me was that there was none. I was blinded by the universal migraine called love.

'How's the leg, Pal?' I said.

'Not too bad.'

'Pity he didn't do to you what you did to Charlie.'

'He didn't have time.'

'Oh yes. I remember. We were in a hurry.'

'I got a call from Debbie.'

'So what are you doing here – visiting the sick?'

'She says Japan has the drams, not Charlie.'

'And not me,' I said and turned to look out of the window. The van was still parked in its usual place. Sweat was beginning to break out on my body. I kept hold of the glass, cold under my fingers, and reached one-handed for my cigarettes in my duffel bag, turning the mouth of it away from him.

'You want to get dressed?' he said once I'd lit up.

'Why?'

'I'm taking you out for dinner. Don't you want to eat?'

'I was thinking of eating in, alone. No offence, you understand. None of this has anything to do with me any more.'

'I was thinking of a threesome.'

'And if I don't want one?'

Pal smiled. I didn't have a choice.

I said I wanted a shower. He watched me take it, wouldn't even let me pull the curtain to, watched me wash, told me where there was soap on my back. He sat on the edge of my unmade bed and watched me get dressed, told me to slow down, there was no hurry. He didn't like the jeans so I had to wear a leather skirt but he said that wasn't light enough for summer. I took everything off again and told him I didn't have much in the wardrobe and maybe he should look for himself. He chose a pair of skintight khaki pedal pushers and a black cotton cut-away top, pushed them at me. When I'd dressed, he told me to lift my arms up over my head, higher, no, higher. I was stretched up like a dancer, my waist taut, my stomach tense. Take off the bra, he said, it didn't go with the top. I took off the top and the bra and he reached out his hand to touch me, to round his fingers under my breasts, lean over and lick them. I wanted to strike him; I should have done, of course, but I was still afraid and I wanted him. His hands were warm on my skin, smooth on my hips, his lips ate away at me. I didn't touch him. I tried not to touch him. He said he wouldn't hurt me, that he was sorry he had hurt me and I had to forgive him. I couldn't do that, but I could kiss him. It was so easy to kiss him. I was ashamed at how easy it was, and how simple to say nothing but just to undress and climb into bed when he told me to, telling me that it was a good way to relax. My arms were circling around him when he said that I had to be relaxed that night, we both had or someone could get killed. I had my head back on the pillow where the bullet holes were and I wondered if they were listening down there in the van. Pal kept talking, kept saying what he was doing but I kept quiet, as if I wasn't there at all.

Fifteen minutes of sex might be relaxing in other circumstances but that night it did nothing but screw the tension up a notch. The flesh had triumphed only to find the same terrors it had left behind. Nothing was going as he had planned and he was uneasy and bad-tempered walking to the cab office round the corner. The van overtook us as it had done before but this time Pal didn't smile. He was irritated that there wasn't a cab available right away and that we had to wait. At one point he started walking away from the office, in the direction of the main road twenty minutes away, but he changed his mind. We had to wait ten minutes and once we were in the car his irritation increased. The driver kept asking which way we should go, that he didn't know his way around up west. Two minutes into the journey we bundled out at the Mile End cab rank where we had to wait another ten minutes for a black cab to turn the corner and take us up town.

'I've been here too long,' he said, lighting yet another cigarette. The cabbie pulled back the partition and reminded us that there was a sign thanking us for not smoking. Pal slid the glass back with a slam and opened his window. I was beginning to think that

187

maybe I should have faked it. He hadn't liked me asking if he'd finished.

'You think you might perhaps be wearing out your welcome?' I said. He said nothing, his hand covered his mouth as he held the cigarette to his lips.

'Maybe if you told Charlie what you wanted in the first place . . .' Pal didn't answer.

'What is it you want?'

'You're just kids. You don't understand.'

'Kids?'

'All of you.'

'Shinichro?'

'He's not a kid, no.'

'None of us are.'

'In this business, yes, you are.'

'So how come you're still here, looking . . . for whatever it is.'

'I had to be sure what was going on. Now I know you're just kids but this one, the one born middle-aged, is making it a point of honour.'

'Shinichro?'

'Shinichro, yes.'

'We're going to see him?'

'Yes.'

'So what am I here for?'

'I'd rather trade than shoot the guy,' he said and, looking at me for the first time, not smiling at all, added, 'Stupid, isn't it?'

We waited in the foyer of the Intercontinental Hotel for ten minutes before Pal got a call on the hall telephone. He took it, tucking the receiver between chin and shoulder and keeping one arm around my waist. I wished the man repulsed me a little more but it felt good in the crook of his arm. I reminded myself of his fist in my belly and the cosh tucked down the back of his trousers. I could feel the gun too, hard by his chest.

'He's changed the place,' he said putting down the receiver. He was smiling, more relaxed now that he was in play.

'Don't tell me.'

'The Savoy. He's got a sense of humour, your boy.'

'Why don't you guys just get on with it? Leave me out.'

'You don't think you're dressed for the Savoy?'

188

'Frankly, no, but that's hardly my main worry.'

'You look fine. Don't worry. I think he is playing with us.'

I didn't like the word 'us' but what choice did I have? I got in the cab and let him squeeze my nipple under my top, let him lean over and kiss me, his mouth bitter as ash, and mine too, no doubt. What the hell, I was along for the ride.

We waited in the pink lounge long enough to order gins and not be able to drink them. Pal got another call, this time it was a message for Pal to go to a little Japanese restaurant in Brewer Street. Another cab but no squeezing now, no feeling up. Pal wanted to concentrate since he realized that this was the last trip. He kept looking out of the window, checking out the journey, keeping track. The restaurant was west of the sleaze that drew the tourists at night, and the Soho crowd thinned out at this end of the street to where the cabbie had muscled efficiently through the traffic and pulled up outside the door. It was a plain building next to a material shop and a new fashion outlet that sold leather caps and waistcoats to the unwary. The lights inside the busy restaurant were quite bright and the decor plain as the outside. There was no attempt at recreating a phony Floating World in London's West End, no ritual of removing footware and sitting around low tables on the floor to the sound of Oriental musak. Nor was there any attempt at Occidental sophistication by way of a kidney-shaped chrome and vinyl bar that offered aperitifs and salted nuts while we waited to be seated. The square room was furnished with scrubbed wooden tables laid with white tablecloths and cane chairs or plain wooden trestles tucked under. The customers were mostly Japanese but there were a couple of tables around which sat some Westerners. Probably what the guides call the theatre crowd, but if they were they were going to be late. In the middle of the room Shinichro sat alone at a table for two, drinking soup that steamed up from a cone-shaped bowl. He looked up after the diminutive waitress, dressed simply in white shirt and black skirt, had welcomed us. If he was surprised to see me, he didn't show it. Pal made a big deal of putting his arm around me as we stood by the door, and made sure I sat next to him when the extra chair was brought, with the table's corner leg between mine and opposite Shinichro. I didn't say a word, not even 'Hello'.

This was where Shinichro had his lunch. The plastic-covered

board menu indicated a set meal for £14.50. Not bad. I supposed it was the closest he could get to his patch. He dabbed his dark lips with a napkin and looked over to the waitress, said something in Japanese and she came hurrying over.

'Would you like to order?'

Her manner was sweet and polite. I had been hungry but how could I eat? I wanted that pizza, deep pan, all on, to go, as they say, washed down with that honey-coloured Chardonnay. It seemed incomparably appetizing and appealing as I sat in the company of these two fighting cocks and their hidden spurs.

'I'll let our host order,' I said, handing the menu to Shinichro.

'Good idea,' Pal said.

I got teriyake salmon with flower-shaped carrots and cucumber strips but Pal got something dubiously fatty, drowning in too much liquid. I noticed that Shinichro dispensed with the usual politeness of detailing what we were eating, though in Pal's case I'd rather not have known. The few times I'd dined out with Shinichro he was always faultlessly courteous, but he expected the same in return. I swore never to go to a French restaurant with him again after he made the waiter detail the content, cooking method and recent history of the ingredients of just about every meal on the menu. That night in Brewer Street we ate and no one spoke at all, though I was tempted to scream. I was tempted to order a bottle of warm saki and just one glass, let them get on with it while I slid mercifully unconscious under the table, out of it. Shinichro pre-empted me by dabbing his mouth one final time and calling to the waitress to clear the table of our unfinished plates. When the tablecloth was swiftly and efficiently made white and smooth again, Shinichro lifted a Harrods green and gold carrier bag on to it and slipped out a couple of familiar-looking waffle packs.

'May I have the bag?' Pal said, taking it and the packs and pulling them over to his side of the table. He held one pack and then another up to the light, checking the pattern of the circuits, and when he was satisfied he slid them with a smile into the bag. He tapped a cigarette from its red and white pack and offered one to Shinichro, who took one and accepted a light from Pal's gold Dunhill lighter that glinted like the precious semiconductors had in the bright lights overhead.

'Where are the rest?'

190

'You have the full amount plus these.'

'I do?'

'I delivered ten packs of one-megabit drams to your friends. One million dollars. With the addition of these two you are now better off by 2K times two at, say, one dollar per chip, that is four thousand dollars.'

'A dollar a chip.'

'That is the market price for eproms, I believe.'

This was new. This was what it was all about. Eproms. Charlie had taken off with four thousand chips that were memory chips but not *dynamic random access memory* chips – not *drams*. The glinting squares on the table were infinitely more versatile. *Erasable programmable read only memory. Eprom.* I tried to think why they should be important. They were different, for sure, no mere scratch pads for a hard-working microprocessor. For one thing, once something was stored in such a chip, it wouldn't disappear if the host machine were switched off. Like the pilot light of a gas fire, it stays alight. Any program or information stored in an eprom is permanent until someone chooses to erase and replace it. The chip would have to be physically removed and ultra violet light shone down on it to disrupt the electrical contracts etched upon its silicon layers. It would then be as clean as a whistle. The ones on the table had to contain some information. If they contained nothing, what, then, had all the fuss been about? As a rule, eproms were no big deal. Hell, Esther's washing machine probably had one. Little electronic miracles they may be, but common as muck. They're everywhere – cookers, microwaves, video cassette recorders, TVs, digital radios and toys, the cartridges of home computers, petrol pumps and Post Office weighing machines. They store passwords in computer terminals and the answerback code in automatic telex and fax machines. They hold the personalized ID and network code in cellular telephones, and unscrupulous diallers have enormous fun and minuscule bills because they take them out and reprogram them with someone else's. Put an eprom in a toy that says the word 'Mummy', take it out, reprogram a line to say 'Daddy'; in half an hour, you get a politically correct doll. Competitive and cute, but not worth killing for. Eproms. Drams. Who could tell the difference? Maybe that was it. Maybe the scam was in selling one-dollar chips for fifty dollars. Packages in a little black case with its pin legs, the eprom chip does look very different. Unlike a dram, it must have a little window in the plastic like a sun-roof to let the ultra-violet light through. Unpackaged, as raw fingertip-sized chips, who could tell the difference between a one-megabit dram and an eprom? Not me and not Charlie, even if he'd thought to look. Pal might, but of all of us only Shinichro certainly could. He'd have checked with his naked semicircular eye and pushed them under a microscope to be sure. They might all look alike to some, but not to him, not to anyone who knew what they were doing.

I took a cigarette of my own from my bag, lit it with my own lighter. I reckoned Pal would accept, which meant the trade would be finished and I was out of it, free – as a ringed pigeon, maybe, but free. This thought kept my hands from shaking but it didn't keep the twinge of curiosity growing to an ache in my head. Things had got pretty nasty back there for the sake of four thousand cheap chips. I looked down at the table. Something stored on these things had to be worth the pain, some little ace of a program. But if that were the case, and if these were eproms twinkling there on the table like raindrops in sunshine, they were not the ones Pal really wanted. The ones he really wanted were in the duffel bag that hung over the back of my chair.

Me, Charlie, forget Sano, who had it coming from elsewhere, we'd suffered for these things and I could have reached back and walked out with them while these two guys eyed each other for love bites. Shinichro was getting on with his cigarette quite well, a study in contemptuous nonchalance, but Pal had started to smile again, that folksy, pitchfork-between-the-eyes grin that rarely got to a laugh.

'Where's the test chip?' Pal said, tapping a missing square in one pack. Each wafer of silicon chips had a few test chips for quality control checks. Shinichro said nothing, moved nothing and Pal grinned and said, '*Kao*, Japan. Big *kao* for you.'

Again Shinichro made no visible response. He kept his elbows planted on the table. A minute edged by until Pal turned away and in a big brash gesture called for some salt. The tiny waitress hurried over, at the table in seconds and away again, so there was just us. Pal picked up the tiny glass bottle and slowly began to pour salt into his hand, watching it fall and pile up in the well of his palm until he closed his fingers slowly around it and let it run through his fist on to the tablecloth. Tiny white crystals flowed out like sands of time crusting the smooth expanse between himself and Shinichro, who sat perfectly still, saying nothing.

'*Kao* for me too, which in this business, believe me, counts for a great deal,' Pal said, spreading the salt out in ripples with his broad shovel-fingered hand. Shinichro kept his gaze steady and strong even as Pal clapped his hands together and rubbed a few more grains from his palms, purifying the space between them, clearing any spare devils away. A little more salt, a little more silence, a little steadier Shinichro's gaze, a little more fixed Pal's friendly smile, a little drier the roof of my mouth. Shinichro made his first move, placing his cigarette carefully in a clear ashtray beside me, rubbing it methodically into the glass to extinguish it fully before spreading his fingers along the rim of the table until they were a shoulder width apart. Pal's voice was full of reason and good humour.

'And dollars too. I get dollars, Japan. I can't see you getting so much as a yen for this, but me, I get dollars. I get a free ticket out of here. I get a good fuck, too.'

There was one moment when the eyes connected and the two men knew but Shinichro wasn't quick enough. It wasn't his business, it was Pal's, after all. Shinichro moved up and forward with brute force but the lightning knife, so quick to appear in Pal's hand, caught his lip and sliced his pitted cheek up in a terrible raw grin of flesh and blood. Pal lunged forward again but this time I caught his arm with both hands and hung on, throwing my full weight back as hard as I could but still Pal lifted me right off the seat, tore his arm from my grasp. I jumped up almost immediately, knocking the table over and finding myself, stiff with horror, between the two men, one rocked back helplessly in his chair, blood running down his chest like spilled paint over a wall, and one razor sharp with the cutting blade. Mine was an idiotic act of spontaneous bravery that I would never care to repeat. Pal crouched, caught the green and gold carrier bag off the tumbling table with one hand, stood upright and reached forward towards my throat with the other. I flinched but there was nothing, no cold sharp metal or wet rip of skin. He chucked me tenderly under the chin with his empty bloody fingers, and then wagged them in admonition at the manager who was edging closer. No one moved again as Pal stepped round the upturned table and pulled at Shinichro's jacket, stuffing his hands inside the pockets, in and out, and then down to his trousers, immobilizing the injured man by gripping his neck as he did this. When he'd finished, he backed away towards the door and grinned broadly as he called out to me.

'And he was healing up so nice, don't you think?'

Chapter Seventeen

Shinichro's face seemed to be flapping apart and my clothes and the tablecloth were crimson red with his blood. The waitress began wrapping a towel around his head, bundling it up to staunch the flow, while the manager tried to calm his distraught customers. Shinichro didn't make a sound. His eyes were squeezed tight, and his fists clenched, tight and white, as the little woman hopped about him, reassuring him as best she could in their own tongue. I saw the telephone poking out from an inside pocket of Shinichro's pocket and grabbed it, pressing the buttons like he showed me and dialling the emergency code. Not fire, no, ambulance, yes, police, yes, and then another number. I needed more help than what was on offer.

'Robert, he's got to be stopped.'

'Have you got something, *for me*, Mrs Powers?'

There was something I wasn't getting. What was it he wanted from me to loosen his leash? My voice was high pitched with tension. I felt like screaming; I thought I was but it wasn't me. Some other woman's sound was in my head, *she* was screaming, one of the theatre crowd.

'I don't *know* if I've got something for you.'

'Mrs Powers, calm down.'

'Shinichro's cut. He's cut him.'

'Please, Georgina . . .'

'I don't know if I've got something for you, God damn it. I've got something for Customs and Excise. Call them, I mean it. This guy's a denied party leaving this country with a million dollars' worth of one-megabit drams, four thousand eproms and a record as long as both your arms. If you don't I'll write it. I will. I'll screw you all. I don't care.'

'Eproms?'

'Drams ... and ... eproms ... eproms.'

'What's on the eproms?'

'I don't know. Oh God.'

Someone was gripping my arm. Shinichro's hand was around my wrist. His eyes were open, bloodshot and bleary but conscious enough to communicate.

'Shinichro knows. He knows.' I screamed and the phone went dead as the ambulance siren wailed in the distance. Robert Falk's bulk seemed to propel itself through the door almost as soon as the phone disconnected. He stood by the table behind me as I held Shinichro's hand. The restaurant was empty now except for the owner, his family and staff standing in a silent single row by the door, the young waitress holding Shinichro's head in the bloody towel. When the ambulance came they stretchered Shinichro out but left me on the pavement blinking in the blue lights that spun in the yellow darkness. Robert said we could follow. I should go with him, he said. I looked up the street. There parked on the double yellow lines was a familiar dark grey van with its mirrored windows reflecting the police car, the ambulance and me. I pointed at it, my hand shaking with shock and anger, and I started towards it.

'Get them. His friends. Get them now.'

Robert held me back and I began to cry and pull at his arm.

'Tell them there's nothing more to listen to ...'

Robert put his hand gently over mine, his face discoloured by the unnatural light to a sallow yellow. His purple lips affected a smile.

'Mrs Powers, that is what they call in the trade my wheels.'

'Your what?'

'It's my van, Mrs Powers. My van.'

I felt more than one emotion sitting in the front seat of that van on the way to the hospital. The clothes I wore, which Pal had chosen with such carnality, were stained with blood. It was drying brown under my fingernails as the hot summer air streamed in the open window with the petrol fumes of the night traffic. Eproms, a dollar a chip. Four thousand dollars. It was cheap, nothing, for all that had happened, all this. Shinichro'd need forty, fifty, sixty stitches

196

in that cut, and he would have a grin more permanent and crazy than that of the man who had given it to him. And he would count himself lucky, because Pal had come for his face, all of it and nothing more, because there wasn't anything more.

Robert swung down a quiet side road into the Coca-Cola neon night of Shaftesbury Avenue, lit up by the shows and the traffic easing its way to late-night gridlock nose to tail up to Cambridge Circus and down to Piccadilly. I could see the light of the ambulance swinging out into the middle of the road for a clear run and still it didn't get it, in the jam of two-lane vehicles. This was no place to be in an emergency. Robert tried to follow its achingly slow progress, spinning the steering wheel through his big hands. He was wedged uncomfortably in the driver's seat, peering out through the windscreen with hunched shoulders, his straw-coloured hair pressed flat against the roof of the van.

'Why didn't you tell me it was you down there. I could have brought you tea or something,' I said.

'Mrs Powers, I was just keeping and eye on you.'

'I'll say.'

We both peered out of the windscreen for another gap in the traffic. The ambulance pulled out again and two cars in front took the opportunity to follow in the clear passage it offered up the road. Robert wasn't quick enough and we lagged behind in the dense mass of cars squeezing along the busy road with them.

'I wasn't the only one, you know that,' he said, breathing a little heavily with the exertion of the stop-start drive and more than a little embarrassment. He smelled a little of warm bread and Right Guard deodorant. I lit up a cigarette without asking.

'You're all bastards,' I said and Robert said nothing for a while. Fifteen minutes had passed and we'd gone less than a mile.

'He's on special work. I found out that much,' he said when we started to move.

'Don't tell me. For us.'

'Not directly.'

'Oh, for the Yanks, then.'

He didn't reply to this.

'It means immunity, doesn't it? We can't touch him,' I said.

'Well, no one's actually told me that, Mrs Powers. I'm just doing my job. I'm allowed to do that.'

'What about now?'

'This is extra. A personal service for a friend.'

I relaxed a little. Check out the white knight, I said to myself. Good news. Better than I could have hoped for, even though the vision was more Friar Tuck than Launcelot. Where did I think I was, anyway? Camelot?

'Tell me about him, Robert. Something I don't know. Something you didn't learn from me.'

'Pal Kuthy is a – was a – spy, a smuggler of high-tech to Eastern Europe.'

'I said something I don't know, Robert. What is he now?'

'Well, he's been privatized, hasn't he?'

'He's freelance.'

'That's right.'

'So what? He's still wanted by just about everyone.'

'Not when he's on special work, I'm trying to tell you.'

'What's special about special work?'

'Special work, Mrs Powers, is work that helps us out, helps our political friends and allies, and wipes his dirty slate a little cleaner.'

'Special work means unaccountable work, then. No comebacks.'

'Think about it. This man has been sentenced in more than one country, this one included. His passport was in the custody of a German court but he somehow got it, boarded a plane and disappeared. When I checked him out, his name and various pseudonyms were on a "watch list" at numerous international airports and yet he buys air tickets, boards planes. He's made himself very useful to someone, that's for sure. No one I work for wants to touch him . . . yet.'

'You could have said something.'

'I wasn't told anything. I got the word. I couldn't do anything but my job.'

The van was beginning to clear the West End and enter the darker zone of the City to the east. The brash lights gave way to quieter streets of closed shops, dark pubs and designer uplighting in the foyers of the finance factories of the Square Mile. Only the meat market at Smithfield was alive, with red-faced workers in bloodied aprons and wellington boots hoisting carcasses on to hooks. The hospital was just around the corner.

'What about the cocaine?' I said.

'I contacted Drugs. They weren't doing anything on Sano – a mite pissed off about it, too. They said it was linked to a DEA cover.'

'A cover for whom? Pal's laundering drugs money, Robert. Don't tell me that's legit, or is he one of theirs?'

'The DEA does do business with another firm. It has been known.'

'Capital F?'

'Capital.'

'The CIA? No shit.'

'As I understand it . . . as our lot understand it, but who knows? There is always some ambiguity in who the employer ultimately is in a freelance job.'

'In my line of business I always reckon it's me,' I said.

I watched burning red flecks of tobacco shoot from my fingers into the night. The van slowed and Robert began to peer this way and that for a space to park.

'You may be right,' he replied, 'but I believe Kuthy gets to keep his money-laundering scam if he comes across for them – his enablers, let's call them – and their interests must coincide with our interests, otherwise why's he getting away with so much? They know him from the good old days when they worked on opposite sides. Maybe they worked together, who knows? Got his CV. Know what he can do. Desirable contacts on both sides of the Curtain and wherever his old employers had influence. He could have a great career in private industry, never mind government, with his skills in high-tech appropriation.'

'But what do they want from him this time? They didn't let him come over here and cruise around just so he could play a game of cards and screw me, surely?' I said and Robert smiled without much enthusiasm.

'I admit he did seem a little diverted, Mrs Powers.'

'Well, why didn't someone warn us? I could have been killed. Shinichro nearly damned well was, and what about Charlie? What about the gun he stuck to my head? As it is I might as well be sitting here with my clothes off. I mean, what's the point of putting them on? All that watching and listening. Christ, I might as well just have done it in the street.'

The van pulled up in a meter space and Robert yanked up the

handbrake, twisting his body as far round as he could to face me.

'I'm sorry. I had to know what was going on at the sharp end, without you telling me directly. I had to do it to help you,' he said.

'Well, you didn't. Not when I needed it.'

'I'm sorry.'

'You could have warned me about him.'

'Oh, what difference would it have made?'

Our discussion screeched to a halt. He sighed wearily and I put my hand out quickly to squeeze the great ham of his arm in instant regret. It wasn't his fault, and he was right, what the hell difference would it have made?

'The chips going missing. that's what threw it. While they knew where they were, it was OK. Kuthy would just walk in and get them. When they went, everyone was a suspect. I wasn't the only one plugged in to your flat, and yours wasn't the only flat. I could only do my job, and there was nothing for me to do. You were closer, I thought you'd come up with something,' he said.

'You watched him leave the restaurant?'

'Yes, and I was going to follow him . . .' he said, opening his door and ambling around to open mine, helping me out on to the pavement '. . . but I got a call, didn't I?'

We stood outside the room with a couple of other uniformed coppers while Shinichro's face was stitched together. He'd lost a lot of blood, they said, but Robert said he had to speak to him. He outranked the other two anyway. I didn't see the point any more. Pal Kuthy was probably at Heathrow Airport. He'd have got there in the time it had taken us to travel two miles across town, if he'd been smart and taken the tube. It occurred to me that I should phone Hanae, but I didn't want to explain. She'd find out soon enough anyway.

Shinichro's left eye was swollen under the thick bandanna of bandage that covered half his face and cushioned his head. He lay flat on the trolley bed, his bloodied white shirt pulled open, exposing his smooth hairless chest, his chin tilted up at an unnatural, uncomfortable angle. The nurse in the room wanted to clean up the rest of him but Shinichro had struggled with them. He wanted to talk to us. He kept asking for me and swearing, she said.

Robert's surname, I assured her, was a problem. I leaned over Shinichro and as I placed my hand on his chest, his hand came up to squeeze it.

'You were foolish to be so brave,' I whispered to him.

'You were foolish, as foolish as any *gaijin* could be, as any woman I have ever met,' he replied. It was really hard to understand him now but I got his drift. There was no point in trying to explain how I came to be with Pal. He was right anyway. I was foolish. I should have left him in the Rock Garden, crying in his beer.

He grunted something else but it was so hard to understand him with his mouth numb and immobilized. The anger and frustration showed in his eyes and in the grip around my hand. I put my ear closer to his mouth.

'My bag? I've got them. Why? Jacket?'

'Jacket.'

'Jacket,' I said to Robert. 'In his jacket.'

Shinichro's jacket wasn't there. It was on the floor of the restaurant.

'We'll get your jacket,' I said.

Shinichro's eyes squeezed tight and opened wide again, bright with effort.

'I had to give test chip,' he said.

'Why?'

'Virus.'

Shinichro was struggling with the language. He was in pain and it was taxing him more than ever.

'Virus,' he repeated breathlessly.

'What's that?' Robert asked.

'Virus? Computer virus?' I interpreted, unsure, but Robert's huge face lit up like the sun.

'Got the bastard,' he said. I looked down at Shinichro. A little triumph would have eased his pain but there was none.

'I don't think so,' I replied.

We called the restaurant and the manager said that they had the jacket. I couldn't see the point of it but Robert wanted the chip that Shinichro had not had the time to palm off on Pal. He wanted to have something in his hand when he explained to Customs and anyone else who was listening that he wanted Kuthy held for questioning because he believed he had four thousand eproms in his possession, all infected with a computer virus program. Computer viruses were within his brief. They couldn't deny him. It would buy time, he said. But time for what? An explanation, half of one, that's all we'd get before they slipped Pal's leash. I looked at Robert's face. He wasn't just buying time. He was doing his job.

'I'll stay here,' I said.

Robert nodded and went to leave but I called out, 'Why bother? He'll be in Rio, God knows where, before you can do anything.'

'I called Customs when you asked me to. They'll be checking him out, if nothing else. They said they've already had one call about the chips anyway. Chips believed to be stolen. A woman called the police, insisted they contact . . .'

'Debbie.'

What a girl.

'What about the two outside?' I said.

'I'll tell them.'

As he went to leave, an argument began. Shinichro wouldn't let the nurse take his shirt off. He told her he wanted to go home, that I would take him, with the policeman. Robert shook his head at me.

'You have to stay,' I said.

'No.'

Shinichro was adamant in the face of a strict explanation from the nurse that they would want to keep him under observation for at least the night. The man stubbornly refused. He swung his legs round and pulled his soiled shirt together, buttoning it up with determined fingers. I put my hands on his shoulders.

'You can't do anything now,' I said.

'Tie my laces. Quickly.'

While I was on my knees, the nurse was calling the doctor.

'Shinichro. Please. You can't. The cut's too bad. Rest. You don't need to go,' I said.

'No.'

He was on his feet, unsteady then firm, and all the pale young Indian doctor who arrived could do was press some painkillers into my hand.

'Mr Saito is with you?' he enquired. He clearly wasn't reassured.

'Yes. And Detective Inspector Robert Falk.'

The doctor turned to the big policeman with the steel glasses who was standing by the door and said, 'Plain clothes, sir?'

The archness of the remark made me look hard at Robert for the first time. Until then, I'd never seen him dressed in a track suit. He always wore a shirt. I'd never remembered him wearing anything else. When he took me out, a shirt, checked sometimes when he deemed the occasion to be casual, and at least a blazer. I'd never seen him in a bottle-green Fred Perry sweatshirt, extra large, unmatching orange joggers and plum-coloured leather bedroom slippers. It was like I'd caught him in his pyjamas; in fact, I think they *were* his pyjamas, and I don't think he had shaved for days. His face reddened under a sandy crust of regrowth as he caught my eye and held his ID up to the doctor, who dutifully checked it out and shrugged. He could only offer his advice, he said, but Shinichro didn't hear, he was already marching out of the door.

There wasn't enough room for us all in the front of the van so I volunteered to sit in the back.

'There's a bed in the back, as you can see,' Robert said, opening the doors wide. I stared at the mess of coffee cups on the floor and banks of surveillance equipment on both sides and turned to him.

'Back-to-back shifts?' I said. 'Did you ever turn it off, man? Give yourself a break?'

I ended talking to his lumbering great back as he took off towards the driver's side. I looked at Shinichro, who stared back with one dark reproachful eye.

'Get in, and tell me about this chip,' I said.

I sat among the empty polystyrene cups and McDonald's cartons and listened as Shinichro described, through clenched teeth, what he had done. He lay uncomfortably on Robert's sagging camp bed, sweating hard. He said he had looked at all the chips he had taken from Debbie and had realized immediately that they were not all drams. He had then spent twenty minutes setting a single test eprom in a plastic casing with a standard pin out before plugging it into a universal programmer: a grey box of tricks the size of a shoebox that plugs into a personal computer and lets the user check the circuits on an eprom and reprogram them if needs be.

'It was programmed for use in communications equipment; in a computer network controller,' he explained.

'How can you tell?'

'It has an advertised function in our catalogue. I load the database . . .'

'You mean it was one of yours?'

He was offended, of course. He took what I said as an accusation rather than an exclamation of disbelief.

'Our company makes communications eproms; like many other chip manufacturers we make many different chips in our fabrication plants,' he said.

'Oh, really? The virus brand is some sort of loss leader, I suppose.'

'Anyone can reprogram an eprom if they have the right equipment.'

'But these were fresh from the fabrication plant. Your company's fabrication plant. They hadn't been packaged. They were raw chips. Do me a favour, Shiny.'

Shinichro sighed loudly.

'I see extra code in the chip. It came up on screen. A couple of lines.'

'But what's the chip for?'

'I told you. Networking. Basic set-up.'

I understood. Each of the eproms had been designed to plug into the central controller of a computer network and hold all the details of whatever piece of equipment was linked into that network. This would mean that whoever was in charge, the network manager, would not need to input all that information every time the network was switched on – stuff like: 'Over here is Tom Brown's PC, it works like this, the hard disk is in room five, it works like this, over there is the fax machine, it works like this, that and the next thing.' The network controller would need to be set just once, like a table set for the same guests every day, and the information would be stored in its permanent memory bank – the eprom – unchanged and unaffected until it was reprogrammed with new information, a new place setting, so to speak. If there was a bit of extra code in the eprom – extra programming, that is – that did something else, then whoever was in charge wouldn't be as in charge as he thought he was. Eproms, I remembered, also stored passwords. Interesting. Whoever owned the network would have purchased a seed for its own destruction.

'The question is, what's it for?' I asked, thinking to myself but talking out loud.

'I told you. Network.'

'Yes, but a network for what – banking? Funds transfer? Databases? The military? And what's the virus, the bad code, what's that going to do? Did you have time to identify it? Are you sure it's a virus?'

He didn't answer. The conversation and the ride had exhausted him, so I sat leaning back against the bed and pondered the possibilities. Any feature on computer crime will carry a list of electronic techniques that sound like a shopping list for mafia bagmen: the Salami Trap Door, the Trojan Horse, logic bombs, worms, viruses. Some are little bits of fun, some are programming with extreme prejudice but whatever their *modus operandi* the outcome is invariably one or all of three things: one, the computers affected by them don't work the way you expect them to; two, they may not work at all; and, three, someone gets access who shouldn't. What intrigued me is that, while all these techniques are relatively commonplace in software, they were unheard of on a chip. But an eprom is a programmable chip, and a virus is a program, so why not? They weren't made in heaven. No, indeed. They came from Shinichro's honourable *on*-man.

The van rattled quicker going westwards than it had done coming east. Shinichro lay with his arm covering his eyes, and me? I was staring at the bank of tapes and electronic scanners that had monitored these past few scummy weeks of my life. I pressed a button on one tape machine, rewound it a little way and pressed play. Pal's excited voice whispered out and Shinichro's finger fumbled over and stopped it. It was very quiet in the back of the van for the rest of the journey.

Robert Falk called through to Heathrow but Pal hadn't shown. It was past midnight. We stood by the dark grey van in Brewer Street, Shinichro bandaged and zombie-like but with his jacket buttoned and his soiled shirt fastened against the chill of the early morning. Robert flapped the portable phone shut and leaned against the van, shoving his pudgy finger up against the bridge of his glasses.

'No point in going there to wait. He'll be held,' Robert said.

'But I have got the right eproms, haven't I? Shiny? I've got it right. You gave him a clean batch. Did he get the test chip with the virus or not?'

Shinichro held an inch-long plug of plastic in his hand.

'The test chip with virus. I have it.'

I'd thought the worst back there in the hospital and the worst had been right.

'Is there a problem here?' Robert enquired. Shinichro showed him the little slug of plastic.

'I have the virus on this test chip. The test chip from the clean batch I delivered tonight, he has. I make mistake with this.'

The chips that Pal had wanted had been in my bag when we three had sat around the table. I'd guessed that much but I hadn't known then what was in them. At first, like Debbie, I'd suspected that Shinichro had walked with one million dollars' worth of drams. When I got the delivery he'd sent to *Technology Week*, I knew that he had a plan. It was a good plan, but it had gone wrong.

'You wanted to give him a test chip that didn't match the batch you gave him,' I said.

'Of course. This virus chip, it matches the batch I gave you. All his eproms are clean. I wanted him to have the test chip with the virus, so he would believe all had the virus. He would have used that chip to check; he would not have wasted time taking out another.'

'Thought you'd make a fool of him, eh, Shiny?'

Shinichro's good eye blinked once and stared. He turned his head away and spoke to Robert.

'He will know quickly and easily that he does not have the right chips. This was not the plan.'

'You think he's tested it already?' I said to Shinichro. He nodded. Robert looked wearily first at Shinichro and then at me.

'Are you saying that this guy has nothing I can do him for? I've got nothing on him? Not even one bloody test chip for him to answer for?' he said.

Shinichro had wanted to spoil it for Pal Kuthy, wipe that semi-permanent smile off his face. Swap the test chips, package them, draw attention to the fact that he'd already done some quality control and make sure Pal got the wrong chip when he asked for it. Shinichro had bet on the certainty that Pal, under pressure, wouldn't waste time separating another chip from the pack. He'd run a test on the chip that Shinichro had given him and assume that he had his eproms, fully infected with the virus he had been commissioned to deliver. He would have nothing, and that's what he would have delivered, nothing. Big *kao* for Shinichro. And if there was a happy ending, we would have the eproms with the virus which we would have passed to Robert Falk to do with what he willed and I would have had the mother and father of a story by way of compensation. Shinichro looked as if he could die of shame.

'He's at the Intercontinental,' I said.

'What makes you say that?' Robert replied.

'I bet you I'm right. What's he got to run from? Us? The Three Stooges? Big deal. He's getting a good night's rest, I'm telling you.'

'Possibly. Held tonight, held tomorrow. Might as well sleep on it.'

'Not sleeping, resting. He won't be sleeping much. Sharks never sleep, didn't you know that?' I said, swinging open the back doors of the van. 'They just slow up for a bit and shut one eye.'

Chapter Eighteen

The night porter was disturbed by our appearance and even Robert's ID did little to appease him, though a display of temperament from the big man did. A couple of white-robed Arabs vacating the lift paused momentarily to glance at the fuss at reception before exiting swiftly through the revolving doors into the night and the pleasure domes of Mayfair. That was the extent of the activity; when we arrived and when Robert explained who he wanted to see the night porter began to press buttons on his telephone. Robert grasped the receiver with one hand and pressed the disconnect lever. He was polite with the man, but firm.

'This is not a social call, sir. You do understand?' he said.

'I have to call the manager,' the man replied.

Robert handed back the telephone and waited while the little man explained the situation to his boss. He put the receiver down and gave us the room number. Robert stretched out his hand.

'A key ... just in case?'

'The manager's coming,' the porter insisted.

'But not with us, sir,' Robert replied.

I was right that he'd be there, snug in his room. A bigger room than before, a suite with at least five lamps dispensing a soft subdued light all around. He'd come good. Why not enjoy it? He opened the door with a smile, one of hospitable welcome, and stepped back as Robert instructed him. That's when we saw Debbie, sitting stiffly in a wide, comfortable armchair. The rose curtains were drawn and the large double bed was made but there was an imprint on the lush counterpane where a body had been lying, a body propped up against the pillows; maybe there had been two, one on top of another. I glanced away to dispel the creeping jealousy, trying to turn it into sympathy for Debbie. It was so damned hard.

'Debbie and I were just having a drink together,' Pal said. I looked over at her. The desperate look on her face showed that, for once, she was actually pleased to see me. I asked if she was all right, and tears began to well in her eyes. There was no coarse wetting of cheeks or anything like that, but the girl looked as if they would start with a vengeance when she felt sure her ordeal was truly over.

'I'm OK,' she said.

Pal grinned.

'Hey. Why not? You OK, Japan?'

Shinichro didn't move a muscle.

Robert began his reason to believe stuff and Pal nodded.

'Drink?'

Everyone except me said no. I had a gin and tonic. Debbie had a drink in front of her but it looked untouched; the ice had melted to miserable lozenges around a yellow crescent of floating lemon. One gin was not going to take away the pain that was squeezing me inside, the hurt I felt just watching Pal, because he was so good, and no good. He'd had a soul, but he'd sold it, and not once but in classic salami style, over and over, shaving off one pure slice at a time so as no one would notice.

'Debbie thinks I have some stolen property belonging to her: drams. You think I have stolen eproms, dangerous ones, even. But where is the proof? Debbie has a piece of paper. Show the policeman your paper, Debbie.'

Debbie reached into the smart black semi-circular basket that was on the floor by her side and, hand shaking a little, brought out a sheaf of documents stapled together in one corner. Robert walked over and took them from her, flicking through them as he walked back into the centre of the room.

'Where are they?' he said.

'I don't know where *they* are,' Pal replied, walking towards the rack where his suitcase lay, a slim dark briefcase above it. He grasped the briefcase and held it up. 'I just have these.'

He smiled but no one smiled back, until I started to laugh and sat down on the edge of the big bed. Suckered. Debbie had been suckered. Pal opened the briefcase and, sure enough, it was choca-bloc with waffle packs, drams and documentation that Robert checked and handed over to Shinichro. Shinichro barely glanced at them before handing them back with a nod.

'I have export documentation for these drams which are certificated by the NC Corporation's subsidiary based here in London and signed by Mr Saito here. As you can see, it states that these drams, according to the EEC export regulations, will not be leaving the EEC. Everything is in order. I just pick up the phone and they're sold. I have no idea where this young lady's stolen chips are.'

Well, he did, as I did and so did Shinichro. Debbie did too but she was saying nothing. Pal had well and truly shut her up. Shinichro had appropriated the stolen chips that afternoon and had returned four thousand fresh untainted eproms to Pal, who now only had a case of legitimate drams and was giving notice that he fully intended to keep them.

'What about the eproms?' I asked.

Pal released the catches on his briefcase and lay it open on the bed next to me. A million dollars' worth, less nothing, delivered by Shinichro to the Colombians who had delivered it to him. Could have been two million, maybe much, much more if Shinichro had not tried to save face by keeping a little compensation for his company. His pride had not allowed him to give all Charlie's winnings to Pal. We would have had him easily by now if he had done. As it was, we had to do what we were doing, riffling and shuffling chips. Maybe Debbie'd get her drams after all, back from Shinichro and the NC Corporation, though not from Pal Kuthy. Maybe. If we all got out of there.

'What eproms?' Pal said.

'Shinichro?' I said.

'These drams are the legitimate property of Mr Kuthy as far as my company is concerned. All the documentation is in order, you will find.'

'The eproms, Shinichro,' I said.

Shinichro did not reply. He stood like a statue, a blank figurine from an alien land that had crumbled at its extremities with the passing of the years and the weight of layered earth above it. Shinichro's shoulders were firm and straight, as were his arms and legs. There was no sag of discomfort or unease apparent in a single

210

sinew of his body. It was a stance inherited for just this purpose, to bestow confidence and comfort on the vessel, however timid, however brave, that was called upon to fulfil an obligation no matter what. One eye was slanted shut, swollen from the trauma of the cut, but the other was open and glinted, dark and baleful in the dim lights of the room. Robert faced him.

'The eproms, come on,' he said.

'The documentation refers only to drams,' Shinichro replied.

'I saw it go down, Robert. Did you hear it?' I said.

'How many places do you think I can be?'

Pal lit a cigarette. He was enjoying himself, loving the fresh humiliation he was piling on his amateurish Oriental adversary. We were pretty convincing. He was relaxed about the whole thing. If he could be relaxed, so could I. I took a cigarette from him and a light. I took a good look at Shinichro making a show of emptying his pockets for Robert again, finding no chip, nothing. In Pal's eyes, it had to look as if that's why he'd come along, to save what face he had left. Any sane person having finished a night's work like he had for his company would have taken the opportunity to stay in a ward for the night, get his head down, keep his head down. But he had to make sure that the chip was there in his jacket and when it was not, that Pal, and consequently his company, could not be blamed. He'd made one mistake. He should never have tried to defeat Pal for personal *kao*, never have gone for him, as he had done, on a personal matter, out of vanity and male pride. No good had come of it. He had paid with pain and defeat, but his company could not be permitted to. He had been alone among the *gaijin* with no trusted colleague to restrain him, and he had weakened. Now, he had a chance to cover his mistakes and save the *kao* of his employers, and his *on*-man, to shame his enemy. Pal would understand this and enjoy the beaten Japanese man's ball-breaking stoicism.

'No virus, then?' I said to Robert and Pal's face dropped. I smiled sweetly and corrected myself.

'Sorry, no *proof.*'

'Am I in a tight spot?' Pal enquired. His face was barely troubled now. He was like a shoplifter with a receipt for goods he had, being asked for one for those he didn't.

'When are you leaving?' Robert said.

'Tomorrow morning.'

'For?'

'Amsterdam. From Heathrow.'

'Thank you for being so co-operative, sir. Would you mind if I searched the room?'

'Do you have a warrant?'

'I'd say I was in pursuit, wouldn't you, sir?'

Robert bashed about the room a bit, pulling out drawers and tearing off bed covers. When he'd finished, he was sweating. There was nothing there.

'That's it?' Pal said.

Robert made for the door and turned to Debbie as he opened it.

'Would you like to come with us?'

Debbie was up like a shot, threading her way out of the square area of sofa and chairs towards the comforting presence of the big solid British policeman. Shinichro bowed from the hip, stiffly and courteously and stepped outside, waiting for me by the door. I hung back.

'I'm staying for a while,' I said and Pal smiled genially at the sullen trio in the corridor.

'This is great,' he said, pouring me another drink while I walked into the shower. He didn't watch this time, he sat back on the bed, leaving me alone to soap away the flakes of blood from my skin and scrub my fingernails clean. I came out naked rubbing my hair. I had another drink and pointed to the pile of clothes I'd brought from the bathroom.

'I need these washed and pressed.'

'Now?'

'Please.'

He telephoned, got a refusal, made an offer and the house-keeper made it to the room in five minutes. When she'd gone, I sat at the end of the bed in the towel.

'You're a clever bastard.'

'You didn't want me to win?'

'I didn't take them, you know. Debbie had them all the while. She took them from Charlie.'

'She told me.'

'You didn't hurt her?'

'Do you care?'

'You hurt me. My baby.'

'I'm sorry, but you're no mama. It was OK, small, made your body more . . . womanly. But big, out here. No. Not you.'

'What did you do?' I said. I controlled my voice, smiled, even, as if agreeing with him.

'I spoke to her.'

'You did something to her, to make her afraid. I have to know.'

'You think I raped her?'

'I have to know.'

'I took her knickers off with my knife, that's all. She undressed. I cut them – she had no brassière, no *bra* – cut them, under there . . . and then here . . . and here. She had nothing more to say then, so she put her clothes on again. That was it.'

'You're disgusting,' I said, pushing his sliding fingers away from me.

'Still jealous?'

He kissed my cheek, bit at my lip. I drew back and took up my glass, draining it.

'You didn't have to cut him, not like that,' I said, lying back. Pal did, too, supporting his head on his arms.

'It was an old-fashioned duel, only I didn't have to kill him. He understands, better than you.'

'Have you killed anyone while you've been here? You have to tell me,' I said.

'No.'

'Not for the *yakuza*? Tell me.'

He didn't reply.

'But you couldn't kill Shinichro.'

'No. He was a company man. Anyway, I thought I might have to use him.'

'What about me?'

'You too.'

'Use me?'

'No. Well, sometimes, only when I had to. I couldn't kill you, no. Why should I? I like you too much.'

'What's that got to do with it?'

Pal laughed. 'OK. I could kill you if I had to. But I wouldn't like it at all.'

I let him touch me then, let his lips move over my damp skin.

'When did you deliver your eproms?' I said.

'I never had them.'

'Liar.'

'It's done. All right?'

'So quick?'

'Yes, quick.'

'Did you test them?'

Pal stopped for a moment and looked up at me with curiosity.

'The buyer will, with that little chip I took from Japan.'

'Who's the buyer?'

He rolled over and leaned his head in the palm of his hand.

'You want to write a story, mama? You want me to give you a story you can write?'

'Yes. Why not?'

'Is this why you stayed?'

'I don't know why I stayed. I'm sick of losing. Sick of losers, I suppose.'

'You want money?'

'I've got money. Don't offer money.'

'OK. Ask me,' he said, reaching for his cigarettes on the side table.

'Who do you work for?'

'Myself.'

'Who's contracted you?'

He stopped for a moment, considering how to describe his employer, and whether he should describe them at all.

'A multinational entity,' he said.

'Not a government?'

'No.'

'Not any government?'

'No.'

'A government agency? Any government's?'

'A major multinational. Good as government. You cannot depend on nation states, not as economic units, not any more. You talk business with business.'

'Which multinational?'

The smoke poured from his nostrils and I could see a smile start to stretch across his face.

'Come on. We haven't got all night, Georgina. Ask me where I'm going after I get home to Budapest.'

'Where?'

'Baghdad. You want to come?'

'Baghdad? Why?'

'AO Electronix is installing an extensive network of computers in Iraq, to deal with, um ... air traffic control. I've supplied friends in the Middle East for years.'

'Civil air traffic control?'

'Air traffic control in uniform. Information on air traffic will be analysed and distributed to a number of special sites around the country.'

He leaned forward, pushing one hand between my legs. 'Have I given you a clue?' he said. I held him still.

'There's a war on there,' I said.

'That's true.'

He looked at my puzzled face reflecting a brain hard at work and laughed. Shinichro's company had fixed it so the controller of this network of computers would have within it a tiny invisible time bomb as destructive as a pound of Semtex. More so, because it was intelligent Semtex.

'But aren't we supporting that bastard Hussein?' I said.

'Who's we? Oh yes, I forgot, *we* are. The West supports Arab oil suppliers. Absolutely. As does Japan. The Soviets fear for their borders, fear the fundamentalism. No one wants Iran to win. No one wants Iran, the Shi'ites, to control the region, or the *oil*. Oil isn't like a silicon chip, you can't suddenly start manufacturing it yourself once somebody you don't trust gets the monopoly.'

'But if Iran does win ...'

'Then no one will want the ... what shall I call it ... communications infrastructure, the *military communications infrastructure*, OK ...? to work very well.'

The telephone rang. Pal leaned back and took the call.

'Your policeman,' he said, handing me the receiver and feeling my breasts. I held my hand over the mouthpiece of the phone and whispered to Pal.

'I can't write that. Not till it happens. Not till it goes wrong.'

'I know. Beautiful, isn't it?'

'You bastard.'

'I told you. I'm one of the good guys now.'

I opened mouth to speak but he shushed me, holding one tobacco-yellowed finger to my lips.

'Tell him you will be at least an hour. He's used to waiting, I think, but this time we don't want him to hear.'

Robert got up from the chair in the foyer.

'Mrs Powers?'

I showed him my empty duffle bag.

'You'll find them in the bathroom, I put them in the bin.'

'Right. You all right?'

'I am. Yes, but . . .'

'What?'

'I don't know, never mind. They're there. He didn't check the eproms Shiny gave him, so he thinks he's delivered the right ones already. You can do your job now.'

'He's nicked, Mrs Powers. In the frame with the virus at the very least.'

'He'll go down for all the high-tech smuggling, from way back?'

Robert shrugged.

'Once we have him in custody for this, if we can persuade Mr Saito, now, and you, we can do him for GBH too. Your friend Charlie . . . and Debbie . . . has a complaint.'

'So what?'

'So what? I don't understand.'

'You'll get a collar for the virus. So what? So what? I think everything will turn out as everyone who paid him wants, don't you? They have to protect their oil supplies and we want them to, don't we? It's in our interest, isn't it? Like the man said, he's one of the good guys. Don't you love the wonderful ambiguity of it all?'

Robert placed his large comforting fingers on my shoulders.

'Maybe, but he's lost face, as they say, especially with those who paid him. He screwed up and he'll do time, I can assure you. This is your revenge; maybe it's not much but it's yours.'

And yours, I wanted to say, against all those people who want you to let the crooks walk away, to save all their powerful faces.

'No egg on your face this time, eh, Robert? You've nailed this one,' I said. Robert let his hands fall and I lit a cigarette.

216

'Where's Shinichro?' I asked.

'He slept on the sofa here on and off, then he said he couldn't wait. You've been quite a while. Was there something you needed him for?'

The big man was already walking towards the lift.

'I had his painkillers in my pocket, that's all,' I replied and the doors closed behind him, leaving me alone in the bright marbled hall.

'Thought we might as well celebrate,' I said.